Dreams
of Eleven

For Dee
Who has always turned a house into a home

and for Meg
Whose comments and insight were invaluable

Crumps Barn Studio
Crumps Barn, Syde, Cheltenham GL53 9PN
www.crumpsbarnstudio.co.uk

Copyright © Michael Bartlett 2022

Cover design by Lorna Gray

Printed in Gloucestershire on FSC certified paper by SevernPrint, a carbon neutral company

ISBN 978-1-915067-17-3

Dreams
of Eleven

MICHAEL BARTLETT

Crumps Barn Studio

A house is not a home unless it contains food and fire for the mind as well as the body.

Benjamin Franklin

PROLOGUE
DEVON

The house clung to the side of a Devon cliff. The drive dropped down from the road, splaying out in front of the building. On the other side a terrace of stone flags curved outwards affording breath taking views over the sea. It was the house he had always dreamed of. A place of safety. A haven.

Richard Kirkwood sat at a round table on the terrace, a glass of vodka and orange in front of him. Soon it would be time to take the car – a Mark V Jaguar no less – and drive down to Dartmouth to meet Mary off the ferry. He smiled to himself as he thought of her pleasure when she saw the house for the first time. Her room was all ready for her. A quiet evening, just the two of them. It seemed like years since that last tearful goodbye in Paris.

Or perhaps it wouldn't be Mary. Maybe it would be his agent, Rhoda. They would have a bite of dinner in the town and then he would bring her back here. They would sit up late with a brandy and talk about his new film script.

Or maybe it would be Ronald who got off the train. Ronald who looked after his investments. Ronald, whose financial skill had made it possible for him to buy this house.

Richard thought for a moment. No, not Ronald. The person he met off the train and brought back here had to be female. The pleasure lay in showing this house which he loved so much to a woman.

It did not really matter which woman, Mary, Rhoda or someone else. None of them existed anyway.

And neither did the house.

1

RICHARD

It's a dark, drizzly evening in early October 2006. I'm driving home to Weybridge from Gatwick after ten long, tedious, tricky days in Stockholm. I'm very tired but the problem is solved. I've informed the office that the risk of legal action has gone away. I've negotiated a slight over-run in the duration of the contract but the project can go ahead. I've found a Kit-Kat in the glove compartment and there's some decent folk music on Radio 2. All is well.

It's around half past eight and I'm approaching the Guildford exit on the M25 when my phone gives two beeps. A text. I assume it's Lauren saying she's been delayed at the office yet again so I wait until I'm off the motorway and can find a safe place to pull over. It's not Lauren. It's Francesca Thompson and the message reads:

> *An issue has arisen with your contractor. Their company is under investigation by police. Situation sensitive. Do not come into office. You're on garden leave till further notice. Will phone tomorrow. FT*

I gaze at the screen in disbelief. I'd heard vague rumours a few weeks ago about possible accounting irregularities with this contracting firm but I'd dismissed them as idle gossip. But now this. And why me? Do they think I'm involved in some kind of fraud?

The wording of the text is final. Non-negotiable. Absolute.

I sit in a layby on the A3 trying to come to terms with the fact that I've been suspended for something I know nothing about. With a single text I am taken out of the loop, all my clients have become someone else's problem. From a full diary I'm suddenly faced with empty days – and I don't know what to do with empty days. If I'm not working I don't have any purpose. Suddenly I find I'm very angry. I know being suspended isn't the same as being judged, but that's the way it feels.

I have no doubt the timing of this text is not accidental. It has been sent after the office has closed so I can't make an instant response. My first instinct is to call Hunky on his mobile and demand an explanation but I hesitate. I push personal anger aside and let my professional self take over. In any crisis, the instant reaction is almost certainly the wrong one, and in any case the message does not even come from Hunky Dory himself, but from his PA, Francesca Thompson.

That's not so surprising though. Vincent Dory, 'Hunky' behind his back, is the Managing Director of my division of *Swamplett, Benson and Dring* and a moral coward. Francesca is his Swiss Guard forming a cordon around his private Vatican. She isn't my favourite person, but then she isn't anyone's favourite person including – I've often suspected – Mr Thompson.

Hunky's not relevant anyway. It's Francesca's views that really matter in our office. If she thinks I've been involved in fraud then she'll show me the kind of sympathy a Rottweiler offers a one-legged burglar.

Anger is now struggling for first place with panic but there is nothing I can do for the moment so I drive on home.

Lauren is in the living room when I get there, sitting on

the sofa with papers spread in a wide semi-circle around her.

"Hi," she says, then glances at the clock. "Hey, is that the time? You're late, aren't you?"

"Contraflow on the M23," I say, "but it won't be a problem anymore."

She glances up, amused. "They've put you in charge of contra flows now, have they?"

"No. I'm no longer in charge of anything." And I tell her about the text message.

She's silent for a moment. "What kinda fraud we talking about?"

"I don't know. It was just a handful of rumours. Something to do with money laundering, I think. Frankly, I didn't pay much attention. I've been working with those guys for years and I find it hard to believe that they were using our contracts as a front."

"Not relevant." Lauren is an American and a lawyer which means she has very few illusions. "You'd probably be the last to know if they were running a scam."

She pauses for a moment in thought. "This garden leave thing – almost certainly a formality. You're the main point of contact for these guys. You need to be isolated so the investigation can go ahead."

"I hope you're right.. Or maybe they think I really am involved."

"But you're not, as we know, so we can kick that into touch."

For the first time I feel a little glimmer of happiness. Lauren's unquestioning assumption that I'm innocent does me the world of good. But her next words dispel that feeling.

"So, they can't prove you're actively involved in any fraud, because you're not, but if it all goes belly up it might not be possible to prove you weren't. Not proven, as your Scottish neighbours would say."

"Not proven?"

"Yeah, you wouldn't face any charges but there'd still be an element of doubt. That can be very damaging."

I hadn't thought of that, and I find the prospect terrifying. "If that were the case then I might not be able to go back to work."

"I guess that's a possibility."

I feel the panic beginning to rise. "But ... but that would be appalling."

Lauren looks slightly surprised. "Well, not ideal, sure, but not catastrophic. They'd probably do some kind of early retirement deal. You should be fine financially."

She doesn't understand. How could she? It's not the money. It's the empty space. Time to brood. Time for unwanted memories to come flooding back. They must be kept at bay, but she has no idea about that. I've never told her.

"I can't let that happen. There mustn't be any doubt. I've not been involved in any kind of fraud and that must be made absolutely clear."

Lauren is clearly a little taken aback by my vehemence. "Well, let's hope it's all wrapped up pretty quickly. Seriously though, you might want to think about getting a lawyer."

"You offering?"

"Not likely. Vested interest."

I think about the suggestion. "Don't think I'll go the lawyer route yet. Bit heavy handed. Let's see how it plays out first."

"Fair enough, but if you change your mind, why not give

8

Max a call? If you can't have me then he's the next best thing."
She grins. "So, what support d'you reckon you'll get from the company?"

"The company in general, no idea, but I wouldn't expect any support at all from Hunky and Francesca."

"I've never trusted Hunky or that bitch who works for him." Lauren, like many Americans, believes in calling a spade a bloody shovel. "So, what's your next step?"

"I don't know, I really don't know. I'll speak to Francesca tomorrow and see where we go from there."

"Sure. Guess that's all you can do."

I nod and she gestures to her papers. Lauren's very good at getting her priorities right. "Well in that case ..."

"You carry on. I'm going to bed."

I lie on the bed but I can't sleep. I'm not so fond of the job that I'd miss the long hours, the stress, the delicate negotiations, but that job is who I am. It gives me a structure, it gives me respect, it gives me a purpose. Without it I am nothing, and left to my own devices all the old insecurities will come back and drown me.

But I have to face the fact that for a while at least there is no choice. How the hell am I going to fill the hours and keep the demons at bay?

I lie there sleepless in the dark. I am very frightened.

2

The following morning I'm tired but I've got myself in hand. The fears have not gone away but I'm determined not to go down without a struggle. I will fight.

Mid-morning Francesca rings but has no more information. The police have removed all the files relating to the contractors and all she can do is confirm that I must stay away from the office until further notice. I want to ask about practical matters, but she hangs up on me.

I'm not standing for that so I ring back and demand to speak to Hunky. She refuses to put me through so I wait until the evening then ring him at home. Hopeless. The moment he hears my voice he says, "This is inappropriate. Speak to Francesca. She'll tell you what you have to do." And hangs up.

The next day I ring Francesca again and make it clear that unless we lay down some rules of engagement pretty quickly then I'm coming into the office whether they like it or not and I will be loud and abrasive. I may even kick over a few chairs and cause as much fuss as possible. Much as I dislike Francesca, she seems to take my point so she agrees to meet me in the office at six that evening when, she says, we can sort out everything that needs sorting.

It's an interesting meeting. Hunky isn't there, of course. I hadn't expected he would be. I know if I lose this battle I'll never see him again but if I win he'll be all over me, maintaining he'd trusted me all along. In many ways I prefer to deal with Francesca. You know from the outset that she hates you. No pretence.

That's how she is this evening. Not judgemental, far too fly for that, but she does outline the case against me. It's far worse than I thought. The contracting company I brought in to try and save a multi-million pound Hydro-Electric project is currently being investigated by the British Fraud Squad, the German and Belgian police and Interpol. The company is apparently suspected, not only of ripping off a number of their clients for years, but also of laundering large amounts of money through their international business links. The police have begun an investigation, not only into the contracting firm but all their clients as well. Which includes us.

I can hardly believe it. I've been using this contracting firm for years. It's always done a good job for me and has always turned in the work on time and on budget. However, according to Francesca, having a few completely legitimate contracts enables a fraudulent company to hide all the fake contracts and confuse the money trail. The problem is that, now it's all starting to unravel, anyone associated with them is tainted – she stops short of saying actively involved – so for the good of *Swamplett, Benson and Dring* I have to stand down while the investigation continues.

Curiously enough I understand this reasoning. Objectively it makes sense, the company has to be seen to be taking precautions. Subjectively though I'm really pissed off. I ask how long the investigation is likely to take. Francesca doesn't know but says they've been told it will probably be months rather than weeks. Great. So where does that leave me? Francesca does have an answer for that.

"You are officially on garden leave," she says. "We'll tell

11

any clients who ask that you've taken a sabbatical to deal with some personal issues. In the meantime you'll be on full salary. If this goes on any longer than six months we may have to review that."

Practical matters come to mind. "What about all the other bits and pieces," I say, "the company car and so on?"

"You may keep the car for the time being, though naturally you cannot use the company fuel card. Your pension rights will not be affected, at least not initially, neither will your private health insurance. You may keep your phone as the office may need to contact you but please don't experience a sudden urge to delete all your historic messages. Is that clear?

"Yes."

"However, we do require you to hand in your business laptop. I'll take that now, shall I?"

"I don't have it with me."

She gives me the kind of look that suggests that not carrying my laptop at all times is akin to going down the pub leaving a six month old baby alone in the house.

"Oh. Well, in that case you need to bring it in tomorrow morning. I will expect you at ten o'clock. Don't be late."

With difficulty I bite my tongue. It's not worth getting into an argument. Not at this stage anyway. Francesca is aware of my struggle and smiles. Not a pretty sight. "Oh, and one other thing," she says, "you will also make yourself available to the police when they want to talk to you."

I leave the room feeling I've been admonished by a strict head teacher. As I'm waiting for the lift I hear someone say "Psst" and I see my PA, Sally, peering round the corner.

"Fox and Hounds in ten minutes," she says and vanishes.

I'm halfway down my pint before she appears looking

flustered. "I shouldn't be here," she says, "we've all been warned not to talk to you."

"Well, I don't have rabies," I say, "and I am not involved in any scam, no matter what the Queen Bitch may say."

"Of course not," says Sally, "but you know what she's like."

"Don't I just."

"The moment I heard what was going on I transferred all the personal stuff from your desk to mine and it's all safely locked away. Let me know if there's anything you need. Now she's spoken to you, she's going to clear your desk tomorrow."

"Thanks, Sally."

"And if there's anything I can do to help just let me know."

I think for a moment. Years working for large organisations have taught me a number of basic survival skills.

"Well, there is just one thing ..."

"Yes?"

"I don't trust Francesca an inch and she has Hunky wrapped round her little finger. I'm not happy about simply leaving everything in their hands."

"What d'you want me to do?"

"I'm going to write a letter saying I understand the need for the investigation and my temporary suspension but I'm completely innocent and therefore expect to be kept informed of the progress of the investigation at all times."

"Who will you send it to?"

"I've been thinking about that. The point is I don't want it to go through Hunky and certainly not Francesca. I want it to go higher so it's on record and can't be denied later."

"How much higher? Gaynor Wiles?"

"I think higher still. Regional Manager is only one step above Hunky."

"Well, the next one up would be the National Director, Kenneth Bannerman."

"He'll do, but we'll send a copy to Gaynor as well. And the Director of Human Resources. Can't remember who that is."

"Don't worry, I'll check. And you want me to make sure they all get it?"

"Please, Sally. I know you won't let it get conveniently lost in the system."

She nods. "It's a bit unorthodox, Richard. You're not meant to by-pass the chain of command you know."

"What have I got to lose?"

"See what you mean. Okay, let me have your letter and I'll make sure it gets to the right people. Now, you've got my personal mobile number, haven't you? Use that if you want to contact me. Don't ring the office."

I watch her go, grateful for her trust but inside I'm feeling very confused. Since my initial panic when I first received the text I've tried to step back and evaluate the problem professionally. My first question when I meet a new client is always, "What outcome are we hoping to achieve?" Having established that, we have a target to aim for and can start planning a route to get there.

But that's me being objective with someone else's problem. Now it's my problem and I'm not sure what I want to achieve. I certainly want the unspoken accusation against me sorted of course, but what happens then? Maybe it's time for a spot of personal re-evaluation. It's been a long while since I felt a true sense of challenge in this job. I travel the world, I face the problems that others in the company have failed to solve and, mostly, manage to find a solution acceptable to everyone.

But these days it's almost automatic. It's a truism but, although on the surface every situation looks different, in fact all corporate disasters mostly come down to the same things: wrong person in the wrong job, lack of resources either asked for or given, insufficient advance planning, no contingency planning, no day-to-day control and, above all, a reluctance to recognise any or all of these reasons and to take positive action. That's where I come in. I am Positive Action Man. I parachute in from the outside world, analyse the problem, deal with it, probably ruffle a few feathers but I'm the outsider so that's what they expect me to do. Nothing personal. I don't do personal.

Well, that's fine as far as it goes but the excitement of non-stop travel has long since faded. Slightly to my surprise I realise that the loss of the job itself wouldn't upset me but the loss of status and security would. And in any case I can't just stop. As I tell clients who are looking to make a change, the trick is to go 'to' something, going 'from' something is not sufficient. But this is long term thinking. For the moment it's what to do with all the empty hours I'm suddenly faced with that is causing me anxiety. I try and explain this to Lauren but she doesn't see the problem.

"Gift horse, I call it," she says when I raise the issue. "Six months paid vacation, what wouldn't I give for that?"

Not a lot, I think. The idea of Lauren sitting round the house or lying on a beach for anything longer than a couple of hours simply doesn't ring true.

"I don't want a vacation," I say, "holidays are fine for a week or two but that's not the same as sitting at home for six months with nothing to do."

Lauren nods. "Guess you're right." She pauses. "Do you

want for me to postpone this trip and stay here with you?"

It's a generous offer but I know she'd be devastated if I said yes. She's about to start a six month stint in the New York office of her law firm – a posting which comes with an automatic promotion. She's waited a long time for this opportunity, and I don't see why this fraud investigation should get in her way.

"Thanks, but no thanks," I say, "no point two of us sitting round staring at the walls."

Her relief is obvious but her next suggestion catches me by surprise. "You could always come with me. Nothing to keep you here, is there."

For a moment I think about it, but I know I won't go. What would I do for six months in New York? Lauren will be working, probably even longer hours than she does here. A week or two over there might be fun, but not six months. Anyway it looks too much like running away and whatever the outcome of this business I have no intention of lying down under an accusation of fraud. No, I need to be here.

I tell Lauren this and she nods again. "Sure, I can see that. Stay in their face. But, hey, Richard, what the hell are you going to do with yourself? Have you thought about that?"

I have thought about that. And I have no idea.

The next few days pass incredibly slowly. Early mornings in our house have always been a bit of a blur. We both get up early, grab a coffee and head off for another packed day. In reality, Lauren still does, but for me there is nothing. I still wake early, of course, and for the first few days, I still get up but I soon discover that all that does is add a couple more hours to a day when I have nothing to do.

The morning after my meeting with Francesca I go into

the office again and deliver my business laptop as ordered. I draft my letter to Kenneth Bannerman, leave it overnight, make some amendments, print it with the 'copy' list clearly marked and deliver it to Sally. There's nothing more I can do except wait for a call from the police.

I'm not good at doing nothing. I tell myself that at last I have time to read all those books I always meant to read but I can't do that all day. I go for walks. I do some shopping. I cook some meals, which makes an interesting change for both of us, but there are still hours left unfilled and the thought of spending several months like this is driving me to desperation. And this is while Lauren is still here. In another week she'll be gone and then I really will be alone.

Alone with no job to keep me occupied. I don't know how I'm going to handle this so, as I always do when I need to talk to someone, I call my brother.

3

SIMON

Simon Kirkwood was sitting in his office checking through the quarterly accounts when his phone rang. He cursed, clicked 'Save' on the spreadsheet and picked up the receiver.

It was Richard and his news came as a complete surprise but he instantly realised the underlying implications and knew he had to do something. Way back in the past, Simon had taken on the responsibility of being the older brother – given the circumstances he'd had very little choice. He didn't always agree with Richard but he loved him and respected him. They were very close.

He also knew this was not a situation that could usefully be discussed over the phone so he pushed aside his plans for the day.

"We need to talk about this face to face," he said, "why don't you come over?"

4

We meet at Simon's office on a small industrial estate between Wimbledon and Morden. I tell him all I know about the situation which isn't very much. When I stop speaking, he thinks for a moment.

"Do they have any idea how long this investigation will take?" he asks finally.

"Not really, but they're talking months rather than weeks. I'm on full salary for the first six months, after that who knows?"

Simon shakes his head. "Can't believe it'll take that long to show you're in the clear."

"It'd better not. I'll go bonkers."

He grins at me. "How would we tell?"

"Gee, thanks."

He regards me for a moment. "Maybe this is a blessing in disguise, Richard, being forced to stop for a bit. No punishing work schedule to hide behind so a real chance to find something else to do with your time, maybe even face the ghosts and lay them to rest."

"I don't want to. I don't need to."

"I know you don't want to, but I'm damn sure you need to."

"Same old record."

"Yes, because you can't hide for ever."

I'm starting to feel a bit defensive. "Look, this is serious.

I'm going to be lost if I'm not working."

"Well, you don't have any choice – so we have to deal with things as they are, not as you'd like them to be."

"Easy to say."

He nods. "True, but think of it as an opportunity. Other people have hobbies, go on holiday, spend evenings down the pub, visit the theatre. What do you do? You work."

"So do you."

"Yes, but not obsessively. Look, you've been given some space. Find a way to use it to advantage."

"Oh, I get it. You're looking for someone to paint the outside of your house."

"Well, as it happens …" We both laugh but then he goes on. "Richard, try and be objective. If this was a management issue with one of your clients would you advise them to pretend the problem didn't exist and just work harder?"

"Of course not."

"There you are then. You're great at solving other people's problems, Richard. Not so hot when it comes to your own."

"Oh, very profound. Have you followed your own advice?"

Simon is silent for a moment, then he says. "Yes, I think I have, but I do acknowledge it was easier for me."

There's a pause, then I voice my real fear. "What if this situation isn't resolved?"

Simon looks surprised. "Oh, come on, they're never going to pin anything on you, are they?"

"No, but there's another possibility." And I tell him about Lauren's 'not proven' theory.

He takes the point immediately. "That wouldn't be good. But in a way it just strengthens my point."

"How d'you mean?"

"If you were to end up in that situation, it's even more important that you make peace with yourself."

I am silent for a moment. This is somewhere I don't want to go.

"I don't think that's possible," I say at last.

"Of course it's possible, but you have to stop hiding."

We've had this conversation, or a version of it, before. But now, the situation's different. I'm reluctant to acknowledge it but deep inside me, I realise Simon may be right. I need to find a way of turning this setback into an advantage.

We sit there for a moment. Simon is very good at knowing when to say nothing.

Finally I say. "Even if I agreed with you, I wouldn't know how to start."

"No," says Simon, "I don't know either. And you certainly won't get there in one leap. The first thing is to decide what you're going to do for the next six months. I think you need to find some kind of challenge."

My brother is the one person in the world I can be completely honest with. "Simon, I'm frightened."

"I know," he says gently.

"What am I going to do?"

"I don't know, but we'll sort something. Look, just leave it a few days, see what happens. Knowing you, I'm sure you can find something to get your teeth into. Just don't go on ignoring the past. That's all I ask."

5

Lauren is clearly thinking along the same lines as Simon because the next evening she comes home unusually early, catching me by surprise. I've only just started to peel the potatoes for the shepherds pie I plan for supper.

"Here, let me do that," she says grabbing the knife. "You go and find a decent bottle of wine. I want to talk to you."

For a moment I watch her. Seeing Lauren acting all domestic is rare but an impatient gesture from her sends me off to the garage where we keep the wine rack. I find a bottle of Rioja and carry it back to the living room.

"I'll open this and let it breathe."

"To hell with that. I need a drink. If that wine's not breathing then it needs mouth to mouth resuscitation. Give it here."

In passing I notice a pile of semi-peeled potatoes which have been abandoned but Lauren under full sail is not be denied. We sit in our respective armchairs, each with a glass in hand. Lauren, as usual, launches straight in.

"So, what's the plan? You just going to sit here on your fanny for six months with nothing to do?"

"Well …"

"Of course you're not. You couldn't. So a dilemma. I can't leave you here like this, but we've agreed I must go and you feel you must stay."

"That seems to be the case."

"That's a 'yes' then." Lauren has no patience with abstract responses. "So what you need is something positive to concentrate on."

I smile. This is more or less what Simon said, but less pointed as Lauren knows nothing about the family background. "You mean I should start collecting stamps or building a model railway?"

This causes her to laugh out loud. "Those I would love to see. No, I meant something with an intellectual challenge of some kind."

They're both right, of course but for now I'm just enjoying the unusual experience of sitting here with Lauren having a serious discussion. Over the past few years we've both become cocooned in our respective work bubbles, we haven't exactly drifted apart but relaxed moments of casual conversation are rare. It gives me a warm feeling to think my problems have been worrying her too.

We decide to abandon the shepherds pie, order a takeaway, pour another glass of wine and kick a few ideas around. I could learn Chinese. Take up golf. Become a prison visitor. Train to run a marathon. Start a business travel website. As the level of the bottle drops our suggestions get wilder and wilder. It's all great fun but there is nothing that appeals to me.

Suddenly Lauren clicks her fingers. "Heh, I've got it. How about researching the history of your family? See how far back you can go and then write it up as a family archive? Didn't you once tell me you kinda liked the idea of being a writer?"

For a moment I freeze. This comes as a shock, not the least because of the echo of the conversation with Simon. It's true that one of my unrealistic childhood dreams was to become a successful writer. I liked the thought of the imagined lifestyle. Freedom to do what I wanted, when I wanted. Recognised wherever I went. Nice house, plenty of money, romantic love. Complete fantasy of course, but in my teens it symbolised the need to escape from the life I had and hated. It was never a serious option, just one of those dreams that never quite went away.

For a brief moment I actually think about it. It'd certainly be a challenge and there'd be a lot of research involved, writing, digging around in old records, piecing together bits of the puzzle. But even as the thought comes, it goes again. In spite of what Simon said, I don't think I'm ready to handle the reawakening of the pain, but as I've never shared that pain with Lauren, it's difficult to put that forward as an objection.

Lauren is full of enthusiasm. "I reckon it's a great idea," she says. "It's the kinda thing people always say they'll do when they have the time but most people never get round to it. Well, the one thing you're going to have for the next few months is time, buster. What d'you think?"

"It's not a bad idea," I say cautiously, reluctant to spoil the sharing mood.

"I think it's a great idea. I'd love to know more about your family. I'm sorry I never met your parents. Neither you nor Simon ever seem to talk about them, do you?"

"No, I suppose we don't."

"And it's just what you need right now. A project. A new challenge. A reason to get up in the morning."

Now is not the moment to go further down that path so on that note we go to bed.

6

LAUREN

She woke at 5:45 as she always did. She slid out of bed, leaving Richard still asleep, and headed for the shower. Five minutes on the treadmill, ten minutes on the rowing machine, a bowl of muesli and by 6:30 she was ready to leave the house. It was still strange to be doing this alone. Usually by now Richard would also be up, packing a case for his latest trip, or opening his laptop to start compiling a report. They would greet each other briefly, have a quick word about evening plans and go their separate ways.

But no more. It had taken a week or so but at last he was managing to sleep for a bit longer. No point in waking him, she thought, nothing for him to get up for today. She shook her head, still grappling with this inconceivable idea.

Her day passed in the usual turmoil of meetings, reports, briefings, discussions and somehow, in between, finalising the plans for New York. She'd worked hard for this six month secondment, laid everything on the line and had been counting the days until she left. Then, just for a second, when she heard about Richard and this fraud investigation she thought it was all in jeopardy. She felt she had to offer to stay, but there was a sense of physical relief when he said no. Deep down she was also pleased he didn't want to come with her. This was her chance, her big chance, and she wanted to be free to concentrate on it without any distractions.

She was still worried about him though and was glad

they'd discussed his situation together and pleased she'd come up with a project for him to concentrate on while she was away. She knew he would have to have something positive to do and the family research project was ideal. He could explore all the sources of information and worry away at them until they yielded answers. And it was something they could share, talk about together, even at a distance.

Result.

She was feeling tired but content when she got home around eight that night, ready to eat, ready to talk, exchange views about their respective days. She would ask him where he would start, mother's side or father's. She was determined to show a positive interest then, secure in the knowledge that he was happily occupied, she could think about her own departure in five days' time.

Then within a few minutes of getting home it all went wrong.

7

It all begins to go wrong from the moment Lauren gets home. I know she's not going to understand but I have to tell her.

"I've been thinking about this idea of researching my family," I say.

"Good," she says, "I can see it'll take some planning but —"

"And I'm not going to do it."

She stops and looks at me. "You're not?"

"No."

"But I thought we'd agreed."

"No. We didn't. You put forward a suggestion, a good suggestion, one worth thinking about, but now I've thought about it, and I don't want to do it."

"Why not?"

"Well, it's difficult to explain, I don't know, it just doesn't appeal. I don't particularly want to know more about my family."

I can see the questions running through her mind. I've never told Lauren anything about my life before I met her, something she has never understood, but she stopped asking some time ago. For a moment I wonder if she's going to push me but she doesn't. After a pause she simply returns to the main question.

"So we're back to square one?"

"Not quite. I've come up with another idea. It's going to be one hell of a challenge but a challenge is what I need."

Lauren looks sceptical. "What kind of challenge?"

I take a deep breath. This is where it's going to get difficult, especially as I can't really explain it to myself. I'm not lying to Lauren, the family history suggestion was, theoretically, a good idea – but, for me, facing my family life head-on is dangerous territory and I know I can't do it. However, while thinking about her suggestion my mind has, inevitably, gone back to my childhood and that has sparked a completely different idea – an off-the-wall idea, but the more I think about it, the more I want to do it. Back then, in the bleak desert of childhood, there was one, just one, beacon of light. That's what I'd like to go back to, but it's going to be difficult to sell it to Lauren.

"I want to try and trace a girl I knew at primary school."

"Primary school? You mean Elementary School? You want to trace a child?"

"Well, she won't be a child now, will she? This was over forty years ago."

"Sure. So why now? Who is she? What's so special about her?"

"She's just someone I remember from my last year at primary school."

"And you had the hots for her?"

I wince. There's something about the Americanism that clashes with a tender memory.

"I liked her, yes. But it was a long time ago."

"It sure was. What do you want to do – find an old bed companion to keep you warm while I'm away?"

"Lauren, for heaven's sake. We were eleven years old."

"Sure, but as you've already pointed out she's not a child now and neither are you."

"Look. I don't know where she is, I don't even know if she is still alive, I don't even know if she'll remember me."

"Not that hot a romance then."

"It wasn't a romance. It was … it was … an attraction."

"An attraction." Lauren takes a deep breath. "Okay, let's suppose I buy this nostalgia angle, what do you hope to gain when you find her?"

"I don't know. I suppose I'd just like to know what she made of her life. How she got on after school. Is she happy."

"Is she happy? Are you nuts? I wouldn't bloody well be happy if some guy suddenly jumped out at me after forty years and asked me if I'd had a good life. I'd call the cops."

"It probably won't come to that. It's quite likely I'll never find her."

"So why do it then?"

"It's a challenge, as I said."

"Sounds more like a complete boondoggle to me."

I'm starting to get impatient. "Well, if I want to spend my time doggling boons, whatever the hell that means, then why shouldn't I? It's no skin off your nose. You won't be here."

There's an uncomfortable silence then Lauren turns away. "No, I won't, will I?" she says. "Five days from now and you can screw who you like."

She walks out of the room. I slump. I knew it'd be bad but I didn't think it would be this bad. Perhaps I shouldn't have told her. Perhaps I should have let her go off to New York thinking I was happily immersed in old family letters and church records.

The door opens and Lauren's head appears. "I'm putting a

fish pie in the microwave. Okay with you?"

"Fine."

"Right. Five minutes." And she disappears again.

It's a silent meal. At the end of it I gather up the plates and head for the dishwasher. Then I come back with the scotch bottle and two glasses.

"You're going away in a few days. It seems a pity to fight."

She nods and I pour two measures. She takes a drink then puts the glass down rather hard.

"You're right. I'm sorry. What you do while I'm away is entirely your business."

"Yes, but for the record I have no plans to screw anyone, as you so elegantly put it."

"I didn't really think you had."

"I just need a challenge. I can't stagnate."

"So you keep saying." She takes another drink. "I don't think you'll find her, you know."

"Maybe not. We'll see."

"I don't think you'll find her because I don't think it's her you're really looking for. I think you're searching for your lost childhood."

"Oh, spare me the pyschobabble, please."

"Call it what you like. That's what I think. You never talk about it. You have no family photos. I've never met any relation of yours other than Simon. Somewhere along the line, buster, you broke a connection and now you're trying to join the bits up again."

Only one bit, I think – the part that's bearable. We sit in silence for a moment then Lauren drains her glass and stands up.

"Well, I've got some paperwork to finish. You do whatever

you want but I think you're nuts."

At the door she pauses and turns. "What's the name of Love's Lost Dream anyway?"

I think back to that classroom – wooden desks, dusty blackboard, blurred faces, old memories.

"Her name's Julie. Julie Orford."

JANUARY 1962

A crowded classroom. Thirty-eight children. Thirty-eight 11 year olds in a classroom designed for around twenty-five. Desks tightly pushed together. Narrow gangways. It's nearly the end of the morning. The arithmetic lesson is drawing to a close. At the next desk to Richard is Suzanne Duncan. Behind him is a boy, name no longer remembered, but from time to time he stretches out his legs and kicks the back of Richard's chair.

Richard finishes his test. Closes his book. Sits back. Glances across the room and there she is. Julie Orford. She wears a neat, green skirt and a white blouse. Her light brown, almost but not quite blond hair just covers her ears. Her face is oval, not round, slightly longer than you would expect. Not flashily beautiful in the way that, say, Suzanne next to him is beautiful, but Julie has what in memory he thinks of as elegance, though whether his 11 year old self would have used that word, is unlikely.

She is sitting next to her friend, Linda, who is a complete contrast. Small, very blond, perky. Always chattering. He knows that Linda, and Suzanne for that matter, are attractive, but he only has eyes for Julie. He doesn't have the words for what he is feeling — not then — but there is a calmness about her, something in her bearing, her personality that touches his heart. He thinks she is lovely.

At that moment — he remembers it so clearly — she

looks up. Sees him watching her and smiles.

She smiles at him and his world is changed.

SIMON

Simon was emptying the dishwasher when Rita came through to the kitchen to say that Lauren was on the phone. He liked his sister-in-law and assumed she was ringing to say goodbye before she left for New York. But it wasn't that. He listened as she told him about the conversation she'd had with Richard and the way he intended to use this unexpected and unwanted free time.

He heard the exasperation in her voice. "Gee, Simon, I don't know what to say to him. This idea is kinda crazy. It's not the girl – the woman, I mean – I'm not bothered about her. It's just the whole thing is so pointless. A complete waste of time. I know how much he likes a challenge but he's chasing some kind of childhood fantasy and even if he finds her, which I doubt, he'll be disappointed. He'll be in a worse place than when he started. Will you have a word with him? Please? You know what I mean, don't you? The whole idea's nuts."

Lauren thinks I'm nuts. Simon also thinks I'm nuts but he takes me to the pub to say so.

"You're nuts."

"I know."

He looks at me thoughtfully for a moment. "Is this crazy idea of yours my fault?"

I give a little laugh. "I suppose it is. Look at the past, you said, and you'll find something to get your teeth into. Well I have."

"Hmm. Not quite what I had in mind. Do you seriously intend to try and hunt down some girl you haven't seen for, what, forty odd years?"

"Thought I'd give it a go."

"But what's the point?"

I pause before answering. It's a fair question but not easy to explain. "I can't just pull a hobby out of thin air, Simon. We agreed I need something that's a real challenge. 'Garden leave' they call it – well, can you seriously see me spending six months tending the garden?"

He grins. "Hardly, but I don't think you're meant to take it literally. Your boss's PA isn't going to expect a bunch of home-grown flowers when you're finally reinstated."

"She wouldn't get them anyway. I wouldn't give that bitch anything."

He raises an eyebrow. "Fair enough – no gardening then

– but why this?"

"Why not?"

"I just can't see what you hope to gain. Lauren says you discussed researching the background to our family. Write a short history about us."

"Is that such a good idea? Really?"

"I don't know. I must admit I suspected it was her idea rather than yours, but you might find it cathartic, bearing in mind what we were talking about the other day."

"I don't think so. Even if you're right, and I'm still not sure about that, maybe this my way of edging my way into it somehow. Lauren's research idea is more of a head-on crash."

"Maybe it needs a crash."

"Well, if it does I'm not ready for it."

There's a long pause. Simon looks at me, I look at him. Finally he says, "No. Pity though. Real research is the kind of thing that'd suit you down to the ground. You're the one who can string words together and make sense. I'm just a guy who mends fuses."

Considering the fact that Simon is a partner in a chain of very successful electrical wholesalers which stretch right across south London, I think this is something of an understatement. I grin and then shake my head. "I'm not a writer. I came to terms with that long ago. Childhood dreams, ways of escape, fantasy houses, that's all."

"Fantasy houses?"

"Yes. It was a bit silly really. I'd lie in bed, imagining these amazing houses where I could live. Have a luxurious lifestyle and … and …"

"Be safe?"

"A sanctuary, yes."

"Security."

"All very silly. Just dreams."

He nods. "Yes. But we needed those dreams didn't we?"

There's a pause, then I say, very quietly. "I still do."

We share a silence. Memories vivid to both of us but seldom discussed even now. It is not a comfortable silence, but then we both look up and catch each other's gaze. Simon speaks first.

"Richard, I've never asked. It's not my business, but have you ever told Lauren ... about ... about Anne ..."

"No. Did you ever tell Rita?"

There's a pause and then he gives a tilt of his head which is halfway between a shake and a nod. "Yes and no. A little. I told her about how Mum was and having to be the responsible older brother."

"Has she ever asked about it since?"

"At first, yes, but I've only ever said as much as I want to say." He looks at me steadily. "What about Lauren?"

"Oh, she asked. She's American. Americans always ask."

"What did you say?"

"Nothing. I clammed up. Wasn't as tactful as you."

"And was that it?"

For a moment I'm lost in thought. Finally I say, "No, that wasn't it. There were other occasions, one in particular. Came out of the blue and I lost my rag. It wasn't good."

"Ah. Not easy, is it? It's not something I've ever wanted to share. Except with you, of course."

That comment pleases me but then he goes on. "But the difference is, I've put it all behind me. You haven't."

"Oh, here we go again."

"I meant what I said the other day. You have to let it go

37

sometime, Richard. It's not worth it."

"I can't."

"You mean you won't." He pauses for a moment and looks at me. "Or perhaps I'm wrong. Perhaps you are starting to face it in your own way. This idea you have of trying to track down Julie. What's that except revisiting the past?"

"That's different."

"Is it? I wonder."

I say nothing. I have an uncomfortable feeling he may be right. Simon is usually right. I don't know. At this stage I don't want to know. I want to keep it simple.

"It's just something to do. A problem to worry away at, a challenge, an intellectual puzzle to solve. That's all."

Simon sighs. I'm not sure he believes me. "Have it your own way. But what was so special about this Julie? I don't remember her."

"Well, you wouldn't, would you? You were two years ahead of me. You'd already left Modbury Road."

"True."

"It's odd, isn't it. No idea why, but I can remember a number of names from back then. Though I can't put faces to all of them."

"But you remember this Julie."

"Oh, yes. I remember Julie."

"What was so special about her?"

"Hard to say. She smiled at me. I liked her."

"How did she feel about you?"

"Much the same, I think. Maybe. Who knows. Looking back it's hard to realise how innocent 11 year olds were then. I know she liked me but I suppose neither of us knew what to do about it. Although there was one afternoon in the park ..."

My voice trails off. It's easy to massage memory but I don't want to feed any latent suspicions that Simon or Lauren might feel about why I want to find Julie.

I cover it up by saying briskly, "I don't know why I want to find her again. Perhaps because she was the first girl who ever smiled at me, perhaps it was some kind of light relief, contrast to life at home. I really don't know. I've just never forgotten her."

"Okay." He eats a few crisps. "let's suppose you do find her, what then? You're not hoping to revive a forty year old embryonic love affair, are you?"

"Don't be silly. Of course not. And it never was a love affair."

"She's not still the 11 year old willowy girl of your childhood dreams, you know, Richard. She's fifty plus, like you; probably overweight, probably lots of kids, probably tired and disillusioned."

"You're a right weary wally, aren't you?"

"Just trying to be realistic. Why not just leave the memory intact?"

He pauses, glass in hand. "Everything's all right between you and Lauren, isn't it?"

I shrug. This is hard to answer. "There's nothing particularly wrong, if that's what you mean. To be honest we don't see much of each other these days, long hours, demanding jobs, and so on. Only now I won't have a demanding job for a while, and she's going away for six months."

In his usual way, Simon gets straight to the vulnerable point in my defences. "You're going to be on your own in an empty house."

"Yes."

"So why don't you just go with her?"

"She suggested that, but I don't want to spend six months in New York. If I'm going to just sit around, I'd rather do it here. Anyway I need to be on hand with this investigation and everything."

He nods. "Yes, I can see that."

"So think of this Julie thing as a task, a quest if you like. It won't be easy but that's the point and at least it'll stop me getting bored. It's either that or paint your house for you and I'm not that keen on ladders."

I'm trying to reassure him for once, rather than the other way round. There's a pause, then Simon says, very gently. "Nice try, Richard but whatever you say, I think this *is* about our childhood and you're starting to look for a way back – an indirect way maybe, but a way back all the same."

"I think you're reading too much into it."

"I hope not. I know I've said it before, but guilt is very corrosive, especially when it's unjustified. You can't bury it under long hours and work-related stress for ever."

I flinch and he goes on.

"One day you'll retire. Then you really will have time on your hands. Permanently. I hope you're ready for that?"

"Oh, come on. I'm a long way off retiring."

Simon gives me the kind of look that passes between brothers when they both know what's not being said is more important than the out loud words.

"Okay," he concedes, "I can see you're set on this. I still don't think you're being honest with yourself but it's worth remembering that any action inevitably causes some kind of reaction."

"You what?"

"Let me put it another way. You start tracking down people from your past, people you haven't seen, or even thought about for forty years or more. They won't have thought about you either and then suddenly you pop up. Whether you're asking questions or just being there, you're bound to cause ripples and who knows what those ripples might do."

I am silent. I hear the warning but I'm fixated on this search now. I am not ready to let it go.

"They might not all be bad ripples ..."

Simon laughs. "You've made your mind up, I can see that. Okay, let the ripples take care of themselves." He finishes his beer and pushes his glass across the table. "Your round. And I'll have another packet of cheese and onion."

When I get back with the refills Simon has obviously been doing some thinking. "If you really want to find this girl, why not use a private investigator? They'll know where to start digging. In fact, I could even put you on to someone. We've used him once or twice to pursue bad debts."

"I don't want to get someone else to do the work. The whole idea is to give me something to do."

Simon grins. "Just as I thought."

"What?"

"Oh, come on, Richard, you could take up golf or ballroom dancing if you just wanted something to do. There's more to all this, even if you won't admit it. Oh, and you forgot the crisps."

11

Later that night lying in bed, Lauren still downstairs working, I think over what Simon had said. Am I just looking for a safe way back to face those childhood memories? Although I've spent most of my life trying to bury them I've never succeeded. Simon is right. Guilt – real or imagined – is corrosive.

Those memories are part of me that I've always refused to share with anyone, except Simon of course. Although, even there I've held back. No two memories are ever the same, of course, but even so we don't talk about them.

Superficially, I am good with people – I couldn't do the job I do otherwise, but I don't let anyone get close. I don't talk about myself, not even to close friends. I'm not actually sure I have any close friends.

There's Lauren, of course. Meeting her was one of the best things that ever happened to me, although I didn't realise it at the time. Over the years, I had superficial relationships, but deep involvement – no way. Then somehow Lauren slipped under my guard and I've never regretted it. But even with her I've never been completely honest. And now, as she prepares for her trip to New York, there's a slight barrier between us, barely acknowledged before in the frenetic lifestyle we both lead, but there all the same.

Sometimes at night when I can't sleep or when I'm dozing on a plane, my childhood comes creeping back, insidious, demanding, inviting despair. Over the years I've learned how to fight this – and one way is to remember Julie Orford.

I'm not stupid of course. The memories I have of her probably bear very little relationship to the reality of that time but that's not the point. When I was rehearsing in my mind how to explain this to Lauren I thought of Julie as a beacon of light. Perhaps that's a good way of looking at it. Perhaps, in my lonely, soon to be lonelier, existence I need a beacon – to guide me through the unfamiliar territory I'm now facing.

Or maybe I just want to prove to myself that I'm not finished, that I can still rise to a challenge. And trying to find Julie after all these years will certainly be a challenge.

I'm not sleepy so I get up again and go down to my study. I sit at the desk, open my personal laptop and type a heading:

THE SEARCH FOR JULIE ORFORD

I begin to map out a strategic plan the way I would do for a project at work. First, what hard and fast information do I have? Not a lot. Her name, or her name back then. She may well have married, perhaps more than once, so her surname may not be much use. Her age. Not her exact age, but she was obviously roughly the same age as me because we were in the same year at school. Her address. That I remember, why after all these years I don't know, but back then I went to some trouble to find out where she lived. 26 Cumbernauld Court, a block of flats down by the shops. I wonder if they're still there or if they have been re-developed. Well, it'll be easy enough to find out.

I think for a minute. What else do I know? Very little. After Modbuy Road, I went on to an all boys grammar school but I have no idea where Julie went. However she did have a close friend, another girl who sat next to her in class. A girl smaller than Julie, with blond, fluffy hair, used to wear tartan skirts. Linda, I think, yes Linda Montgomery. That was it.

Surprised at my own memory I begin to jot down the names of others I can remember from my class that year. Rodney Montana, of course. We'd been close friends, both went to the same grammar school but drifted apart after a few years. Then there was the very tall, thin boy, what was his name, always polite but rather aloof. No good at football.

Heather Westcott, also tall and conventionally attractive. Terry Baldwin, lean and rangy, always looking for a fight, often in trouble. Suzanne Duncan, Frank Lomax, Mary Jenkins, Roger Fisher. Where are all these memories coming from?

I count up the names. Including Julie that makes ten people I can remember from a class of over thirty. Not bad going after forty plus years, though how much good they will do me I have no idea.

I study the screen but can't think of any other hard and fast facts. The basic data is pretty slim. I think for a moment. What sort of things can one do to try and find someone after all this time?

Start from the basic data.

The school. Assuming the Modbury Road School is still there they might well have records of which schools the various pupils went on to. Whether they'll give me that information is another matter but I can ask. There's the internet of course, I've never actually used social media but it'll be worth trying, though the surname would be a problem if she married.

Then there's the Electoral Roll. Back in 1962 I went into

our local library and used the Electoral Roll to find out Julie's address. Presumably those rolls still exist so I could perhaps discover how long her family had stayed in Cumbernauld Court. The final course of action, or the only one I can think of at the moment, is to try and find some of the others who were in our class and see if they remember her, perhaps even stayed in touch.

To be honest, none of it looks very promising but I have to start somewhere.

Meanwhile I decide I won't do anything until after Lauren has left for New York. I don't want to exacerbate the situation and I'd like to spend some time with her – or as much time as her work allows – while she's still here. Time enough to turn detective when she has gone.

I close the laptop and go back to bed.

12

LAUREN

The departure hall at Heathrow was as chaotic as ever. Lauren had asked Richard to drive her to the airport but once she'd checked her baggage she said there was no point him hanging around. The truth was that she didn't like protracted partings and he seemed to agree. There was an awkward moment but then, almost at the same time, they reached out for each other and hugged tightly.

"Don't let the arseholes get you down, Richard," she said. "Kick 'em where it hurts."

He grinned. "Too right, I will." Then he very gently kissed her. "Text me when you get there. Take care of yourself and I hope it all goes well. I know it will."

He turned and vanished into the crowd and for a moment she felt all the old loneliness return. Then her practical common sense kicked in. For the next few months she was on her own again, and work was the answer to that as she'd learned long ago. She picked up her hand luggage and headed for security.

Now she sat nursing a cup of coffee waiting for the flight to be called. The last few days before her departure had been a little strained. They hadn't spoken again about Richard's plans. They had concentrated on the practical arrangements of living apart for six months, separated by an ocean and perhaps by more than that. She was surprised and a little upset to realise that leaving felt like being left. However, her professional side knew there was no room for emotional upheaval if the next six months were to be a success.

Her flight was called. She picked up her bag and headed towards the gate and, as she went, she gradually began to fade out all thoughts of Richard and Weybridge and became focused on what lay ahead. By the time the plane was gaining height over Windsor she had herself well under control.

13

It is strange leaving her there, just walking away, but I realise she doesn't want to protract the parting and I don't either. We're both used to saying goodbye, but today it feels different. Whether that's because she's going for a longer period this time or whether it's because of my plans while she's away, I have no idea. It's just different.

I feel at a loose end. I wonder if I should call Sally at the office but resist the temptation. If there was any news she'd have called me and I recognise the impulse as no more than a need to reach out to the world I know. It would be to seek comfort, but ultimately would offer no comfort.

I'm definitely restless and I don't want to go home so in the end I rescue the car from the short-term car park and head south to the little village of Bosham Quay on Chichester Harbour. Lauren and I came here for a day out together when she first arrived in the UK so that seems kind of appropriate today. It is one of the most peaceful places I know and, as it is a mid-week autumn day, I have it almost to myself.

I sit on the stone wall overlooking the harbour, watching the ducks and the gulls. After about ten minutes I feel the urge to get up and go and do something else but I fight it. I have to learn to linger. I need to get used to having time to spare.

I force myself to go on sitting and after a while a small miracle occurs. I have sat here, briefly, many times before, enjoyed the view and moved on. Now, sitting with no time pressure other than my own impatience, I begin to notice details. I realise I'm not looking at 'ducks' but at a variety of different swimming birds. Presumably they're all ducks of one kind or another but I've never noticed the differences before.

That little boat over there with its name painted on the bow. As it swings to its anchor in the outgoing tide I see that the name painted on the other side is not the same. Why would that be? Has the owner changed its name and only got round to painting one side? Was he called away in the middle of the job and forgot to come back to it?

I have lunch in the village pub and I take my time over it. Afterwards I walk along the shoreline for a while and then head for home. With time on my hands I decide to try and get back to Weybridge using as few main roads as possible. It's an interesting exercise and I get lost more than once but it doesn't matter, there's no hurry and the effort of unravelling myself from narrow lanes leaves no time for unwanted thoughts. In the late afternoon I find myself somewhere near Dorking so on the spur of the moment I give Simon a ring.

"Hi, it's me. I saw Lauren off to New York this morning."

"Oh, of course, it was today, wasn't it? What you doing now?"

"I'm on the edge of Dorking. Do you fancy a drink? It's almost on my way home."

"Good idea, and you can do me a favour too."

"What's that?"

"My car's been in for service. I'm at home and I need a lift to go and collect it. Rita's out this evening."

"No problem. I'll pick you up in, what, twenty minutes?"

I collect Simon from his home on the outskirts of Epsom

and he directs me to a small industrial estate near Ashtead.

"Why d'you come all the way down here to get your car serviced?"

"'Cos Gus is very good and not expensive. He's a right nutter but what he doesn't know about engines isn't worth knowing."

"What sort of nutter?"

"He's in the TA. Loves all that army stuff. Fascinated with guns, weapons, anything that will do maximum harm. Did a stint in Afghanistan and loved it."

"Loved it?"

"That's what he said."

"He does sound like a nutter."

Gus turns out to be very tall, very thin and very shy. Can hardly meet my eye when Simon introduces us. Apart from the fact he's wearing camouflage trousers and a once-white T-shirt with the legend '*Come back Guy Fawkes, all is forgiven*' plastered across it, he doesn't seem to be scary at all.

I ask him what it was like in Afghanistan and his eyes light up.

"Amazing."

"Really?"

"Oh, yeah. It's what we train for. It was a real buzz. You can't imagine what it's like."

He's right there. I can't.

We collect Simon's car, I follow him home and we go out for a curry together. He asks me about my quest and I say, now Lauren has gone, I'll get started on it tomorrow.

When I eventually get home I watch the ten o'clock news and then as I'm preparing for bed I get a text from Lauren.

"Arrived safely. Apartment small but fine. Will call soon."

It is signed with a capital L and two "x"s.

Somehow the brevity of it fits this rather strange day.

14

The first few days after Lauren leaves are not fruitful. It doesn't take me long to discover that actual detective work is nothing like stories on the TV. Not that I ever thought it would be, but I had expected to turn up something. I'm now five days in and haven't made much progress.

On Day One I do nothing, or nothing connected with my project anyway. I do some shopping. I buy a lot of stuff that I like but which Lauren doesn't. I do some washing, then some ironing. I tidy my study, including washing the windows. Our cleaner, Mrs Atkins, is going to have a surprise when she comes tomorrow. I put last week's papers in the recycling bin. I rearrange the books on the shelves. I oil the hinges on the garage doors – a job I've been meaning to do for the last five years.

I am procrastinating.

I know I'm procrastinating and am determined to do something about it so I go down the pub for scampi and chips.

On Day Two I take myself in hand. I'm at my desk by eight-thirty and work solidly on my strategic plan, breaking it down into possible lines of enquiry: internet searches and social media sites, Modbuy Road school itself, old pupils from that last year in primary school, electoral roll searches.

Using those headings, I draw up an Action List. It pays to be methodical but after a while I run out of ideas.

I make a coffee for myself and Mrs Atkins, who is already marvelling at the clean windows. I don't know what to do next so I take my coffee into the conservatory with a plain digestive biscuit and sit there looking out at the rain.

I've never really watched rain before. Well, you don't, do you? You're either indoors where it isn't relevant or outdoors trying to stay dry until you can get indoors again.

It's quite interesting actually. When the rain is heavy you can actually see the drops moving sideways, caught in the wind. When the rain is light you can hardly see the individual drops but you can see the way they splash onto the window, flatten into two dimensions and trickle down the glass. Sometimes they hit a horizontal surface and then they bounce like an aqua-acrobat. Fascinating.

And I'm procrastinating again.

I go back to my laptop and check my emails. Normally there'd be dozens of them by this stage of the day, but all the office ones have been diverted so there's very little. I check the BBC News website. I play three games of solitaire – none of them come out. I re-read my strategic plan and adjust the punctuation on page three. I make another coffee. How on earth do people pass the day when they have nothing to do?

I take an early lunch. Read the paper. Then I close my eyes and think about my next step? I have to crack this block. Even if my search is going to fail at the first hurdle, I can't spend the next few months playing solitaire and making coffee.

I need fresh air so I get in the car and drive down to Byfleet. An hour walking along the side of the Basingstoke Canal and not only do I feel refreshed, virtuous and ready to get going again, but some practical ideas are starting to come.

I've remembered the names of several people who were

in that distant class with me, but I haven't seen any of them since my teenage years. This is going to make finding them as difficult as finding Julie herself. Never mind. When you hit a dead end you have to move sideways to find a way round. Who else of my age do I know who might have stayed in touch with one of my old classmates?

The trouble is I don't really have friends, only people I know. It's odd really. My annual appraisals always bang on about how good I am with people and I am, so long as they stay at arm's length. Lauren is the same. Professional. Maybe we recognised that in each other. She was very much a solitary figure when I first met her and, although I knew I loved her forthright nature from the very beginning, we circled each other warily for a long time before deciding we could trust each other. That had been a defining moment for me. In previous relationships with women I had always shied away at the last minute.

Shying away makes me think about Tina. She was my first betrayal, or at least that's the way I remember it. Teenage is such an intense time, everything seems larger than life. In later years whenever I broke off a relationship with a woman I just shrugged and moved on. But Tina was different.

Although it turned out that we lived quite close to each other, we didn't meet until our teens, at the local youth club, a kind of dance hall above the Co-op in the High Street. A table tennis table, a half-size snooker table, a record player, a small kitchen where we made coffee, a harassed and out-of-his-depth Youth Club Leader, a lot of noise and exuberance.

I don't know why I went really. I was never at ease with other people my own age and I wasn't much good at dancing, couldn't shed enough inhibitions probably. But I did enjoy table tennis. It was about the only sport I was ever any good at, and that was what tempted me.

The first time I went to the club, sidling uncomfortably into the hall, Tina came across and welcomed me, made coffee for us both and started chatting. She was so open, so friendly that I almost relaxed. I was eighteen, she was sixteen or seventeen, but gradually over the next few months we kind of drifted together. I think she hoped it might develop but I wasn't willing to lower my defensive shields and anyway I was about to go off to university and didn't want to take any commitments from home with me.

"But you'll be coming home in the holidays, won't you?" she asked.

"Vacations, not holidays," I said in an unnecessary put down. "And no, I don't think I will."

I was determined never to come home again but I couldn't tell her that.

I know Tina was sad to see me go. I know because she told me so. My own feelings were more a sense of relief which is why I call it a betrayal. However, strangely enough she stayed in touch with me and several years later when she got married she asked me to be an usher at her wedding. I still get Christmas and birthday cards from her but I haven't seen her for years. Thinking of her now though, something comes back to me. I can't remember what primary school she went to but I am pretty sure that one of her friends had a brother who was with me at Modbury Road school.

Could be worth a try. I'm pretty sure I've got a phone number for her somewhere so I could give her a ring in the morning.

15

TINA

Tina Cummings heard the phone ringing as she staggered up the front path with the first load of shopping but by the time she'd put down the bags, delved into her handbag, found the key and opened the door, the phone had stopped.

She made three more journeys to the car, dumping the various bags on the kitchen table. She flicked the switch on the kettle, rummaged around for the frozen stuff and got that into the freezer then, leaving the rest for a moment, made herself a cup of coffee, sat down, picked up the phone and punched in 1471. She didn't recognise the number but she pushed 3 anyway and heard the distant ringing tone start.

"Hallo, this is Richard Kirkwood."

16

I can hear her astonishment when I give my name. Only to be expected really. It must be at least ten years since we last saw each other.

"Richard. Good heavens. What a surprise. How are you?"

"Fine, how about you?"

"Mustn't grumble. Got the grandchildren coming this weekend so I've been doing a big shop."

"Grandchildren? You've got grandchildren?"

I hear her laugh. "Three of them, don't you ever read the Christmas cards I send you."

"Yes, of course. Sorry."

"How's your wife?"

"Lauren. Oh, she's fine too. She's away at the moment. In New York."

"New York? Golly. Work or pleasure?"

"Oh, work definitely."

"Isn't she a … solicitor? Have I got that right?"

"A lawyer, yes. She's normally based in London but right now she's on a six month secondment to their head office."

"Six months. Golly. I hope you can cook."

"'Course, I can." I refrain from pointing out that this is the twenty-first century and we share the cooking. "It's a doddle. Just one button on the microwave, isn't it?"

She laughs. "Well, it'll keep you alive. Anyway, what can I do for you? Is there something particular or are you just feeling lonely and want a chat?"

Lonely? Of course, I'm lonely – always have been – but I skip that and hurry on.

"Well, yes, there is something particular as it happens, though it's going to sound a bit strange …"

"Try me."

"Think back to our primary school days—"

"Golly, that's ancient history. You went to Modbury Road, didn't you?"

"Yes – and I think you went to that school up by the station. Is that right?"

"That's it. Crossways. Why the sudden interest?"

"Well, this is a pretty distant memory, but didn't you have a friend who had an older brother in my year at Modbury Road?"

"Several, I think. It was either Modbury Road or Crossways for most of us in that area."

"The one I'm thinking of had an elder brother who was in my year. She would have been younger, of course."

"Golly, let me think … Older brother in the year above … that narrows it down. Ah, I know which friend you mean – Gillian Armstrong. She had a brother, Phillip I think it was."

"That's it! Phillip Armstrong. I remember."

"Okay, so what about him?"

"Are you still in touch with Gillian?"

"Well, sort of, on and off. Bit like you really, Christmas cards, you know. Haven't seen her for yonks."

"I'd rather like to get in touch with her brother. Do you think you could ask Gillian if she could get me an address or phone number or something?"

"Oh, I see. Well, yes, I can try. But I think I need to know why."

So I tell her. Not the full story, just the headlines. About my garden leave, about needing something demanding to get my teeth into and a bit … just a little bit … about Julie.

Bless her, Tina doesn't laugh. If anything there's a touch of sadness about her response, but she agrees to get in touch with Gillian and see what happens.

"I'll let you know how I get on," she says. She pauses for a moment, then goes on. "Richard, as you're on your own why not come down here for a few days and let me and Paul take care of you."

"That's very kind," I say, "but I don't need taking care of."

"I think you do," she says. "You'd be very welcome, only wait till the grandchildren have gone. There's a limit to my nurturing strength."

17

Day Three starts well with my conversation with Tina. I know she'll help if she can and perhaps this is the breakthrough I've been looking for. I won't visit her though, I wouldn't feel comfortable. It's been too long. Perhaps it always was.

I have another look at my Action List but can't think of anything to add. Planning is all very well but I know from experience that there comes a time when you need to stop theorising and do something practical, so I make a decision. I get out the car and set off to rediscover Modbury Road school.

Ever since I decided to pursue this search for Julie I knew that I was going to have to revisit the area where I grew up. I haven't been back there since I first left home, never wanted to, never had a reason to. Now I've got a reason. I'm not looking forward to it but it's unavoidable.

I turn off the by-pass and almost at once I'm in familiar streets. However, when I reach the school I see it has changed quite a lot. Part of the original building has gone, a couple of large extensions have been added and it now has a high fence all round with gates which are firmly locked. Whether that's to keep pupils in or undesirable visitors out is not clear.

I use the intercom by the gate to ask if I can speak to someone but once the tinny voice has established I'm not a parent and don't have an appointment the gates remain firmly shut. In vain I plead that I only need five minutes chat but as

I'm reluctant to shout the full story into a tin box in a public street, the best I'm offered is to go away and write for an appointment.

I drive down to the shops and establish that Cumbernauld Court is still there. More in a spirit of optimism than expectation I knock at the door of number 26 but there's no answer. I can't believe that any of Julie's family still live here but, as our science master at school used to tell us, every hypothesis should be tested.

I walk round the corner to the small branch library I belonged to for so many years. I go in and once again savour the smell of silence and expectation. This was the place where, from the age of eight, I devoured books like a starving man faced with a banquet. First the children's shelves and later the adult ones, taking books almost at random and losing myself in them. I always preferred reading to dancing, another thing that set me apart from many of my peers.

I ask the librarian if they still have copies of the Electoral Roll but apparently they're now kept at the main library. Possibly. Or they might be at the County Registry. However, he suggests I try the internet as most official records are available online these days.

I haven't achieved a lot but I suppose you could call it a 'recce', an up-to-date look at the place where it all began. I ought to call it a day now and go home but I hesitate. There's one last location I ought to see but I don't want to. I tell myself I'm being stupid. My mother's long since dead. It's close on forty years ago. And it's only a house for heaven's sake.

I make up my mind. I drive back to the school and park just outside. It's early afternoon and the roads are empty. I lock the car, take a deep breath and begin walking, following the route I used to take all those years ago moving from a disciplined world to a cold one.

I turn the corner into the street we used to live in. The houses, all alike, sit there quietly familiar under the pale afternoon sun. The main change here is that most of the front gardens have gone, converted into parking spaces. I walk slowly along, lost in memory, but when I finally come round the bend and see our house, I stop. The windows stare back at me, I don't know what's behind them but I can't go on. The memories here are too painful. I turn and almost run back to the car.

I go home, cook a pork chop with mushrooms and eat a whole bar of chocolate. Comfort food.

18

On Day Four I decide it's time to try the internet. A Google search of Julie Orford gives me a number of hits but none look hopeful. I click on a few but either the age is wrong or I can't tell from the limited amount of information offered whether it's the Julie I am looking for or not.

I decide to put a toe into the unfamiliar waters of Facebook so, rather reluctantly, I set up an account and start searching. I find several entries for 'Julie Orford' but most of them are clearly far too young. There is one faint possibility so I click on it but all I get is a picture of a goldfish and an indication that she last posted two years ago. Everything else in her profile is blank. I appreciate the need for privacy but that's no help to me.

I try LinkedIn which is one of the few such sites I'm registered on as my company insisted on it. I hardly ever look at it but I give it a go now. Result – zero. I tell myself that I couldn't really see Julie as a professional woman but then give myself a slap on the wrist. The truth is I know nothing about her since schooldays. She could be alive or dead, she could be in the next street, or in Scotland, or in Australia. She could be married, she could be running a bank or a house of ill repute, or all three at the same time. I have absolutely no idea.

She isn't on LinkedIn though so I come out of that and have another think. The problem with internet sites is that the person you're looking for has to have taken the first step and registered. If they haven't, then you're stuck.

The post this morning brings a letter from my company *Swamplett, Benson and Dring*. I'm slightly surprised to see it's a personal letter written, or at least signed, by the head man himself, Kenneth Bannerman. It's brief but not discourteous. He doesn't refer to the fact that I've by-passed the normal channels by going directly to him over the heads of Hunky or Francesca. He simply says that he's received my letter, he understands why I wrote it and he will ensure that I am kept in the loop. Not quite those words but that's what he means. That's good. At least the situation is now public and I can't just be brushed under the carpet.

I'm beginning to appreciate the scale of the task I've taken on in this search for Julie. I'm happy to put in the graft, I have nothing else to do after all, but where to put it, that's the problem. The only person I stayed in contact with from Modbury Road – and that only for a year or two – was Rodney Montana. I'm sure he'd remember me as I remember him, but I have no idea where he is now.

I think for a moment. I remember quite clearly where Rodney used to live. 23 Fortescue Drive, off Swindon Way. I often went there to tea back then. I liked going there. His mum made a great chocolate cake and was always very welcoming. A stark contrast to my own home life.

The chances of any of his family still being there are pretty slim but, following the 'test every hypothesis' rule, I go back online to a phone directory site and enter the name and address. To my amazement the name 'Montana' appears. C. Montana with a phone number. Could be a coincidence but it's worth a try. I reach for the phone, then stop. Just suppose this really is Rodney's parents they must be getting on a bit by now. It might not be easy to convey who I was and what I wanted on the phone. Probably better if I went and knocked on the door. Job for next week.

Day Five is Sunday. I lie in bed until I know I'm not going to sleep again then I go down the road, buy all the Sunday papers, get some bacon and eggs and come home for a real fry up. I read the papers, I watch some television. Basically I do bugger all for the whole day and find it surprisingly difficult. I've never spent so much time in the house before, certainly not on my own, and I'm surprised to find how unwelcoming it is. I can't think of the right word. Sterile, perhaps? A roof, not a refuge.

I think of Simon and Rita's house, chaotic but welcoming. In spite of our shared childhood, Simon has managed to create a relaxed and happy home while as for me, well, I suppose I just didn't try. Perhaps being on the move all the time relieved me of the need to try. Too many maudlin thoughts. I go to bed.

Day Six and I'm back in the Modbury Road area. I find Fortescue Drive easily and stop outside number 23. It's a little down at heel, paint not peeling but reaching the stage of needing some attention. Garden gate squeaks. Someone ought to oil that, I think, as I walk up the path.

I don't recognise the elderly lady who answers the door but I can't really remember what Rodney's mother looked like back then so that's hardly surprising. What is surprising is her reaction when I say who I am.

"Oh, yes, I remember you," she says in a voice far stronger than her physical appearance would suggest. "You used to come and play with Rodney's train set?"

"Well, yes, I did."

I really did. I remember those days so well. My own train set was kept in a box and I had to get it out every time I wanted to play with it. Rodney's was properly laid out on a baseboard that folded down from the wall in his bedroom. His was much bigger than mine and he had the Hornby Dublo Duchess of Montrose locomotive in green. I lusted after that. All I had was the black Triang 0-6-0 tank engine.

"Yes, you and that other boy, the one with the quiff."

I struggle to remember anyone in our year who had a quiff but she is already moving on.

"Fancy seeing you again after all this time. You'd better come in and have a cup of tea."

Not sure if this is an invitation or a command, I follow her into the house. In the course of the next hour over a mug of the strongest tea I have ever tasted, accompanied by what I take to be last year's custard creams, I learn a number of things, most of which are of no interest whatsoever.

I learn that this really is Rodney's mother. She tells me that Mr Montana – Albert – died about ten years ago, that the wallpaper in the bathroom is always peeling, that the man who kept the toy shop down the road was done for indecent exposure sometime in the 1970s, that the BBC weather forecasts offer much better weather than ITV so if she wants to go out she always watches the BBC, that her sister moved to Wales in 1984 and became very strange, that the man who repaired her roof last year made an inappropriate suggestion to her but did a good job with her tiles, that her shopping bag which was meant to be a 'bag for life' broke on its third outing and that her cat was eighteen years old when it produced a set of kittens.

Judging by the fact that only some of the tea goes into the

mugs when she is pouring, I reckon her eyesight might not be up to scratch so possibly the cat who had the kittens was not the cat who was eighteen years old, but there doesn't seem much point in pursuing that further.

She is clearly lonely and I feel sorry for her. However, I've come with a purpose so I try to steer the conversation in the direction of Rodney, but without success. Eventually, feeling slightly wild-eyed, I decide it's hopeless so I stand up and make a move towards the door.

"Oh, must you go so soon?" she says, "I've enjoyed our little chat, catching up on the old days. You and Rodney and your trains."

Your days, not mine, I think. Then I relent. She really did make the most amazing chocolate cake back in those days. And it isn't her fault that she's grown old. Seizing the opportunity I ask her where Rodney is living now.

"No idea," she says, shaking her head, "but I have a nasty feeling he might be in prison."

My heart sinks. "Prison? Why do you think that?"

She sits there gazing into space. "I do hope he's not in prison," she says, "but he's not been in touch with me for a very long time."

"But why would you think he's in prison? What's he done?"

"I don't know, but he called me a few years ago. Said he wouldn't be seeing me for a while and gave me the number of his cell phone. If it's a cell phone it must mean he's in prison."

I take a deep breath. "Not exactly, Mrs Montana," I say. "A cell phone is just another name for a mobile phone."

I'm not sure this helps her much but at least it's a possible lead. "Do you happen to have the number handy?" I ask. "I thought I might give him a call, chat about old times, you know, train sets and things." I am starting to get desperate.

She looks doubtful. "Not sure where I put it. You might try the coal scuttle."

I'm getting used to her zig-zag train of thought so instead of saying: "coal scuttle" in tones of complete bewilderment, I take a quick look round the room. Sure enough there's a coal scuttle sitting on top of the sideboard. I go across, open it and see it's full of books. I rummage around and find an address book and sure enough under 'R' for Rodney there's a mobile phone number.

Bingo. Or possible bingo. I still don't know if it's a current number. I scribble it down, thank Mrs Montana for the tea and leave. I sit in the car and think. Shall I ring him now or wait till I get home? Remembering my new-found skill for procrastination I decide it's best to get on with it so I dial the number. There is a short delay and then it rings.

RODNEY

Rodney Montana was sitting in a bar in the North Point district of Hong Kong when his cell phone rang. He liked to meet new clients in out of the way places, places where no one he knew was ever likely to see him. This small bar in a narrow alleyway behind the street market was ideal.

He wasn't expecting any calls unless it was the Frenchman cancelling their meeting. He peered at the display but it showed no number. For a moment he considered ignoring it but then curiosity got the better of him and he pressed the button.

"Hallo."

"Is that Rodney Montana?"

"Who wants him?"

"This is Richard. Richard Kirkwood. From school – remember?"

The incongruity of it caught him off balance for a moment. Richard Kirkwood was from another life. Shared homework, train sets, discussing the merits of various saddles in the bike sheds behind the school. Untouched innocence. Another world.

For a moment his innate caution kicked in. Was this a trap? Why would Richard Kirkwood be ringing him after all these years? He hesitated and the voice on the phone went on.

"Look, I'm sorry to disturb you. I'm sure you're busy but I wondered if you could spare me half an hour if I came to see you."

He sounds distant on the phone, distant in manner I mean, but when I ask if I can come and see him, he laughs. I recognise that laugh. We shared many laughs together at Modbury Road and later for the first couple of years at grammar school until we drifted apart.

We even started a '*Laugh A Minute*' club at school to collect the silly things people said. It didn't last long but it was fun for a while. Out of the blue I remember one of them. Our form master: "Boys are forbidden to get wet in the rain."

Presumably he meant "Don't go outside if it's raining" but it struck us as hilarious that the rain would be forced not to land on us because our form master had forbidden it. Amazing what a 12-year-old can laugh at.

Rodney seems tense when he first answers but the laugh relaxes us both. "Richard, good God, you're the last person I'd have expected. How are you?"

"Fine, fine. It's been a long time."

"It certainly has. Must be … what … forty plus years ago …? Another life."

Another life. I suspect I'm going to hear that phrase time and time again during this quest. But Rodney is already moving on.

"Look, now's not an awfully good time …"

"Sure, I understand. So could you spare me a few minutes when it's convenient?"

Again the laugh. "Where you calling from?"

"My home. Well more or less. I live in Weybridge."

"It'd be an expensive few minutes then. I'm in Hong Kong."

I wasn't expecting that. "Oh, I see. When will you be back?"

"I won't. I live here."

"Oh, right. Pity. Wish I'd known. I've been to Hong Kong a couple of times. Work you know."

"Yes, sure. Look, Richard, I'm in a bit of a hurry."

"Oh, yes, sorry. It was just I wanted to ask you about our time at Modbury Road."

"Modbury Road? Primary School? What on earth for?"

"It's just to ask if you remember anyone else in our 11-plus year there?"

I can almost hear the brain cells whirling over the satellite link. Then he says casually.

"Not really, apart from you, of course. No, wait, wasn't there a guy called Baldwin, Terry Baldwin? Was that his name?"

"Yes, I remember him too. Always a bit wild".

"Yeah, he was. I seem to remember being around him was never safe but always fun".

"Not sure I remember the 'fun' bit. Anyone else?"

"Can't think of … No, hang on … Clive … no, Chris … Christopher Everett, I think his name was. Plump guy with specs."

"Oh, him. Yes, I remember. He was always mooning after that blonde girl …"

"Blonde girl?"

"Yeah, the one with the fluffy blonde hair. Quite short,

71

tartan hair band, sat over by the window? Linda something, Linda Montgomery, I think. I've been trying to remember."

Rodney laughs again. "Hey, do you know. I think you're right. Yes, Linda Montgomery, that's it. Never stopped talking. Bit tasty though. Not surprised old Christopher was smitten. Mind you, he never got anywhere. She never reckoned him much. She's great though. Lots of fun."

"Linda Montgomery, yes. Do you remember her friend, Julie Orford? They sat next to each other."

The half beat before he answers is excruciating. Then, "Julie Orford? No, can't say I do? Why do you ask?"

"Oh, nothing really."

"Come off it. You don't start raking up the past from forty years ago without there being a reason."

I think on my feet. I should have been better prepared for this. "Well, actually, don't laugh, I'm writing a novel and I'm just trying to do some research about our early schooldays."

Even from six thousand miles away I can sense the disbelief. Suddenly he sounds distant again. "How did you get this number by the way?"

"From your mum. I couldn't think how to find you but then I remembered where you used to live and just on the off-chance popped round there. Amazing she's still in the same place."

Silence in Hong Kong for a moment and then a muffled mutter which sounds like: "Bugger, never thought of that." Then he's back at full strength.

"Look, I've got to go. Good to hear from you, Richard. Good luck with the ... er ... novel ... Sorry I couldn't be more help."

The phone goes dead.

21

Looking coldly and dispassionately at the facts, I have made no progress in my search for Julie Orford, but Day Six ends with me feeling quite positive. I'm rather puzzled by the conversation with Rodney though. It's not surprising he can't remember much about Modbury Road but I only half believed his "good to hear from you after all this time" voice.

Day Seven. On Day Seven I decide I'm going to stop numbering the days. It serves no useful purpose and it's beginning to look rather freaky.

I phone the office for an update. Francesca is her usual self, that is she spares me thirty seconds of her time to say – with obvious satisfaction – that no progress has been made but the police will be in touch with me this week. I call Sally's mobile but she has no news either. Rumours are flying around but no one seems to know anything. The Regional Manager, Gaynor Wiles, has been in the office and delivered a rah-rah speech about how everything is under control and life goes on as normal and please answer all the questions from the police. Hunky has not been seen in the office for days and Francesca is ruling the roost with a rod of iron.

Sally does give me one piece of information though. They've recalled Mervyn Wilby from Puerto Rico to stand in for me while I'm suspended. Sally can't believe it and neither can I, but it makes me laugh. Old Mervyn is about as efficient as a Formula One racing car with a broken piston, that's why they buried him in Puerto Rico where he could do no harm. I wonder whose bright idea it was to bring him back. Good news for me though. When I'm reinstated I won't have to fight off competition from my stand-in.

The day ends on an odd note. Just after ten as I'm dozing off in front of the television news, my mobile beeps. A text. A short text.

We strongly suggest you say nothing. To anyone. You have been warned.

No sign of who it's from. Number not one I recognise. Doesn't come up on Google either. Decide it's probably been sent to the wrong person and go to bed.

The next day Tina calls.

"Well, I've got what you wanted, Richard. Gillian's given me her brother's phone number."

"That's brilliant! Thanks very much." I grab a pen and scribble it down on the bottom of my shopping list. "Is it an office number or home?"

"Home. He's a barrister apparently, so Gillian says it's probably best to avoid the office. Catch him at home."

"A barrister. Hmm! He'll probably end up asking me questions. Oh, well, thanks, Tina. I'll let you know how I get on."

"Righty ho. And don't forget our invitation. Any time."

"Thanks." And I ring off.

After my experience with Rodney I'm not optimistic about this idea of contacting old pupils from Modbury Road but I decide I might as well give it a go. At the moment I'll grab at anything to fill the hours.

22

PHILLIP

Phillip Armstrong was polishing his third best pair of black shoes when the phone rang. He liked highly polished shoes and had a number of pairs, all identical, though some he found more comfortable than others, an illogical disparity that had always worried him. He sighed, gave a final rub to the shoe he was holding and went to answer the phone.

He was expecting it to be his clerk about the case that was due to start next week but it was an unfamiliar man's voice. "Oh, hallo. Is this Phillip Armstrong, the Phillip Armstrong who used to go to Modbury Road Primary School?"

Modbury Road. It was years since he had thought about Modbury Road. He had a quick flash of memory, standing forlornly on the football field, uncomfortable in shorts, jersey and ungainly boots, hearing the cries of derision from the other boys for kicking the ball in the wrong direction. He had hated football ever since.

The voice on the other end of the phone went on. "This is Richard Kirkwood. I don't know if you remember me. We were in the same class at Modbury Road."

Richard Kirkwood? The name was familiar even after all these years, but he couldn't put a face to the name. Modbury Road. He had travelled a long way since then, physically and mentally. Kirkwood, Kirkwood? Wasn't he the boy who always had his head in a book? And something to do with the school magazine?

The voice was speaking again. "Look, I know this is a bit odd but I'm on a kind of quest. I wonder if you could spare me half an hour if I came to see you."

23

I smell money the moment I arrive at the house. Highgate never comes cheap but this is a beautiful place. I already knew he was a barrister and he made it clear on the phone that if it was a legal matter I wanted to discuss then I would need to talk to his chambers. I assured him it wasn't.

I don't recognise the man who answers the door but then I haven't seen him since 1962 so that's hardly surprising. We do the usual "it's been a long time" stuff and then he disappears to make coffee. There's no sign of anyone else in the house.

The coffee is served in wafer thin, tiny cups, one gulp and it's gone, but there's a large coffee pot on the tray which promises several more gulps to come. The conversation gets off to an awkward start, not helped by me fumbling to be polite and only succeeding in stating the obvious.

"So you're a barrister, Phillip."

"Indeed I am."

"Must be interesting. My wife's a lawyer. She's American."

"Ah, an American. Their system is quite a bit different to ours."

"Yes, I suppose it is."

"So you live in the States now."

"Me? Oh, no. I ... um ... that is we, live in the UK. Lauren works for their London office."

"I see. And you, Richard. How do you earn your daily crust?"

Pompous twat, I think, but I need his help so I just smile. "I work for an international management consultancy."

"How interesting. How does one arrive in management consultancy from Modbury Road?"

I've had enough of this. Politeness ought to flow both ways. "Much the same way as you arrive in barrister's chambers from Modbury Road I imagine. Grammar school, A-levels, university."

He gives a half smile and takes a sip of his coffee. "Congratulations. I don't suppose many of our 11-plus year went on to university. Where did you go?"

He is beginning to get on my nerves. "Cambridge, actually. Robinson College."

"Ah," there's a pause and then he says. "I was at Kings."

That figures, I think, and decide to quit. I'm clearly not going to win this old Modbury Road pupil pissing-up-the-wall contest.

"About Modbury Road," I say.

"Ah, yes. How can I help you, Richard? That was a long time ago."

"It certainly was. How well do you remember the place, our last year in particular?"

He considers before answering. I've already noticed that everything he does is controlled and deliberate. I make a private bet that he's the kind of man who never leaves the house without polishing his shoes first.

"I don't remember it terribly well. Little flashes of memory of course. Football practice where we stood in a circle and the teacher threw the ball at each of us in turn and we either had to head it or trap it with our feet, depending on where he threw it."

"Good Lord, yes, I remember that too. I was rubbish at football."

A thin smile crosses his lips. "Yes, so was I. Preferred cricket. Still do. I'm a member of the MCC."

Yes, you would be, I think. I'm not warming to this man but I persevere.

"Anything else?"

He puts his hand up to his chin in a gesture of thought. A well-rehearsed gesture I think unkindly. "I remember the headmaster," he goes on, "chap called Blenkinsop. Rather pompous I thought. Do you remember School Assembly? The teachers up on the platform, all of us sitting on benches down below clutching our hymn books. Blenkinsop would announce the hymn number, glance at the pianist to make sure she was ready and then say 'Commence'. Never 'let's begin' or anything like that. Always 'Commence'. I've never forgotten that. Pompous."

Pots and kettles come to mind but aloud I say. "I remember the hymn books. Red covers. Dozens of hymns but we only ever sang about six of them."

He nods. "Not very imaginative, were they?" he says, "I've often wondered if they were the only tunes that teacher at the piano could play."

"What about other pupils in our year? D'you remember any of them?"

"Not really. It's so long ago. There was a boy called Martin Green I used to play chess with. We carried on playing for a while after we left Modbury Road but that sort of stopped after a year or so." He thinks for a moment. "I seem to remember someone called Terry Baldwin. He was always in trouble, bit of a rebel as I recall. Then there was a kind of frizzy girl, now what was her name? Sue, was it, Sue Duncan?"

"Suzanne Duncan, yes, I remember her too. And Terry Baldwin as well but I'd forgotten Martin Green."

"Suzanne Duncan, that's it. Quite popular, wasn't she?"

"How about Julie Orford? Do you remember her?"

"Julie Orford? No, I can't say I do. It's all a very long time ago."

There is a pause. He finishes his coffee, proffers the pot and in answer to my nod fills my cup with another gulp. He places his own cup carefully in the saucer and sits back.

"I'm not entirely sure what you're after, Richard, unless it's just a nostalgia trip. Wasn't it Wordsworth who said something like '*The child is the father of the man*?' Curious thought, isn't it, to think our future destinies may already have been settled in that 1960s classroom."

"What a load of bollocks." The vehemence of my response surprises us both. I spoke without thinking, from instinct, and now I'm deeply embarrassed.

"I do apologise. That was very rude of me."

He regards me thoughtfully for a moment. "Oh, I don't know. You get to recognise honesty of response in my profession. Am I to assume they were not happy days for you?"

I am fighting to get myself under control. "If I had thought my destiny was settled when I was eleven years old I would probably have killed myself."

There is a short silence. Then he says. "I appear to have inadvertently touched a raw nerve." I say nothing and he goes on. "I'm sorry if I've upset you but in view of your reaction I don't quite understand why you want to revisit those Modbury Road years?"

I take a deep breath. Since speaking to Rodney I've thought long and hard about how to answer this question. I have my new story all prepared and, although it doesn't sound convincing, I find I don't care. Let the man think what he likes.

"Well," I say, "I've recently been granted a sabbatical from work and I was looking for a project to occupy my time. My wife suggested I should research the history of my family, perhaps write a short piece about us, for the grandchildren, you know."

He nods, his face impassive.

"Well, I started digging around in all the stuff I got from my parents' house after they'd died and I found some letters that seem to suggest that I may actually have been distantly related to one of the other pupils in our 11-plus year. I just thought it might be worth trying to find them to see whether or not this is true. At the very least it's an interesting intellectual exercise."

He nods again. "I presume the person in question is this Julie Orford."

"Well, yes, as it happens." He may be pompous, but he's astute.

"Well, I'm sorry I can't help you. I don't remember any of them very well and I don't remember her at all. The only person I was really friendly with was Martin Green and I haven't heard from him for years. We stopped playing chess together but we did correspond occasionally right up to my first year at Cambridge. Then it just came to a natural end."

"No contact information at all?"

"None recent."

"Well, even an old address might help. I might be able to

81

track him down."

He thinks for a moment. "I suppose that can't do any harm though I think it's a pretty remote chance."

"Everything I'm trying at the moment is a pretty remote chance. I don't suppose this is any more so."

He nods. "Just a minute."

He goes out of the room. After a moment, when it's clear he is not coming back instantly, I lean across the table and pour another thimbleful of coffee. I feel quite shaken, not just at my angry outburst but at the realisation of how raw those feelings are.

It's a good ten minutes before he comes back but when he does he is holding a large blue book.

"Old address book," he says, "took some finding."

"I'm impressed. I doubt I could find anything like that of mine."

He smiles and opens the book. "Let's see, Martin Green. Ah, yes, here we are. 37 Ravensbridge Hill, Uxbridge. No post-code, they didn't have them then."

"Any phone number?"

"Three. All crossed out. Can't help you there."

"Well, thank you anyway." I get to my feet. "As you say, it's a long shot." I fish in my pocket and pull out one of my business cards. "If you do think of anything else, perhaps you'd give me a call. My home number is on there."

He takes it, smiles and shows me to the door.

"Goodbye," he says, "it's been interesting. I hope you find your ... er ... relative."

As I walk down the path I have a strong feeling that I have left the witness box with all my lies exposed.

24

The morning after my visit to Phillip Armstrong I'm woken by the phone. I struggle up towards full consciousness but come wide awake when I realise I'm speaking to a Detective Sergeant Williams. He is perfectly courteous but wants to make an appointment to come and see me. He makes no apology for calling so early. We agree he can come to the house at 11:00 this morning and he rings off.

I shower, shave, have breakfast and wonder how you prepare for a meeting with a policeman when you've done nothing wrong. I decide the smell of fresh coffee is a good start so I rummage around and find Lauren's posh percolator and set it up on the kitchen worktop.

I still have some time to spare so I decide to do a bit more basic research. I go through to my study, google Modbury Road and discover the school has a website which includes a list of staff. The head teacher is Mrs Gina Pitts so I draft an email, explaining that I'm an ex-pupil, making out that Julie Orford and I were actually close friends, and ask if she can tell me what school Julie went on to after the 11-plus. I ping this off without a lot of hope but at least I can tick it off my Action List.

At 10:55 I turn on the coffee percolator. At 10:57 a car pulls into the drive and a man gets out. I'm watching from the window and judge he's in his early thirties, tidy though not unduly smart, clean shaven. He walks across the gravel and as he rings the bell – on the dot of 11:00 - my mobile beeps with a text message.

I open the door and beckon him in, pointing at the phone. "Go through. Won't be a tick."

He nods and smiles and walks past me into the living room. I look at my phone. No indication of who the message is from, but the meaning is clear.

You are being warned. So far you are safe. Say nothing to the police.

Now here's a dilemma.

I join Sergeant Williams in the living room and offer coffee but he declines.

"Thank you, Mr Kirkwood, but you wouldn't believe how many coffees and teas I get offered in the course of a day's work." He sniffs appreciatively. "Wonderful aroma though, isn't it? Don't let me stop you."

I lift my hands to say no. We sit, him in an armchair, me on the sofa. He seems in no hurry to begin which gives me a chance to think. Do I tell him about the text message or not? And what about the one from a few days ago? I'm still pondering this question when he speaks.

"I'm sorry to intrude on your time, Mr Kirkwood, but I wonder if we can just get a few formalities out of the way."

For a moment I half expect him to say: *You do not have to say anything but it may harm your defence ... etc. etc.* But he doesn't. All he says is: "Do you have some identification, sir, just so I know you really are Mr Kirkwood?"

"Of course. Passport okay?"

"Fine."

So I go and get my passport and hand it to him. He looks

at it, looks up at me to compare the photo, then hands it back with a smile.

"Thank you, Mr Kirkwood." Then silence. I wait. There's clearly something else I'm meant to do or say. I don't know what it is but I do recognise the tactic. Stay quiet long enough and sooner or later the other person will break the uncomfortable silence and that's the moment when they say something they shouldn't.

However, I'm a veteran of difficult negotiations so I say nothing and eventually he gives in.

"You should really be asking to see my ID at this point, Mr Kirkwood, in fact you should have done that before letting me in."

"I suppose I should. Okay, let's see it then."

He pulls out his warrant card and hands it to me. I look at it. It looks genuine but then how would I know? I'm starting to feel a bit irritated so I decide that two can play games.

"Seems fine, but I've never seen one of these before. How do I know you didn't run this off on your laser printer this morning?"

He smiles. "You don't, but I can give you a number to ring if you want to check I am who I say I am."

"Ah, you mean a number where your mate is sitting ready to do his gruff policeman voice 'Evening all, I understand you have that nice Sergeant Williams with you. No problem, squire, he's a real copper, honest as the day is long.' Something like that?"

His smile slips a little. "You've been watching too much television, sir. 'Evening all' went out with Dixon of Dock Green."

I smile and he takes a deep breath. "If you really want to

be sure, call the general enquires number for the Police in your local phone book, explain your problem and ask them to check the warrant card number for Detective Sergeant Bruce Williams."

I feel that honours are now even, maybe even slightly in my favour, so I shake my head. "No, that's fine. How can I help you, Sergeant Williams?"

The next half hour is really quite scary. Not that it's threatening or anything like that, it's just the amount of detail he wants. Some, the general stuff, is no problem. How long have I used this contractor? How did I first find them? Who did I deal with there? In which countries did they work on projects for us? Did we always pay them in sterling? What were the different stages? Did they, to the best of my knowledge, use sub-contractors?

Then he starts to get down to detail, wanting dates, sums of money paid, how it was paid, stuff like that. There my memory breaks down.

"I'm sorry, Sergeant, but if you want that level of detail you'll need to go back to the office. I don't keep all that in my head."

"No notes here at home, sir? I understand from your office that you do quite a lot of work here."

"Preparation of reports, assembling project notes, listing costs incurred, that's the kind of work I did here."

"Why here? Why not in the office?"

"Often wasn't time. I'd get back from say, Athens, in the early evening and was probably booked on another flight the next day. No point in trailing into London. I'd write up what needed to be passed on immediately, make a note of the expenses for that trip, email those to the office and go and pack another suitcase."

"I see. A real jet-set lifestyle."

"A really exhausting lifestyle. Some weeks I did more sleeping on planes than I did in a bed."

"And you kept notes of all those reports and things here?"

"I did."

"Do you have them to hand?"

"No. They were all on my business laptop and the company reclaimed that when they put me on garden leave. If you want to see that you'll need to talk to Mr Dory or his PA, Francesca Thompson."

"I see. Would it surprise you to learn that Mrs Thompson says she's still waiting for you to return your laptop?"

"Yes, it would, as I handed it over to her three weeks ago."

"She says she doesn't have it."

"Then she's either going senile or she is lying."

He seems taken aback by my direct reply. "That's a very unambiguous response, Mr Kirkwood."

"There's no need for ambiguity. After all this first blew up, I had a meeting with Mrs Thompson at the office on 7th October at 6:00 pm. That meeting is recorded in my business diary. When we met she laid out the conditions of my garden leave which included the return of my company laptop. She wanted it immediately. I didn't have it with me so it was agreed I'd go into the office the next day, 8th October at 10:00 am and hand it over then. This I did."

"Did you get a receipt for it?"

"No. I asked for one but, as I expected, Mrs Thompson said it was not necessary as I was returning company property not taking it out."

"As you expected?"

"Yes. Mrs Thompson is always, how shall I put it, very precise, but over the years I've learned how she operates. On this occasion, she also gave me strict instructions not to talk to anyone else while I was in the building. In case I muddied the waters with this investigation. So I took the lift up to the third floor, I knocked on Mrs Thompson's door, she said come in, I went in, handed her my laptop as requested, she took it, she didn't say 'thank you' because she doesn't do courtesy, I walked out of the room, went down in the lift and left the building."

"You don't like her very much, do you?"

"No."

"So really this is your word against hers?"

I stand up. "I think I will have that coffee now. Will you change your mind and join me?"

For a moment I think I see a half grin, quickly suppressed, then he says, "Why not?"

I pour two coffees – Lauren's posh percolator keeps its contents warm for eternity – and bring them back to the living room.

Sergeant Williams takes a sip, then says. "Shall we cut to the punch line, Mr Kirkwood."

"How do you know there is a punch line?"

"Well, I wasn't born yesterday. You stated just now that you were told very clearly to deliver the laptop without talking to anyone. I presume you were relating those instructions exactly as they were given to you? No casual rephrasing?"

"Exactly. No. I took that laptop in and handed it over exactly as I told you just now ..."

"And ..." he says encouragingly.

"And as I walked along the corridor holding the laptop in

my hand I was watched from one end by my own PA, Sally Mountford, and from the other end by Tom Curtis from the post room. They will tell you that I had the laptop in my hand when I went into the room and I did not have it when I came out a few moments later."

He looks me straight in the eye and I meet his gaze unflinching. After a moment he says. "I see. And no doubt it was just a fortuitous coincidence that those two people happened to be there at precisely the right moment."

"Not exactly. I've learned to take precautions in all sorts of situations over the years, Sergeant, and not just with our clients. I spoke to Sally on the phone on the morning of the 8th and she organised Tom."

"I thought you just said you'd been instructed not to speak to anyone."

"I was told not to speak to anyone while I was in the building and I didn't. I did wave to Sally and nodded to Tom, but I didn't think that contravened my instructions."

Sergeant Williams puts his coffee cup down on the table. "I see. Would it be fair to say you're a man who likes to plan for all eventualities?"

"I wouldn't be much good at my job if I didn't."

"No, I suppose not." He pauses for a moment then observes, "So if you were involved in this fraud in any way you'd have made sure your tracks were well covered."

I feel the anger rising in me but I take a deep breath and bring myself under control. "I am not involved in any kind of fraud and I resent the implication that I might be."

"Of course. I appreciate that, but you must also appreciate that at this stage of the investigation I have to keep an open mind."

He has a point and I calm down a little.

"Let's get back to the question of your laptop, Mr. Kirkwood. Why do you think Mrs Thompson was lying?"

I shake my head and say unguardedly, "No idea. I think she's a poisonous bitch but let's be generous and say that perhaps she was busy at the time and simply forgot my visit."

He eyes me thoughtfully for a moment and I realise I shouldn't have spoken like that. Comments about conflict with colleagues are the sort of foolish thing that could be taken for a motive. But he only says, "Are you suggesting there may be something on your laptop that she doesn't want us to see?"

"I wouldn't have thought so. She may, of course, be hoping you think there's something on it which *I* don't want you to see, even though there isn't, but it does seem extreme behaviour just because you don't like someone."

"And did you also foresee the possibility that there wasn't anything untoward on there when you handed it over but there might be now?"

I don't like the sound of this. "No, I hadn't thought of that. But this is all starting to sound a bit 'conspiracy theory', isn't it? I don't like Mrs Thompson and she doesn't like me, but I really can't see her attempting to incriminate me for something I haven't done. It's just incredible."

Sergeant Williams nods his approval. "And yet you took precautions to make sure you could prove you'd handed the laptop over."

"Common sense precautions for anyone who works in a large organisation and takes their work home with them. No one takes your unsubstantiated word for anything anymore. It becomes instinctive after a while."

"And they say the police are suspicious. Ah, well." He gets to his feet. "Well, I think that's it for the moment, Mr Kirkwood. We'll probably want to talk to you again. Not thinking of going abroad at all, are you?"

"Not at present. Are you telling me I can't?"

"No, but if you do it would be a good idea to let us know. I'll give you my number."

I take his card. "Thank you, Sergeant. What are you going to do about my laptop?"

"Not sure. I'll talk to my boss. We could apply for a search warrant but it seems a bit heavy-handed – and we'd probably find nothing anyway."

I see him out and go back to collect the dirty coffee mugs. I suddenly remember the texts. Should I have shown them to him, I wonder? There's no reason for it but I'm starting to feel uneasy about the whole business. It all seems rather surreal. I wonder if I've strayed into a parallel universe, like a writer who has somehow ended up in one of his own plots.

Except I'm not a writer, despite Simon and Lauren's best efforts to turn me into one. And why would Francesca deliberately lie about my laptop not being returned?

25

LOS ANGELES

He sat on the balcony of the apartment in LA overlooking the Pacific Ocean, glancing through his notes. Time for another hour's work before his American agent arrived to collect him for the premier of his new film. He was quietly confident about the reception it would receive, the sneak previews had all gone well and he was already being tipped for an Oscar.

Richard hoped it wasn't tempting fate but he'd booked a table for supper at Nobu Malibu after the showing and was expecting a group of friends to join him. Sylvia would be there and he had every expectation that she would come back to the apartment with him.

He dragged his thoughts back to the current script. His central character was in a tight spot. The police had been interrogating him, they suspected he was involved in large scale fraud. They had just found the incriminating financial records on his laptop but he knew he hadn't put them there. Someone was trying to frame him. Was it the beautiful Marlene, so apparently warm, supportive, with pouting lips and long eyelashes? Or was it Marvin, his boss, loud voice, loud suits, apparently harmless and yet ... Or then again was it Griselda seeking a divorce but making sure she didn't walk away empty handed from their marriage.

Richard glanced up. The view across the city was stunning, the twinkling lights, the moonbeams glittering on the ocean. He had no idea how he was going to untangle his central character from the maze of plot lines that enmeshed him. He knew it was far easier to create complications than to resolve them.

It didn't really matter though. It was only fiction after all. Just like the Los Angeles apartment, the premier of the film, Sylvia, Marlene, Marvin and Griselda.

None of them actually existed.

26

Overnight I think about my options. I can't see any point in confronting Francesca. I have witnesses who saw me hand over the laptop. It seems to me I can only make things worse by interfering, so I decide to do nothing.

I wonder if I should try to ring Lauren, see how she's settling in, but if I'm being honest with myself I don't really have anything to say. Plus, if I tell her about Sergeant Williams, she'd probably tell me off for agreeing to an interview without legal representation. I compromise by sending her a text. Usual platitudes, but I stick an 'x' or two after my name.

The day stretches out ahead of me. Somehow Saturdays seem longer than ordinary days. I turn on my laptop, open the file and update my strategic plan. At the beginning of any project you have no idea what will turn out to be important so the discipline is to make a note of everything. I take comfort from applying the professional approach but I'm aware of one big difference between a management problem and my quest. When I'm working with a client, everyone involved is trying to find a solution. In my quest I'm the only one who is looking for answers, it's of no real interest to anyone else, so I'm on my own.

I update the entries for Rodney and Philip Armstrong, record the fact that I've emailed the head teacher at Modbury Road, and then run out of ideas so I close the file and go and put some washing in the machine.

On Sunday I transfer yesterday's washing to the tumble dryer and set that going. After that I have nothing to do again. I struggle through to lunchtime and then I just have to get out of the house so I drive down to Portsmouth and walk out on the Farlington Marshes. Not the warmest place to be in late autumn but the smell of the sea does me good. More ducks, more gulls. I still don't know what any of them are, but at least now I'm noticing them and the fact that they're different. I enjoy the walk. I seem to find it easier to relax in the open air.

My mood changes when I get home. I feel very restless and the house is silent, cold and unwelcoming. I try and rationalise my feelings and, slightly to my surprise, I discover I'm missing Lauren. I'm surprised because it's been years since we spent much time together doing nothing. We haven't exactly drifted apart, just exist in occasionally overlapping separate bubbles.

Perhaps it's the walk by the sea that's brought this on. Back in the days when she was newly arrived in the UK and neither of us were working quite so hard, Bosham and Farlington Marshes were the kind of places we'd go for an afternoon. We would walk for hours, holding hands, talking about all the things we wanted to do. And over the years we both achieved them, but not together.

I sense I'm in danger of becoming morbid so I sit down and give myself a good talking to. I'm really struggling with enforced idleness. I'm not comfortable on my own, especially when I have nothing to do which is why the quest for Julie has become so important.

And that is not going well. What have I done? I have stood outside Modbury Road School and been refused admittance.

I have knocked on the door of her old address – no answer. I have spoken to Rodney's Mum and then Rodney. Nothing useful gained. I have talked to Philip Armstrong and got one faint lead to another pupil, so faint I wonder if I have the energy to pursue it. It's all pretty hopeless but just as I'm wondering where the hell I go from here, the phone rings. I answer it and hear Phillip Armstrong's voice at the other end. How weird is that?

"Hallo. Is that Richard Kirkwood?"

"Speaking."

"Phillip Armstrong here. You remember you came to see me the other day trying to track down a ... possible relative, I think you said?"

"Yes, that's right."

"Well, I have a couple more Modbury Road names for you. Don't know if they'll be any help. There was a boy called Norman Huggett and a girl called Heather Westcott."

"Oh, I see. Well, thank you. I'd remembered Heather but not Norman. Norman Huggett. Let me think. Was he the tall boy, sat at the back of the class, wore a green pullover?"

"I'm afraid I have no idea about the colour of his pullover but my memory – such as it is – suggests that he was tall, yes."

"Well, thank you for taking the trouble to ring—"

"Wait, don't be precipitate, there's more. I've been talking to my sister, Gillian. In fact it is she who came up with these names."

"Oh, I see."

"One of Gillian's friends at school had a brother who went around with Norman Huggett. I suspect Gillian was rather smitten with this brother and got to know Norman a bit as well. She thinks he got married quite young and moved to

Oxford. She tried to use him as a go-between to keep in touch with her friend's brother. Didn't work, of course, but she still has Norman's Oxford phone number."

"Not his current one?"

"No, no, of course not. So this one's long out of date, but it might give you a start."

I frown. All the leads I'm getting seem to take me backwards. Still I shouldn't be ungracious. The man has taken the trouble to ring me when he could easily not have bothered.

"Okay, thanks a lot, let me just grab a pen."

He gives me the number and I think that's it, but apparently not.

"Now, about Heather Westcott."

"You don't have a number for her as well?"

"No, I'm afraid not. But Gillian says she's certain Heather went into nursing. Don't ask me how she knows, I've never understood women."

Out of sight at the other end of the phone I raise an eyebrow. That comes as no surprise.

"Gillian says she thinks Heather did her training at St Thomas's so that might be worth investigating too. You know St Thomas's. On the river, near Waterloo station."

"Yes, I know."

"Well, that's about it, I'm afraid. Hope it's some help. I'd be quite interested, in a purely academic way you understand, to learn how you get on in this search for ... for your possible relative. Set yourself quite a challenge, haven't you?"

"Yes, I have, but I am making some progress. Thanks for your help. I'll let you know how I get on."

Maybe, I think, as I replace the receiver, or then again,

maybe not.

Then I pull myself up. I keep being angry when these people aren't able to immediately make my search easier. But I know they don't owe me anything. And at least it's another small step forward. If Heather Westcott really did go to St Thomas's that would seem a good firm lead but I suspect that simply ringing them up and asking about someone who did their nursing training there in the late 60s and early 70s isn't going to get me very far. Probably easier to start with Norman Huggett and the Oxford number even though it is so old that after the area code is discounted it is only 4 digits long. Hard to remember how simple phone numbers were back then. I'll have to rummage around to find the modern equivalent.

The next day I turn to the internet again and, after a bit of searching, I come up with a site that sets out the history and development of telephone numbers in great detail. Using this, it doesn't take me long to work out what is probably – I'm very aware of the 'probably' – the current six figure number for Norman Huggett's old house. Nothing ventured, nothing gained, so I dial it.

I find myself talking to a very courteous gentleman, a Mr Stonham, who seems totally unfazed by my reason for trying to trace Norman Huggett. The bad news is that he's never heard of him. But the good news is that he's lived in that house for over thirty years and is still in touch with the people who sold it to him. In fact they're friends with Mr Stonham, live nearby in Abingdon and he thinks they may well have bought the house from Norman. I ask if he'd be kind enough to give me their number. He hesitates a bit at that but offers to ring them for me and see if they'd mind if I call.

I sit at my desk and think about the next step. There is

still Julie's old address, long since out of date, of course, but there may be some people in that block of flats who might remember the family. I fall back on my youthful detective experience and decide to have a look at the electoral rolls.

I turn back to the internet and eventually find a site that looks hopeful. I have to register and then buy a number of credits but before long I'm looking at the electoral rolls for the Modbury Road area. Easy as that.

I begin with our 11-plus year just to get my bearings. Yes, there's the Orford family at 26 Cumbernauld Court, just as I remembered. I try the next year and they're still there. I think about how many years there are between then and now and decide to jump ahead a bit. Ten years later they're still there, another ten – they're still there, another ten – and they've vanished, replaced by someone called Foxburrow. Working backwards I come to the conclusion they probably moved out in the early eighties.

I access the current register to see if by any chance the Foxburrows are still there but no, the current name against that address is Siddell. I dip into the intervening years at random and come up with a lot of names, 26 Cumbernauld Court obviously changed hands quite often after the Orfords had moved on.

I think for a moment then decide to work sideways. There were four flats on each level in Cumbernauld Court so I check the current names for numbers 25, 27 and 28, then go back to the early 1980s to see if any of them were there before the Orfords left. To my surprise I hit the jackpot. The entries for 25 and 27 are completely different but the name against number 28 is the same – Bronowski. Might be worth paying Mr Bronowski a visit.

On Tuesday I have to wait in for the man to come and service the boiler. The appointment is for some time in the morning but just before lunch they ring to say he's been delayed by a burst pipe in Chertsey and won't be along until after lunch. He eventually arrives about four, very apologetic but that's wiped out Tuesday. I go to bed grumpy. Don't know why. It's not as though I'm pushed for time.

Wednesday is better. At about eleven the phone rings and to my surprise I find I'm speaking to Gina Pitts, the current head teacher at Modbury Road.

"Mr Kirkwood," she says, "I've seen your email and have been thinking about how to reply. In the end it seemed easier just to pick up the phone."

"Thank you for taking the trouble," I say.

"No, it's a pleasure. I always like hearing from old pupils, though your request is unusually specific."

"Well, yes, I suppose it is. But can you help me?"

"Well now," she says, "what you're asking is technically not allowed. Certainly if it were information about a recent pupil I would give you a flat 'no' without hesitation."

"But as it isn't a recent pupil ...?"

"Well, strictly speaking the answer should still be no, confidential records and so on, you know."

"Yes, I understand, but I can hear a 'but' coming."

"Oh, can you? Well, yes, I suppose ..." There's a pause and then she seems to go off at a tangent. "This might seem a strange question, Mr Kirkwood, but may I ask what you do for a living?"

I can't quite see what she's getting at but I tell her about my work, omitting the fact that I'm currently on garden leave.

"I see ... so, you travel widely and you're a problem solver."

"Well, yes, I suppose I am. Problem solver. Trouble shooter. A sorter out of other people's messes. Call it what you like."

"It sounds very interesting."

"It can be. It's certainly varied."

"Yes …" Another pause. "I was wondering, Mr Kirkwood, if I could persuade you to come and talk to our Discussion Group about your work."

This I was not expecting. "Well, I don't know. Discussion Group? Children, you mean?"

"Certainly children, this is a school."

"Well, I suppose … How old are these children?"

"Ten, eleven years old. Year Six - the last year before they go on to senior school."

"And you think they'd like to hear about my work?"

"Not in huge detail, no, but I'm very keen that my children should learn about the real world. How it works. What people do. Not just school, home life and computer games. I like to get people to talk to them about a range of things and answer their questions. Now you're an old pupil from this school which is a positive link and I'm sure you could find something interesting to say to them, couldn't you?"

"Well, I suppose so … To be honest it's not something I've ever thought about."

"And while you're here," Mrs Pitts goes on persuasively, "you could see your own entry in the old records of the school – all written records then of course."

I suddenly see where this is leading. "Okay, yes, I'd like to see that. Very interesting."

"And I'd leave you alone to have a look, of course."

"Of course."

I grin to myself. This is a lady after my own heart She's basically offering me the chance to browse through the book without actually putting it into words. "When did you have in mind for this talk?"

"Well, the discussion group meets on Tuesdays after school for about 40 minutes. As it happens, I do have a gap next week if that's any good."

We settle on next Tuesday and I ring off. Knowing what senior school Julie went on to might not help much in the long run but it's something positive and at least gives the illusion of progress.

The next development comes the following day. I'm tossing up between making myself a sandwich for lunch or going down the pub when Mr Stonham rings from Oxford sounding what I can only describe as 'courteously excited'.

"I believe I may have an answer for you, Mr Kirkwood," he says. "I spoke to my friends in Abingdon and they not only remembered buying their house from your friend, Mr Huggett and his wife, but they know where they moved to. And they're still there, or they were last Christmas, as my friends had a Christmas card from them. '*Merry Christmas from Norman, Polly and the girls*' it said apparently."

"That's amazing."

"Well, maybe, but that's what comes of not moving about, you know. I've been in this house for over thirty years now and I've had the same neighbours on the left for nearly as long, and on the other side for well over twenty."

I cut short the flow of detailed neighbour data and ask for the address which turns out to be in Cromer.

"It seems your friend, Norman, is a music teacher," says

Mr Stonham. "I suppose that's what they call a 'transferable skill' these days. He plays the flute apparently."

That sounds odd, but then I stop and think that all I actually know of 'my friend Norman' is what he was like aged eleven, running round the playground playing cowboys and indians, wearing a green pullover and being taller than the rest of us. Why shouldn't he have become a flute player? He might equally have become an oilrig engineer, a nightclub bouncer, a politician or an insurance adjuster.

I make a note of the address, thank Mr Stonham for his help and ring off.

I do yet another internet search and find a phone number for Norman Huggett in Cromer but I'm uncertain whether to call him or not. I'm having second thoughts about whether talking to old classmates will ever lead me to Julie but, I have to admit, it's quite interesting discovering what happened to some of those 11-plus hopefuls I once rubbed shoulders with. I decide it's worth pressing on, for a while at least.

And I really do have to do something to fill the time.

27

POLLY

Polly Huggett was taking a cake out of the oven when she heard footsteps on the gravel path. She liked her gravel path, better than a dog for letting you know someone was approaching and a gravel path didn't need feeding or taking for walks.

She heard the steps stop, then a pause. The bell push on their front door was hidden away, low down off to one side and had been painted over. Norman had always said he was going to do something about it, but he never had. Many people never found it and knocked on the door with their knuckles.

However this visitor must have been made of sterner stuff because after a few moments she heard the soft 'ting-tong' of the bell echo in the hallway. For a moment she hesitated, then she had an image of the long empty weekend stretching out before her. Any diversion was welcome so she took off her apron, tidied her hair and headed for the door.

She had a quick look through the peephole. She didn't recognise the man who stood on the step but he looked perfectly respectable so she opened the door. He was smartly dressed in casual slacks and a fawn jacket and had a lovely smile. So lovely that she found herself smiling back even before he'd said a word.

"Good afternoon," he said, "My name's Richard Kirkwood and I'm guessing you'd be Mrs Huggett. I wonder if I could have a word with Norman, please. I'm an old school friend."

28

It's a spur of the moment decision to go to Cromer rather than phone. I know I'm trying to find reasons to get out of the house but I also think it would be better just to turn up and see Norman in person. I'm finding it increasingly difficult to explain to people the reason for my quest, but at least face to face you can see a person's reaction and judge if they think you're completely off your trolley.

So now it's Saturday afternoon in Cromer and I'm standing on the doorstep of the Huggett's bungalow wondering if this was such a smart move. The woman in front of me – presumably Polly – is, I would guess, in her early fifties, well turned out, 'clean and neat' as my aunt Elsie would have said. She obviously wasn't expecting me, that's the whole point, but her smile is friendly until I speak so I'm surprised when she stiffens and her fingers turn white where she grips the door frame.

"Are you all right?" I say but she just stands there, gulping and staring. "Did I interrupt something?"

When she speaks, she sounds as if she's barely able to catch her breath. "Have you seen Norman? Has he sent you?"

This is even more puzzling. "No, I haven't seen him. I was given your address by another ... um ... another old friend and I happened to be in the area so I thought I'd look him up. Look, are you all right?"

She shakes her head vehemently. "No – I mean yes, I'm

fine." Then there's a pause. She is clearly making a real effort to pull herself together. She takes a deep breath. "Look, I'm sorry, you caught me by surprise. You say you're an old friend of Norman's?"

"Well, yes, but—"

"When did you last see him?"

This is always the tricky bit. "Well, to be absolutely honest, over forty years ago. At our primary school."

"Oh."

"I know it's a long time but ..."

"And you haven't seen him since then?"

"No."

"Or heard from him?"

"No."

"Well, then I don't see ..." She stops and gathers herself together. "Look, I think you'd better come in Mr ...".

"Kirkwood. Richard Kirkwood."

"Then please come in, Mr Kirkwood, this isn't a conversation for the doorstep."

I step inside rather doubtfully. My antenna is twitching. I'm sensing trouble here. Polly leads me straight into the kitchen, a large bright room with a view over the fields behind the house.

"Please, do have a seat. Cup of tea?"

The last is phrased as a question but she doesn't wait for an answer, just fills the kettle and plugs it in.

"Your timing is good, Mr Kirkwood. I've just made a lemon drizzle cake. Would you like a piece?"

It isn't that long since lunch but I know the right answer.

"I'd love some. Thank you."

Plates, knives, a cake stand, cake forks get whirled round

the kitchen like a dervish on speed. The kettle boils, tea bags are spun into mugs, milk poured into a jug and suddenly – silence.

I find myself with a mug of tea and a slice of cake still warm from the oven, sitting opposite this woman who is gazing at me expectantly across the table.

I don't know where this is going so I take refuge in the cake. "Mmm, this is awfully good." I struggle to think of the right thing to say about cakes and another memory of my aunt Elsie comes back to me. "Yes, this is wonderful, very light, beautifully moist."

For a moment a hint of a smile touches her lips. "It was one of Norman's favourites."

Was? The word is not lost on me. Is this bereavement I am faced with?

"Er … I see … so Norman is …?"

"Gone. Yes."

"Oh, I'm so sorry. Was it sudden?"

She looks rather surprised. "Well, it was sudden for me but he'd obviously planned it."

Planned it? For heaven's sake, has the man killed himself?

"The first I knew was when I got up to let the cat out around six that morning. I noticed Norman wasn't in bed and then I found a note on the kitchen table."

Oh, the poor woman, I think, but her next line is a complete surprise.

"Apparently he left at five that morning. He's gone to Thailand where I understand he's living with a teenage girl. I've had one post card from him. From a place called Phuket – strangely apt. He did say sorry, but no indication of why or what she's got that I haven't."

Youth, I think unkindly, but clearly that isn't the whole story.

"I didn't hear his car start or anything. God knows what he's done with it. Left it at the airport I suppose. Well, he needn't think I'm paying the parking fine when they eventually discover it."

My sympathy is genuine. "I'm so sorry to hear this. Was it recent?"

"Oh, no. He left last February. On Valentine's Day would you believe? That was the final cruel twist of the knife."

I raise an internal eyebrow. After eight months or so, I doubt the overdue parking fee is going to be a problem. It's probably been towed. Or maybe he sold the car to finance his playboy lifestyle.

I take another bite of cake, trying to think what to say next that isn't banal or useless and come to the conclusion there is nothing. Polly takes a gulp of tea. She seems to be calming down. She smooths her hair back from her forehead and is clearly trying to do the polite hostess bit.

"So all this is news to you?"

I nod, my mouth fortuitously full of cake.

"And you haven't seen Norman in ... did you say, forty years?"

I swallow the last few crumbs. "Yes, about that. Not since our last year at primary school."

"Primary school? I'm sorry, I don't understand. Why after all this time—?"

"Yes, I know it's a little odd but I'm trying to trace another classmate of ours from back then. I'm not having much luck but a chance sequence of events put me on to Norman so I thought I'd see if he remembered her."

"Her?"

"Yes, her name was Julie Orford."

She shakes her head. "What is it with men your age? Are you all chasing after young girls?"

"I'm not chasing after a young girl. This girl would now be a woman my age and I do not having any feelings of … of …" I search for the right word and inevitably pick the wrong one. "I don't have any feelings of lust for her."

"Ah, lust. Yes, I suppose that's it. Poor Norman." And for a moment her face softens. "If only he'd had a little more imagination he could have satisfied more lust here than he'll ever manage in Thailand."

Suddenly she realises she's spoken this thought aloud and she blushes. "I'm so sorry, Mr Kirkwood. This isn't your problem and you've had a wasted journey."

"Call me Richard, please. And the journey was worth it, if only for the cake."

It's a clumsy attempt at gallantry but it makes her blush again.

"Thank you, Richard. My name's Polly."

"Yes, I know. The … er … the friend of a friend who gave me this address had a Christmas card signed 'Norman, Polly and the girls'."

"Ah, that was last Christmas, just before …"

"I'm sorry. I don't want to …"

"No, no, it's all right. I don't know how I'll sign the cards this year. Shouldn't really keep putting 'the girls' on them anyway. They're both grown up and long since left home."

"How have they …?"

"Reacted to their father pushing off? Not well. They won't have anything to do with him. They don't even speak about him."

"Good for them," I say rather more bitterly than I had intended. Polly looks surprised and I quickly go on. "Are you in touch with him? Norman, that is."

Polly looks at me for a moment then says. "Emails. Practical stuff, bills and so on. I could give you the email address but I don't think it'll help you. Emailing him certainly doesn't help me."

"Oh, no, that wasn't why I was asking."

I look down embarrassed but I can feel her gazing at me.

"This is a very odd thing you're doing, Richard. I don't think you did 'just happen to be passing'. I think you've made a special journey."

It's my turn to blush or at least feel very self-conscious.

"I thought so." She regards me for a moment. "Are you married?"

"Yes."

"And is your wife with you?"

"No, she's away at present. Working abroad."

"And what does she think about your search for this other woman?"

"She's not 'the other woman', not in that sense, but yes, you're right. My wife thinks I'm nuts."

Polly smiles. "Perhaps we're all nuts, as you put it, in our own way. I know I go stir crazy here sometimes, all on my own."

I'm clearly not going to get any useful information out of this visit so I open my mouth to say I ought to be going but instead, to my surprise, I hear myself inviting her to have a meal with me this evening.

She eyes me thoughtfully for a moment then says: "That

would be very pleasant, Richard. Make a nice change. Where are you staying?"

"I'm in a B & B down near the sea front. I can come back later and pick you up."

"Thank you. Would about half past six suit you?"

"Yes, that's fine. I'll leave the choice of restaurant to you. This is my treat of course."

I spend the rest of the afternoon walking round the town or sitting on the pier, huddled into my coat against the sharp wind off the sea, trying to rationalise what I'm doing.

I've booked the B & B and it would be a pity to waste it ... I'm bored with eating alone ... The poor woman clearly needs to talk ... I might learn something more about Norman ...

But none of this rings true, even to me. Maybe I'm just feeling lonely. Nothing new about that, of course, I've always been lonely, but until recently I've never had time to think about it. Now that I have, I'm not finding it comfortable.

Around five I go back to the B & B, have a shower, give my shirt a shake to get rid of some of the creases and I'm back on her doorstep sharp at six-thirty.

Polly, who I'd already decided was the sort of woman who is always immaculate, has clearly taken some trouble with her appearance. She is wearing a white embroidered blouse and a navy blue skirt. Her hair is held back in a clip and her eyes are brighter than they were this afternoon.

She takes me to a pub with a small restaurant off to one side where the food is very good, plain but well cooked. She has the lamb cutlets, I have the belly of pork. We share a bottle of red wine.

Neither of us want dessert but we linger over coffee and mints. Throughout the meal the conversation has been inconsequential. I tell her a bit about my job, places I've been. She tells me about her work as a doctor's receptionist, part time after the children came along. She asks me a bit more about my search for Julie, but I keep it vague, skimming across all the long shots, all the dead ends.

Finally, inevitably, as all along I've known she would, she begins to talk about her daughters.

"Ruth's married now. Lives over near Kings Lynn." She smiles shyly. "She's just made me a grandmother as it happens."

I force myself to go through the conventional motions. "I can't see you as a grandmother but congratulations."

"Thank you. They've had a lovely baby girl. They've called her Annabelle."

I freeze. Annabelle? Anne ... no, I can't go there. I grit my teeth and fight to try and stop the unexpected emotion from showing in my face. Polly notices nothing and goes on.

"The other one, Emily, lives in London. Software programmer for an insurance company. She's doing awfully well."

I really don't want to hear any of this. I can't handle other people's family trivia but I can't think of a polite way to change the subject.

"We were always a very close family, or so I thought. The girls and I still are. I often pop over to see Ruth or she comes here and Emily gets back home every couple of months or so. They've been a great support in all ... all this."

She drifts off into a private reverie. "Norman always said life was a journey. I thought he was speaking metaphorically. It's odd really, he didn't like it when the girls left home, well, I suppose in a way, neither did I, but you have to let them go,

113

don't you?"

"I wouldn't know. I don't have children."

It sounds curt. I know it sounds curt, but I hate this question at the best of times. I think I'm still in shock after that flash of memory when she said Annabelle. I haven't quite got my mind back in order. And anyway, there really is only so much interest that someone who isn't a parent can be expected to have in other people's tales of their grown-up children. Everybody knows that. Polly gives me a glancing look.

"Ah. Well, I've never believed you own children. You have them, bring them up with as much kindness and sensible discipline as you can manage, then let them go. If you do that, they'll want to come back. Cling on to them and when they finally break free, they're gone for good."

I can't handle this. She might be talking a foreign language. But she is unstoppable.

"I love my girls, Richard, and I know they love me. I don't believe Norman has any idea what he's thrown away."

She is rummaging around in her bag and, to my horror, produces some photos. She flicks through them, selects a few and pushes them across the table to me.

"That's Ruth, very pregnant in that picture as you can see, and that's Emily. Oh, and this one is just after Annabelle was born. That's Ruth's husband, Daniel."

I find myself staring at a picture where the woman is smiling down at the baby with love in her eyes and the man has his arms round her shoulders looking as though he's just won the lottery. I wonder if my parents ever looked like that but my imagination won't stretch that far.

"Very nice," I manage to say.

Polly looks at me rather strangely. I can't take much more of this so I wave at the waiter to bring me the bill. Polly gathers up her pictures but as she's putting them away another one falls out and lands face up in front of me.

This is an older picture. The woman is obviously a younger Polly and she's walking along a beach, laughing, with a little girl clinging to each hand. They appear to be dancing along beside their mother. A happy picture of long ago, full of love.

And suddenly I'm back there again, mistaking her mention of Annabelle for Anne. This is too much. I can feel it showing in my face and I turn away so Polly can't see. The bill arrives, I pay it, the waiter goes away and I start to get up but suddenly Polly lays her hand on my arm.

"I'm sorry, Richard. I've made you unhappy. I didn't mean to."

"It's not your fault."

"It was seeing my photos, wasn't it?"

I sound strangely normal. "Yes, well sort of."

"I thought so." A pause, then, "Do you want to tell me why?"

I shake my head and she says, "No matter."

But then suddenly I can't hold it back. "It was just ... well ... you all look so happy."

If she thinks this is an oddly resentful thing to say, she doesn't show it. "We were. We are."

I swallow. "I'm glad for you."

"But you're not happy, are you?" She takes my hand. "You've been very kind to me this evening, Richard, and I'm sorry I've upset you ..."

"It's nothing. I'm being silly."

Polly is silent for a moment, but when I don't respond she

115

says, "You're a strange man. Why are you really looking for this girl?"

I take a deep breath and force myself to sound normal. "No reason really. It's just … well … oh, I don't know. I've got, well, time on my hands at the moment. I have very strong memories of her and I'd like to know how she got on in life."

Polly shakes her head. "That's nonsense and you know it. I suspect your wife knows it as well. You're looking for something but this girl's only a symbol. What's missing, Richard? What's your equivalent of a Thai teenager?"

When Lauren and Simon asked me this question I had a glib answer all ready, but every time one of my old school contacts ask me, I have to search harder and harder for an answer. Deep down I don't know. Why am I doing this? Why am I edging open the door to those memories so long since buried?

"I don't know, I really don't. It's just, well … those memories of Julie are so … so vivid. I remember that school as a happy place, happier than …"

"Yes?" she prompts.

"No, I can't. I'm sorry. It's just that I was free there. At school. I could be myself. And Julie was … was lovely. Like a light in the fog, a promise, a hope that things could be different."

I run out of words and I turn away as a flare of something like anger courses through me. I didn't expect to tell her this. Ridiculously, I have to fumble for my handkerchief. After a moment I get myself under control again and I turn to face Polly.

"I'm very sorry about that. I'm being stupid."

"No, you're not, but I think you've had enough for one

evening. Time to go."

We go back to the car and I drive her home. When we pull up outside her bungalow she turns to me and I can make out the shape of her face in the light of a distant street lamp.

"Are you going to be all right?"

I nod.

"Then thank you for a lovely evening. I am sorry I upset you at the end."

"You didn't upset me. I—"

She gently touches my arm. "No, not tonight. Get some sleep. I don't know if we'll meet again but if you do want to talk more at any time you know where I live."

She leans forward and surprises me by kissing me gently on the cheek. Then she is gone.

I pull myself together, drive back to the B & B and go upstairs to my room. I sit on the bed and think. I hadn't realised I was so vulnerable. My self-imposed quest is to follow the happy memories of that last year in primary school but I've always known, I must have known, that my brother was right – behind them are all the other memories, memories I'm not yet ready to deal with, but then, when Polly spoke about her children and grandchildren, they came flooding back. Memories and dreams. My dreams are an escape, so perhaps exploding the dreams is how we learn to grow up.

I realise that if this fraud case goes wrong, if I do end up with a 'Not Proven' verdict, then this endless effort to fill my days is what it will be like for the rest of my life. I am not sure I can live with that.

I sit there for what seems like hours until I am very cold then, without undressing, I crawl under the covers and go to sleep.

29
FEBRUARY 1962

Three children have been kept back after school for a meeting. Richard, another boy and a girl, names long since forgotten, though in his memory he thinks the girl had pigtails. Wonders for a moment if he's done something wrong but it's nothing like that.

It's been decided that Modbury Road should have a school magazine. The headmaster has chosen a team of three pupils to run it. Richard and the two forgotten names. The teachers will invite pupils to submit pieces – stories, poems, where they went on holiday, anything that might be interesting to others – and Richard and the other two will choose the best bits and assemble them for the school secretary to type up and put through the duplicator.

Richard is very excited. He writes a story and a poem and offers them to his fellow editors. They choose the poem but say they'll keep the story for the next edition. It's his first writing success. In his dreams, the first of many.

Together the three editors sift through all the other submissions, pick the ones they like the most, and the first magazine is published. It is well received by pupils, parents and staff.

The second edition, with Richard's story included, is also a success. They begin work on the third one. Lots of stuff comes flooding in and the three of them discuss what to include, what to leave out. They settle on the final content but the next day Richard has another life changing moment.

He is on his way out of school when he hears running footsteps behind him. He turns and sees Julie Orford hurrying to catch him up. As she reaches him she smiles. Oh, that smile.

"Hallo, Richard, I'm glad I caught you." She thrusts a piece of paper towards him. "I've written a poem. For the school magazine."

He takes the proffered paper. "Oh, right. Thank you."

"I do like the magazine. I think you do it really well and I'd love to see my poem in it."

"Well, okay, yes, I'll have a look at it."

Julie smiles again. "And I wanted to give it to you personally. You'll see why." And then she is gone, running down the road, her satchel bouncing on her back.

He stands there outside the school gate, leaning on the wall and reads the poem. Later he has to brush the red brick dust off the back of his trousers before his mother sees them. But now, in this moment, dust is the last thing on his mind. Julie has written a love poem. Its tone is general, no names are mentioned, it's a poem about love, not people, but he has no doubt in his heart that it's meant for him.

He is elated but then suddenly reality strikes. The magazine is already full, the contents of the next issue decided. There is no room for this poem. But she gave it to him. Personally. She wants to see it in print.

The following day he looks through the planned content for the next magazine and makes a decision. He tells his two fellow editors that he now has doubts about one of the pieces they have chosen. He thinks it should be held over so they can think about it some more. They are not convinced.

They still like it and point out that if they take it out they will have a gap.

As casually as he can he says he has found another piece, a poem that came in at the last minute that would fill the gap nicely. They are still not convinced but he is insistent, he stands his ground and eventually they give in. Julie's poem goes into the next edition.

The school magazine has not only given Richard his first chance to see his own work in print, it has also introduced him to the art of vested interests and professional compromise.

30

Sunday morning in Cromer. I'm feeling very embarrassed about last night. Breaking down like that in front of a complete stranger is out of character, but something about the combination of hearing her talk about her family and the intensity of accidentally stumbling into her own heartache just pushed me over the edge.

And yet, in a strange way, I had enjoyed the evening. I found Polly a very calming person to be with, at least until the photos appeared, and I admire the way she seems to be handling Norman's behaviour.

I feel guilty about just leaving today without saying goodbye but I don't want any repeat of last night and anyway she has problems of her own. In the end I compromise. I buy a postcard of the pier and scribble a note on the back.

Thank you for a lovely evening and your understanding...

I add my phone number and pop it through her letter box on my way out of town. I pass up the chance to remind her about giving me Norman's email, not sure I still want to get in touch with him anyway. A curious weekend and I haven't advanced my search for Julie at all.

On Monday morning I decide it's high time I thought about what to say to Year Six at Modbury Road tomorrow afternoon. I'm well used to speaking in public but my audience is usually a little older.

I start making notes, concentrating on explaining how problems can arise, how you analyse them and then work through to a solution. The structure comes together pretty easily but the next day, faced with an eager group of children, I discover a basic truth. You can usually bullshit adults but eleven year olds are another matter.

The notes I've prepared, which I reckoned should last half an hour, are used up in the first ten minutes. With an adult audience I could have bluffed my way out of it, probably by doing the same thing all over again in a different order and changing the words around a bit. But this group isn't having any of that.

"You've said that already," shouts one boy. "Tell us about your visit to Los Angeles. Did you ever meet Darth Vader?"

Somehow I get through the session with a mixture of facts, anecdotes and occasionally pure invention. In fact I find it quite refreshing. After a few weeks of struggling to find ways to fill the time, the chance to think on my feet again is energising.

Gina Pitts is delighted. We have a cup of tea in her office and then she honours her side of the bargain.

"I've dug out the old records, Richard," she says, "they're over there on that table. I've found the page where you're listed."

"Right. Thank you."

"I've just got to nip along to the staff room. I'll be about ten minutes. Is that okay?"

"Fine," I say and she leaves.

I look down at my name written in ink in this old ledger. It's a curious feeling. There is the date I first came to the school, there is my progress through the different classes and there is the entry saying I had passed the 11-plus exam and the grammar school I went on to.

I browse through the pages looking for Julie Orford. At first I can't find her but then it occurs to me that she didn't necessarily join the school at the same time as I did. I search forward and suddenly there she is. Julie Orford age 9. Her parents must have moved into the area and she transferred to Modbury Road. I follow the record through and discover that she had gone on to Stuart Farm Secondary school, the mixed school on the other side of the park.

I close the ledger. I'm not sure this helps much but it has somehow brought me closer to Julie again.

As I walk out of the school gates it suddenly occurs to me that, as I'm in the area, it might be worth another visit to Cumbernauld Court to see if Mr Bronowski is at home.

31

JANUARIUSZ

At five o'clock each day he fed the budgerigar. At half past five he lit the fire. At six o'clock he sat down to his tea. At half past six he did the washing up. At seven o'clock he poured a small vodka and turned on the television to watch Emmerdale.

He had begun watching Emmerdale Farm – as it was known then – when it first began in the early 1970s. He and Stefania had enjoyed it, the farming story lines reminding them of their childhood in Lower Silesia, though the scenery was very different. They also had some initial trouble with the dialogue because, although their English was good having lived in England since the war, they had not travelled much and the Yorkshire dialect was occasionally baffling.

These days he mostly watched it out of habit and also because, since the death of Stefania, the characters in the story were the closest thing to a family that he had.

At 91 he was still physically fit and perfectly capable of looking after himself. He had a number of acquaintances, but very few friends. This was partly because, even after all these years, he still felt like a foreigner in a foreign land. He and Stefania had always shared everything, work, pleasure, life, and now she was gone it was all down to him, a fact he accepted automatically without ever thinking about it.

But he did like his routine which is why when his doorbell went at half past five one evening, it disturbed him. No one ever came in the evening. He hesitated and the bell rang again. Maybe it was one of the neighbours, maybe somebody needed help. If so, Januariusz would do what he could. He was not a recluse, he tried to be a good neighbour, but since he had lost Stefania he had needed no company other than his own.

The bell rang again and with a sigh he went to open the door.

32

There's no response to my first ring, or the second, so I give it one last try. This time I hear steps approaching the door, bolts are pulled back and then suddenly there he is, a wizened little man peering out at me.

"Yes?" he says. "What is it that you want?"

"Mr Bronowski?" I ask, "Mr Januariusz Bronowski?" I know I am making a mess of pronouncing his name so I smile as warmly as I can to show no offence is intended.

He smiles slightly and I get the impression that over the years he's heard countless variations of his name.

"Yes, I am he," he says, "I am Januariusz Bronowski." When he says his name, I can hear the native Polish accent more strongly.

"I am very sorry to disturb you," I say, "but it's just possible you may be able to help me."

"In that case you must enter," he says, stepping back and holding the door open.

"Thank you." I go inside, he closes the door behind me then leads the way into a back room that seems to be dining room and kitchen combined. I see the table is laid for a meal.

"Oh, I am sorry," I say, "Am I interrupting your supper?"

"No matter. It is okay." He moves across to the oven and turns down the temperature. He gestures me to a chair.

"Now then," he says, "how is it I may be of assistance?"

"Well, I don't know if you can," I say. "Oh, by the way,

my name is Richard Kirkwood. I am sorry I didn't get your name exactly right."

He smiles broadly. "Polish names are very difficult," he says. "Just call me Jan."

"Thank you, and I'm Richard." He nods in acknowledgement and I pause a moment to gather my thoughts.

"I'm trying to trace an old friend," I say, "her family used to live next door here. I believe you've been here for quite a while."

He nods again. "It is fifty years I have lived here now."

"That's a long time."

"Yes. Very long time. My wife and I, we come to England 1939. Nothing left at home. Safer here."

"You were in England during the war?"

"Yes. I fly aeroplanes."

"You were a pilot?"

"We were lucky, we leave Poland in time. I Join Polish squadron. RAF."

"Oh, yes, I see."

"So after war my wife and I decide we will stay here. I leave the air force. Get a job, we save, we buy this flat."

"And your wife?"

"Ah. Dead now. Nine years."

"Oh, I'm sorry."

He smiles. A rather sad smile. "I miss her but this will happen to us all." He pauses for a moment, lost in thought. "It might have happened for me many years ago but I was lucky."

There doesn't seem much I can say to that so I leave a respectful pause then return to the matter in hand.

"Well, as you've lived here that long Mr Bron … Er … Jan … I'm hoping you'll remember one of your neighbours."

"I may. Which one?"

"The family were called Orford and they lived at—"

"Number 26 – next door, yes. Them I remember well."

"You do?"

"Of course. Mr and Mrs Orford and their two children. Mrs Orford and Stefania were always good friends."

"Two children?"

"Yes, girl and boy. I think the boy was a lot younger."

"I didn't know she had a brother. It's the daughter, Julie, I am trying to find."

He gives me a broad grin. "Ah, Julie. Young love. I understand."

His perception surprises me. I'm starting to warm to this old man.

"Something like that. She and I were at school together when we were young. After that we lost touch."

"And now you wish to find her and hope I can help?"

"I know it's a long shot but …"

"I have not seen that family for many years. Mr and Mrs Orford live here until" – he stops to think – "most possibly 1980 something, maybe. But the girl …"

"Julie …"

"Julie, yes. She grown up by then. She go long before they move. Maybe ten years before."

"Did she leave to get married?"

He shakes his head. "No, no wedding. She got job, but not a local job."

"Can you remember where?"

He shakes his head again. "Too long ago. Good job

though, I think, they were very excited for her. But a long way away."

"And you can't remember where?"

"No."

"Did she ever come back to visit her parents?"

"Oh, sure, from time to time. But she never stay long. There is something …" His brow is furrowed with the effort of remembering. "No, no, it has gone."

I sit back in my chair. "Well, thank you for that. You don't know what happened to the brother?"

"Teddy. Ah, he was scamp that one. Up to many things. They said he was bad boy but I think it was just high spirits."

"No idea where he went?"

"Abroad, maybe Australia, maybe New Zealand. Somewhere long way."

"And the parents?"

Jan gives a big beam. "Ah, they go to Yorkshire. Just like Emmerdale."

"They became farmers?"

"No, no, no … they just go to Yorkshire. Very beautiful country there."

"Did they retire?"

He shrugs. "They say goodbye and I get card at Christmas for few years, then nothing."

I think for a minute. "Do you think they moved to Yorkshire to be near Julie?"

"I do not know. They were nice people. Good to have next door. Not so nice there now."

"Are there any other people in these flats who might have known the Orfords?"

He shakes his head doubtfully. "I do not think so. People

do not stay. Many come, then go."

Ah, well, I think, no point in knocking on any other doors. I can't think of anything else to ask. I glance at the clock and see that it's nearly six. Time to go.

"Well, thank you for your help, Jan" I say, getting to my feet. "It's been a pleasure talking to you."

"Was it good?" he asks.

"Good? Oh, helpful, well, yes it was. In a way."

"I am happy then. Childhood times, very sweet memory, yes?" He sees my face and his smile vanishes. "No, not good? Not for you?"

I shake my head. I can't explain, don't want to stumble into trying to explain, not again. His brow furrows, then he says. "But Julie, she good, yes?"

I nod.

"Ah."

He stands up and we move towards the front door. He opens it and holds out his hand. I shake it, manage to mutter a few words of thanks and make my way towards the outer door of the flats. I hear his front door shut behind me but I've only gone a few steps when it opens again and I hear him shout.

"Mr Kirkwood. Richard ... I remember something. Cook school – Julie, she go to cook school."

It takes me a moment. "Cookery school?"

"Yes, cookery school. She was going to be a chef."

"Can you remember where this school was?"

"No, but I think somewhere north. She make joke about needing lots of jumpers."

"The north. Could be Yorkshire then."

"Maybe. There is a lot of north. Don't remember where."

"Well, thank you very much, Jan. I appreciate your help."

"Perhaps." He pauses for a moment. "You know, we have a saying in Polish, *przeszłości nie zawsze jest to dobre miejsce.*"

"Which means?"

"The past is not always a good place to be."

Since I don't quite know which part of my past he is referring to, his warning seems particularly ominous. He goes on. "Good luck with your search, whatever you looking for. Goodbye, Richard, powodzenia."

33

The next day I do yet another evaluation – I now know which school Julie went on to, I know she left the area and went to cookery school, I know her parents moved to Yorkshire sometime in the 1980s. I am acquiring information but none of it is getting me anywhere.

I sit at my desk and run through my Action List. It looks good on paper but so much of it is inanimate – electoral rolls, internet searches and so on. Facts are always useful, of course, but in my experience the answer to any problem comes from talking to people, listening to their views, understanding their prejudices. All well and good, but the only relevant people in this search are our old classmates from Modbury Road and my contacts so far with Rodney and Phillip Armstrong have not been productive. As for Norman Huggett in Thailand, well I think that's best left alone. Then I have a sudden thought. If anyone did stay in touch with Julie, it was more likely to be a girl. The real 11 year old friendships were between people of the same sex.

I think over all the girls I can remember from that time. Julie herself, her friend, Linda Montgomery, Suzanne Duncan, Heather Westcott, Mary Jenkins. Then suddenly, out of the blue, something Rodney Montana said on the phone comes back to me. We'd been talking about Linda Montgomery and how Christopher what's-his-name had been obsessed by her. Rodney had said she was tasty but then he said: "She's great though. Lots of fun."

She's great. She is. Present tense. I was so pre-occupied with Julie at the time that it didn't register but thinking back it must mean Rodney had seen Linda in later years. But if he had, why didn't he say so?

This is a really promising lead. I flip through my notebook and find Rodney's number and dial it. It rings a couple of times then goes to voicemail. No name given but I recognise Rodney's voice. "Leave a message and I'll get back to you."

"Rodney, it's Richard Kirkwood again. Look, I'd like to talk to you about Linda Montgomery. Can you call me please."

I start to feel a bit excited. I wonder if I can take this idea further? The only other girl from back then that I have any hint about is Heather Westcott who might have trained as a nurse at St Thomas's.

I ring the hospital in case she still works there – she doesn't. A tentative enquiry about whether she ever did meets a blank wall. No surprise there so how am I going break through that barrier?

After a few minutes thought the answer comes to me. I can't – but that doesn't mean it can't be done. I pick up the phone again and ring my brother.

"Simon, you remember that night in the pub when we were talking about my … my quest, you mentioned a private investigator you knew."

"Aha, given up already, have you?"

"Not at all. I still want to do this myself but I'm up against a brick wall."

I explain about Heather and the hospital and the impossibility of my finding out the information. "D'you think this is something your guy could do?"

"No idea. Probably. Best talk to him direct. Hang on a tick. I've got his number here somewhere."

I grab a pen and write down the name and address he gives me. Steve Carling, Private Investigator, with an office off the Goldhawk Road.

"And he's good, is he?"

"I think so. Efficient and discreet. What more do you want?"

It still feels like cheating somehow, which I know is stupid, so I put it to one side to think about overnight.

The following morning, at a loose end again, I decide to ring Sally.

"Any news? What's going on?"

She doesn't really know. The police are in and out of the office. Francesca is uncommunicative, Hunky only appears occasionally and Gaynor Wiles, the Regional Manager, seems to have taken command. There's one piece of juicy gossip though. My stand–in, Mervyn Wilby, has managed to offend Knut Mortensen, one of our leading Norwegian clients, to the point where Knut is threatening to withdraw his business. This is no mean achievement. You would have to work very hard to upset Knut. I ask Sally what Mervyn has done but she doesn't know.

"This is all so silly," says Sally. "We need you here, Richard, not this prat. Why don't they just get it sorted?"

Why indeed.

On the spur of the moment, feeling reckless, I ring Kenneth Bannerman at head office. I'm expecting a secretarial brush off but much to my surprise they put me through to him. I apologise for disturbing him but he is very courteous.

"I understand, Richard. It can't be easy for you."

"It isn't. My own office is telling me nothing. My boss isn't available. I'm existing in limbo."

"I know and I'm sorry, but there's nothing I can tell you."

Without stopping to think how rude it sounds I say. "Can't or won't?"

There is a pause and then he says. "How many delicate negotiations have you handled for this company over the years, Richard?"

I'm rather taken aback. "Oh, I don't know. Hundreds I would think."

"And how often have you employed the technique of saying nothing, doing nothing and waiting for the other side to make a move?"

In spite of myself I laugh. "Okay, point taken."

"I appreciate how difficult this is for you, but I'm afraid you'll just have to be patient."

Of course it's difficult, but I realise that he's given me a generous and courteous response to a call which, in his position, he didn't have to take in the first place.

Friday is another frustrating day. Empty hours. Raining hard. Walk not an option. I finally make up my mind, ring Steve Carling's office and arrange a meeting with him for next week.

Then I try Rodney's number again but again it goes to voicemail.

"Rodney, it's Richard again. Did you get my message? I want to talk to you about Linda Montgomery. Can you call me back please. Thanks."

I think about Linda. The 11 year old I remember was small, perky, dancing eyes, full of life to the point where she could hardly sit still. A complete contrast to Julie. As that year progressed, I often caught Linda eying me speculatively. I wondered if she knew how I felt about her friend. Did they talk about me between themselves? Did they share all their secrets? Did Linda know about the note?

34

APRIL 1962

A spring day. Sun shining brightly illuminating all the finger marks on the window. The class is dispersing at the end of the morning, heading down to the hall for their school dinner. He is in no hurry. He is not hungry. After the scene that morning at breakfast he doesn't feel he will ever be hungry again.

He stands up and reaches behind him for his satchel. A crowd of children push past him, nudging his desk as they go. When he looks round he sees a folded piece of paper with his name on lying on top of his books. He picks it up, puzzled. Then looks up. Julie is just passing out of the door. She looks back at him and smiles.

Now the room is empty. He unfolds the piece of paper. The note is very short but, oh, so very sweet. It reads:

> Richard, please don't tell anyone but I lo ...
> I like you very much.
>
> J.

Suddenly the sun seems even brighter. His world has changed again. His appetite returns. Julie has written to him. He doesn't think of it in these terms but he has just received his first love letter.

35

Another weekend passes very slowly. I've never spent so much time in this house before and now I'm doing so I realise it's totally devoid of any personality. It's really only a box where we sleep and store stuff.

I'm starting to understand what Simon meant when he talked about my eventual retirement and how that would leave me with time on my hands. I have time on my hands now but at least I have every hope that it's only temporary. Even so it is almost unbearable. Without my quest to fill at least some of the hours, I don't know what I'd do. The idea of this being a permanent situation is beyond imagining. I daren't even think about it – it's too frightening.

In the dark hours of the night when I can't sleep the fears come creeping into my mind. Guilty. Not proven. No hard and fast conclusion. Doubts about me not dispelled. How could I ever live with either of those verdicts? When Simon said to me, *"Guilt is very corrosive ... You can't bury it under long hours and work-related stress for ever"* I dismissed it as exaggeration. Now I'm not so sure.

Would I feel less unnerved if Lauren were still here with me? I try and tell myself that it wouldn't change anything, we'd still only meet in passing. But then I think again and realise I'm not being entirely honest with myself. She knows nothing of the deep fears that constantly haunt me but, apart from Simon, Lauren is the only person who can keep my loneliness at bay. I would be happier if she were here. Ours is a curious relationship, we only come together for short periods of contact these days, but it works for us. We both need our own space but we trust each other. I think that's the key, I don't trust many people.

I first met Lauren in 1989 when the company I was working for at the time sent me to their Boston office for a few weeks to negotiate a deal with an American contractor. Lauren was working at the law firm that handled the negotiations so our relationship was confrontational from the beginning, at least our professional relationship was. We fought over the contract but found we enjoyed each other's company and spent a number of evenings together. I discovered she came from Charter Oak, a small town in Iowa, and knew nobody in Boston outside her office. Did I sense then that here was someone as lonely as I was? I don't know, I only know that we had a lot of fun for those few weeks.

When the deal was settled and the time came for me to return home, we had a difficult parting. She didn't want me to go and, to my surprise, I found I didn't want to leave her either. I'd always fought shy of any close relationship – to me they were minefields where you could only get hurt – but at that moment, suddenly, I wasn't so sure. However, it wasn't my call, I had to return to London and so I did, thinking it would become an enjoyable memory but that was that.

Except it wasn't. She wrote and, after some hesitation, I replied. We even had a few transatlantic phone calls and then she announced she was coming to London for a fortnight's holiday. She came, we met, after two days she moved out of the hotel and into my flat. I enjoyed those two weeks and the following year I went back to the States for a return visit.

And so it went on for two or three years and then suddenly everything changed. Lauren had joined another law firm by then and was based in New York. I'd gone across to stay with her for a couple of weeks and, as usual, we'd had a good time. But then, on our last night, we were sitting in a bar just off Broadway when she suddenly said.

"I'll be coming to London in a few months' time."

"Great," I said, "I'll look forward to it."

"I mean for good. I've applied for a vacancy in our London office and I've just heard I've got it. I'll be arriving in May."

I was completely taken aback. "Oh, I see."

She looked at me. "Don't overdo the enthusiasm, will you?"

"No, sorry, of course. Excellent news. It's a wonderful opportunity for you."

Her face drooped a little. "I rather hoped it might be a wonderful opportunity for us."

Sitting in a designer armchair in Weybridge surrounded by impersonal possessions, I remember with painful clarity my reaction to this news. My first thought had been *This is all my fault. I should never have let her get this close.*

My three thousand mile buffer zone had been breached and I didn't know how to get out of it without hurting her. I'd been gazing into my glass as I battled with this unexpected situation but then I looked up and I will never forget the look of absolute misery on her face.

"Oh, forget it," she said. "I figured this wrong. Let's just call it quits."

"Lauren, I'm sorry …"

"Don't be. My fault. I guess I misread the situation." Her voice broke slightly. "It's just … well, I was kinda hoping you might ask me to marry you."

I was dumbfounded. I had never ever considered marriage – to me that was yet another, even bigger, minefield. But then I realised I'd been blind and because of that someone I cared about was being hurt. At that moment I hated myself.

Lauren was gathering her things together. "Guess it's time to go."

Someone I cared about. Suddenly, sitting there in that New York bar, the amazing, unexpected realisation had dawned. Lauren was someone I cared about. She was the first woman I'd ever felt safe with. Why throw all that away?

"Don't go." I wasn't even sure I'd spoken the words out loud but I must have done because she paused and looked back at me.

"Lauren, I'm sorry. I'm absolute crap at all this. I'm just not very good at … at …"

"Feelings?" she suggested, and I nodded. "No, you're not, are you."

"It's not I don't have them, I can't … I don't know … I just can't …"

"Express them?"

I nodded again.

"But you want me to stay?" Another nod. "Then let me try and make it easy for you. Richard. When I come to England will you marry me?"

Yet again I nodded but she wasn't having that. "Say it."

And suddenly I threw all caution to the winds and shouted so the whole bar fell quiet. "Yes, yes, yes. Lauren, I want to marry you."

There was an outburst of cheering, glasses were raised all over the room while I fought down the emotion that was

141

threatening to overwhelm me.

Afterwards I'd been terrified at what I'd done. I'd always been so careful to protect myself and now I'd let my guard down with a vengeance. But somehow it had worked. We were married six weeks after she arrived in England, much to Simon's surprise and delight I may add.

Those early years were a revelation to me. My few previous relationships had been enjoyable while they lasted but I never felt any regret when they came to an end. Being with Lauren was different and, although I didn't entirely understand why, my heart lifted every time she walked through the door. We were both working hard, of course, even back then, but we managed the occasional evening at the cinema, cooked some interesting meals together and even had a weekend away from time to time.

Lauren loved to visit the sea. Growing up in Iowa and the mid-west the only large bodies of water she knew were very big lakes, but the sea was different. I think it was the smell of the salt and the action of the tides that fascinated her.

In those early years we often found time to spend a day or even a weekend somewhere by the sea. We sought out the places where most people never ventured out of sight of their cars so by walking a mile or two along the shoreline or a cliff top we could be more or less alone. Then at the end of the day we'd head to the nearest town and eat fish and chips out of newspaper while walking along the prom. Together we explored stretches of the Dorset coast, the Isle of Wight, the shingle beaches of Dungeness, the cliff paths along the North Foreland, the Essex marshes and many more. Lauren loved them all. So long as there was seaweed, salt in the air and the chance of an ice cream cornet, she was happy.

Gradually, as our respective jobs became more demanding, we had less and less leisure time together but the feelings of warmth and companionship between us did not fade. This experience was something totally new to me but over the years I gradually learned to relax into it. Not complete relaxation, of course, that would have been a step too far, but Lauren's love and her acceptance of me as I was, gave me a stability that I could never have achieved on my own. Thinking of her now, like this, I'd had forgotten how happy we were back then and I realise how much I miss her. We text each from time to time, of course, but the messages are usually brief and practical.

On the spur of the moment, I open my laptop and compose a long email. I don't tell her about my search for Julie but I do tell her about my visit from Sergeant Williams, the news from the office, Mervyn Wilby's cock-ups, my conversation with Kenneth Bannerman, the latest bon mots from Mrs Atkins bellowing good advice above the noise of the hoover, and news from Simon and Rita. I end it by saying "Hope all is going well. Take care. I love you."

I can't remember the last time I said that.

36

Tuesday finds me in Shepherds Bush. I haven't been to the Goldhawk Road area for years and it's not as down at heel as I remember. I don't know what I'm expecting, but a smart chrome fronted office with a secretary leading me through to a very comfortable inner room is not it. Neither does the man who rises to greet me conform with my idea of a private investigator. Steve Carling wears a smart suit and is courteous and confident, a mixture that is rare in my experience. He reminds me a little of Sergeant Williams, except his clothes are better quality.

We exchange courtesies. I explain what I want and he makes notes on a pad.

"You just want us to find out what happened to this Heather Westcott after she finished her nurse's training?"

"Yes. Assuming she actually went to St Thomas's, did she stay there? Did she move to another hospital? Stuff like that."

He raises a courteous eyebrow. "That's not going to get you very far, though, is it?"

"How do you mean?"

"Don't you want to know where she is now?"

"Can you do that?"

"Probably. I can't promise, of course, but unless she deliberately set out to lose herself, it should be quite straightforward."

I am rather taken aback. I think of all the time I've spent

trying to get a lead on Julie Orford and here's this man saying that finding Heather should be quite straightforward. For a moment I'm tempted to dump the whole problem in his lap but then I think of why I took on this challenge. Julie is my dream, my fantasy if you like. Getting someone else to track her down defeats the whole object. But I could certainly do with a strong lead.

I look up to discover he's watching me closely. "I think I understand your dilemma, Mr Kirkwood," he says. "And I think I should be honest with you and say I know more about this search of yours than you've actually told me."

Light dawns. "That'll be Simon then."

"That'll be Simon. I daresay he told you we have a professional connection."

I nod.

"Well, it's a little more than that. I owe Simon a lot. He once managed to extricate me from a very difficult situation. I will always help him in any way I can and I'm happy to extend that courtesy to his brother."

"I'm not looking for any favours."

"And you won't get them. Not financial ones anyway. I have a business to run, Mr Kirkwood—"

"I think it's time you called me Richard."

"Thank you, Richard. And I'm Steve. Well, as I was saying, I have a business to run and I will charge you in the same way that I'd charge any client. What I am saying is you're guaranteed the best service I can offer you, complete discretion, and a willingness to do as much – or as little – as you require."

I think for a moment. "Thank you, Steve. I'll bear that in mind but, as I'm sure Simon's told you, I need to do most of this myself."

"I understand."

"But occasionally I may need a little help."

"Like access to official records to trace this nurse?"

"Precisely. I have no idea how to go about that but you probably do."

He smiles but says nothing.

I pause for a moment wondering how to phrase the next question.

"And you can do this without …?"

He finishes the sentence for me. "—Without contravening the Data Protection Act, is that what you were going to ask?"

"Well, yes, but—"

"Don't worry, Richard. We operate strictly within the law. Most people leave traces and when they do, we find them."

"Okay then. So shall we leave it like that for the moment."

"Fine by me," says Steve. There's a pause and I sense he wants to say something further. "I can see why you want to do this yourself, Richard, but don't feel too bad about bringing me in. Think of it in the same way as asking someone to help you solve an anagram in a crossword puzzle. You're still doing the puzzle but you need a bit of help with a tricky bit."

I laugh. "Fair enough."

"So let me just check … Her name is, or was, Heather Westcott?"

"Yes."

"Westcott with a double 'tt'?"

"I think so, yes."

"And she was in your final year at Modbury Road Primary School. Anything else?"

"I'm pretty sure she passed her 11-plus which probably

means she went on to High Oaks, that was the local girls' grammar school."

Steve nods. "I can check on that. Her age would be the same as yours, give or take."

"Yes."

"No suggestion she married before she began her nursing qualification?"

"No idea."

He nods. "Okay, we'll assume not and I'll take it from here. I've got your number. I'll let you know how I get on."

I get quite a buzz from my meeting with Steve but by the next day some of the euphoria has vanished. Having handed the next step onto someone else I'm at yet another loose end and that's when the despair creeps up on me. Then, later that morning when I turn my phone on, it beeps and tells me I have a voicemail message and to my surprise hear Rodney Montana's voice.

"Richard, I give you this for old time's sake but don't call me again. The number you have for me has been abandoned. But if you still want to contact some of our old school mates then try the Cerberus Club in Farnborough. They tell me that they'll be able to put you on to Terry Baldwin, and Terry is in touch with Julie Orford. Good luck. Call the Club soonest. Go, Apache, go."

Now what the hell's that all about? At first I'm excited. Rodney has found someone who knows Terry Baldwin and has learned that Terry knows where Julie is. Amazing. But then I begin to wonder. How did Rodney know to contact this Cerberus Club and if they do know where Terry is why didn't they just tell Rodney so he could tell me? Plus how would the people at this club know that Terry is in touch with

Julie, unless they also know Julie. I suppose it's possible that Julie and Linda Montgomery are still friends and Rodney is in touch with Linda. But then, he hasn't mentioned Linda, even though I asked him about her in both my messages before his phone was cancelled.

It's a very odd message and it all seems a bit convoluted, but at least it's another lead so I go onto the internet and search for the Cerberus Club. Their website states:

The Cerberus Social Club – an excellent place to come to relax and enjoy leisure time with friends and family.

I scroll down further and see they have a function room (weddings and parties catered for), 6 full sized snooker tables and a bar. From the pictures it seems a bit rough, more working man's club than high-end wedding venue. The manager's name is given as Victor Bradbury. Down at the bottom of the home page is a banner which reads: *3-headed dogs welcome*, so someone there has a sense of humour. However, there's no obvious link with Terry Baldwin, or why Rodney gave me such a cryptic message about it.

I try the number but all I get is an answerphone telling me the Club will be open at five o'clock and would I please ring back then.

The more I think about Rodney's voicemail, the more I'm puzzled. Why he didn't mention Linda Montgomery or the message I'd left him? I try his mobile number again but this time it just cuts out each time. As he had warned, the phone has been abandoned, or he has blocked me.

Inevitably I forget all about ringing the Cerberus Club. When you have nothing to do it's hard to find time to do anything. Inertia breeds forgetfulness.

I remember the Club at breakfast the next day and write a note to myself to remind me to call that evening. Then later that morning as I am making myself a ham sandwich for lunch my phone beeps and I have another anonymous text. This one reads:

Be very careful. They are watching you. So far your secret is safe.

What bloody secret, I think? I'm starting to get very irritated by these cryptic messages.

Thursday is Mrs Atkins' day which at least means I have someone to talk to and, inspired by her energy, I set to and wash the car.

That evening I remember I have to call the Cerberus Club but I hesitate. In all my years of trouble shooting for *Swamplett, Benson and Dring* I've developed a sixth sense that tells me when I'm hearing a lie, an evasion or less than the complete story. That instinct has proved very useful on many occasions and it's kicking in now.

Rodney seemed very insistent that I should contact this club, almost as though it were important to him rather than just a tip. I think back over his message, not just the words but the tone of voice. Then suddenly I remember his last words: "Call the Club soonest, yeah. Go, Apache, go."

Go, Apache, go. I hadn't especially noted that on his first message, but now it all comes back to me. The playground at Modbury Road. Morning break, or playtime as we called it in those days. Two teams. One led by that boy, Frank Lomax I think it was, the one with the thin face and red hair, they were the cowboys. The other led by Rodney and me, we were the Indians. It was based on our comics, of course, and was all about hunting and hiding and tracking and ambushing and, sad to say, ultimately fighting. Rodney and I were particularly good at the hiding and tracking bit, we had our own signs and signals, including a warning when danger seemed to be threatening. The warning was "Go, Apache, go."

Across the years that warning speaks to me again. Why did Rodney say that on the phone? Is it just a link with childhood memories or is it a guarded warning? If so, what is he warning me against?

Suddenly my brain is in overdrive. Perhaps he's warning me about the Cerberus Club but then why mention it in the first place unless he was forced to? But forced by whom? Oh, this is crazy. I'm building conspiracy theories out of nothing, but the whole of my professional life has taught me that just because something is unlikely that's no reason to believe it won't happen.

Proceed with caution. Keep an open mind. Later that evening I call the Club. This time the phone is answered and when I give my name I'm asked to hold. I can hear music in the background and then a rather silky male voice says: "Is that Mr Kirkwood? Richard Kirkwood?"

"Yes, I'm Richard Kirkwood."

"Thank you for calling, Mr Kirkwood. My name is Victor Bradbury. I am the manager of the Cerberus Club."

"Yes, I saw your name on the website. The reason I'm calling is—"

"I know why you're calling, Mr Kirkwood, you're trying to trace an old school chum called Terry Baldwin."

"Well, 'chum' is going a bit far, but essentially, yes."

"Well, I think we might be able to help you, Mr Kirkwood. Mr Montana has told us about the research you're doing for ... a novel you're writing, I think he said."

"Um ... yes, that's right, a novel. About childhood so I'm trying to find some old friends from that time to chat to." It is hard for me to think back through all the lies I've told people to explain my search.

"I see. Well, what I suggest, Mr Kirkwood, is that you pop in here sometime soon and we'll see what we can do to help."

"Can't we do it over the phone?"

Victor Bradbury's voice drips with regret. "Sadly, no, Mr Kirkwood. If I'm to put you in touch with Terry then I need to show you some documents first, documents which I have to keep here."

"Documents? What sort of documents?"

"Why not just come and see us, Mr Kirkwood. Then we can sort everything out."

Now the whole thing sounds truly odd, but I don't have a lot of leads to follow up.

"Okay then, when did you have in mind?"

"I think as soon as possible would be best. How about tomorrow?"

I don't like being rushed so I say, "Sorry, I'm not free. What about the weekend? Sunday sometime."

There is a pause then Victor Bradbury says, "Very well, Sunday then. About ten. In the evening. Come to the club and ask for me."

"Can't it be earlier? I have to—" but I am speaking into a dead receiver. Mr Bradbury has hung up.

Go, Apache, go, I think to myself as I replace the receiver.

I eat my supper in a thoughtful silence. I don't like the sound of the Cerberus Club at all but if there's any chance of finding Julie this way then I'm going to take it. I will keep that appointment in spite of my misgivings but I don't have to go alone.

I ring Simon and arrange to meet him for a drink tomorrow evening. He invites me to go back with him afterwards for supper.

37

RITA

Rita Kirkwood glanced at the clock. Simon had said they'd be home around seven so she'd give it another half hour before putting the potatoes on. She was glad he was bringing Richard back to supper. She was fond of her brother-in-law and felt rather concerned about him living alone while Lauren was away.

They arrived home almost on the dot of seven and after they'd eaten Richard thanked her for the lovely meal.

"I bet you're not eating properly," she said to him and he grinned.

"I manage."

"And how's the search for ... for ... your friend going?" she asked as delicately as she knew how.

"Slowly." And she saw him glance across at Simon and she felt an unspoken message pass between them. She had always been aware of the closeness between the brothers, a closeness which she admired and perhaps sometimes even envied.

"I don't want to pry ..." she began, knowing that was exactly what she was doing, but he stopped her.

"I don't mind. Everyone thinks I'm nuts. Even Simon. And you're probably right, but as an intellectual exercise it's quite interesting."

"You haven't found her?"

"No, not yet."

"How about your work? What's going on there?"

"No change, or none I've been told about. I can only assume the wheels of justice are grinding away somewhere. Sooner or later they'll work out I'm not a master criminal and then I'll get my job back."

"That'll be a relief, won't it?"

There was a pause, a long pause, and then Richard said. "Yes, I suppose it will."

38

I like Rita. She and Simon have a good thing going and they always find time to spend with each other, time they clearly enjoy. I envy that sometimes, though until recently I've had no plans to change how Lauren and I live our lives. But as these limbo days grind on I am starting to wonder.

I look across at Rita as she begins to clear the table. The smile she gives Simon, the smile he returns and then he just touches her hand in a gesture I find very moving. I push that thought aside and start helping with the dishes but that moment stays with me, a moment of closeness, of tenderness.

Sitting by the fire after dinner having coffee, I compare Rita with Lauren. Not as one woman against another – I certainly don't have any improper feelings about my sister-in-law – but rather as people.

Lauren is a powerhouse. She can be passionate. She is kind and caring. She is superbly competent at what she does, but her life is lived in compartments. She is working. Or she is cooking. Or she is making love. Or she's discussing the new carpet. But these are all in rigidly defined spaces. She does not flow out of one and into another, instead one stops, abruptly, and the next one, whatever it is, starts.

Rita on the other hand seems to flow through life in one long fluid movement. I've never thought about this before, before I found myself with time to linger, but now I have thought of it I can't stop noticing it. And I discover that her company is very relaxing.

It's peaceful sitting here. I've wondered before why their house seems so much more relaxing than mine. Is it the architecture? The furniture? Or just that the people living in it have achieved a balance in their lives. A balance I was not aware I lacked, but perhaps I do.

I feel calm now. Earlier in the evening, sitting in the pub, I told Simon about the texts I've been receiving. I thought he might laugh but he didn't.

"I'm wondering if I should have shown them to the police," I say, "although they'd probably think I'm sending them to myself or something, to make more of a thing out of the loss of the laptop."

Simon shakes his head. "I think you should tell them," he says, "they might be able to identify the number. You have nothing to hide and you must be as open as possible."

"I haven't been completely open." And I tell him about the messages from Rodney and the appointment at the Cerberus Club. "I might be making far too much of all this," I say, "but I was going to ask if you'd come with me on Sunday."

Simon is silent for a moment. "It does all sound rather melodramatic," he says finally, "are you thinking the '*don't speak to the police*' texts also come from Rodney?"

"I don't know, but I can't help feeling something's going on."

"Mmm. Well, look, I'll certainly come to this club with you on Sunday. I don't think you should go on your own. I think you need a bit of insurance."

"I can't think of anything better than having you with me," I say and he gives me a grin.

"We've faced worse than this, haven't we?" he says, "and

we'll come through this as well."

We arrange that he'll come to Weybridge on Sunday evening and we'll go over to Farnborough together. Then we drink up and go back to Rita's supper.

When I get home later that night there are two messages on the answerphone. The first is from Tina asking how I'm doing and reminding me of the invitation to visit her and Paul in Margate. I still don't fancy that but I'll call her tomorrow. The second message is from Steve Carling saying he has progress to report about Heather Westcott and would I give him a call on Monday. Sounds hopeful.

The following morning I check my emails and find one from Sally and one from Lauren. I read Sally's first. Hunky is back in the office but there seems to be some kind of tension between him and Francesca. The police have been back again but she's not clear why or what they are looking for. I wonder if they've found my laptop yet and, if so, if there's something on it that I don't know about.

I open Lauren's email and suddenly realise it's a week since I emailed her. She acknowledges that and apologises for the delay – pressure of work. The tone of her email is much the same as mine. She tells me a bit about the work (long hours), how she is settling in (very well), how comfortable the apartment is (though she's seldom there) and how vibrant New York still is (though she doesn't have much time to experience its non-working delights).

However, she has been back to the little Vietnamese restaurant in So-Ho that we discovered on our first visit to the city together. Apparently the food is still as good and as plentiful. She doesn't say who she went there with. She doesn't ask how my search is going. She signs off *Lauren xx*.

Ah, well.

I've been thinking about the conversation with Simon last night and decide he has a point about telling the police about the anonymous texts so I ring the number Sergeant Williams gave me and say I have something I want to talk through with him.

"Well, that's convenient, Mr. Kirkwood," he says, "I need to talk to you again as well. How about this afternoon?"

We arrange he'll come to the house at 3:00 and I go down the pub for lunch.

Sergeant Williams is as punctual as ever and by five past three we're sitting in my living room and I am telling him about the texts. He asks to see them so I hand him my phone.

He reads the three texts, his face impassive, then looks up at me. "No idea who these came from?"

Briefly I wonder whether to mention Rodney in Hong Kong but then decide against it. "No, none at all."

"'*So far you are safe …*' Safe from what, Mr Kirkwood?"

"I've no idea."

"And '*Say nothing to the police*'. Why would someone send you a message like that?"

"Same answer. No idea."

"Hmm. What made you ignore this warning?"

"To be honest, I haven't – for the pure and simple reason I have no idea what I'm supposed to be saying nothing about. Unless they're warning me off showing you the texts, you mean? Well, I wasn't sure if I should show you at first but then I thought, this is silly. I haven't interacted with them, or replied or tried calling – because that's what you do, isn't it? You don't encourage them. And I know I haven't done anything, so either these are a wind up or someone's trying to put the frighteners on me."

"Okay. Do you mind if I forward these texts to my own phone?"

"Not at all."

He pushes a few buttons, then hands the phone back to me. "There, I'll show these to my boss. I've made a note of the sender's number. Is that all you wanted to tell me?"

I look him straight in the eye. "Yes, that's all."

"Right then. My turn." He pauses then says. "You might be interested to learn that your business laptop has turned up."

In spite of myself my stomach lurches. "Has it indeed? Where was it?"

"In a drawer in a filing cabinet. We had a call from your Mrs Thompson—"

I interrupt indignantly. "She's not 'my Mrs Thompson', Sergeant. Francesca Thompson is a ... a ..." I pause, lost for words that would accurately reflect my feelings without landing me in trouble. Fortunately Sergeant Williams doesn't need things spelling out.

"Quite. I do understand. I have met the lady in question. However, Mrs Thompson did finally admit the possibility that you may have returned your laptop but she still denies you ever gave it to her personally."

"What does she say happened to it then?"

"The best she can offer is that you put it down when you entered her office without her noticing and then sometime later it must have got tidied away without her knowledge. She says she decided to look for it which is when she found it in this filing cabinet drawer."

"And do we believe her?"

"You may think what you like, Mr Kirkwood, I couldn't possibly comment. All I can say is that it'd be hard to prove either way."

"Yes … So have you had a look at it?"

"We have."

"And what did you find on it?"

"Less than we expected."

"How do you mean?"

"I think you told us you kept all your notes and records of your various projects on that machine."

"Yes, that's right, I did."

"Well, we certainly found a lot of stuff but would you be surprised to learn that there is no record, not even a passing mention, of the contractors we're currently investigating anywhere on your hard drive."

"Yes, I would be surprised. Everything was on there. I told you."

"So you did. So what conclusion do we reach?"

I suddenly see where this is going. "You think I wiped all reference to those contractors before returning my laptop?"

Sergeant Williams picks his words with care. "We think someone did, yes."

"Me?"

"We don't know, Mr Kirkwood. Did you?"

"No, I most certainly didn't."

He nods. "Fair enough." A pause. "Computers are interesting things and most people don't know nearly as much about them as they think they do."

"I'm sorry, I don't follow."

"It's easy to delete a file from a hard disk so it no longer appears when you look for it. However, the chances are that it is still there and skilled technicians can almost certainly access it. Our technicians are currently attempting to do just that with your laptop. How do you feel about that?"

"You're saying that even if all those contractor files are apparently deleted you can still recover them?"

"Almost certainly we can, yes. So, how do you feel about that?"

"I am perfectly happy with that, Sergeant. There is nothing on there that would worry me."

He looks at me for a moment then nods. "Fair enough. Well, I think I've taken up enough of your time." He gets to his feet. "We'll let you know how we get on with your laptop and in the meantime I'll see if anyone has any thoughts about what we can do about these texts."

"Good. I don't understand them. I can't see what they have to do with me and they're starting to piss me off."

"I'm sure they are. Leave it with me. Thank you for your time, Mr Kirkwood."

He goes and I am left wondering what happened to all those contractor records on my laptop. I really am starting to feel very uncomfortable.

39

Ten o'clock on Sunday evening and Simon and I are at the Cerberus Club in Farnborough. We leave the car a few streets away and arrive on foot. I'm nervous but determined. Simon is silent and watchful.

I know it's a Sunday night but the place looks deserted. There's one car in the car park, only some of the lamp posts are lit, two windows in the club itself are showing lights. It all looks very gloomy.

Simon and I look at each other. "All set?" I ask.

He nods. "Let's do it."

We walk across the car park to the main door. We push it open, step inside and find ourselves in a small foyer. No one there. We walk across to the next door and push it open. This leads into a dimly lit room and we see a man in jeans and a check shirt leaning on the bar.

"Mr Kirkwood, I presume," he says and then he sees Simon behind me. "Who's this? I told you to come alone."

"Actually you didn't," I say mildly, "you just told me to be here at ten."

For a moment he looks confused. "Well, it's been a busy week, I've had a lot on my mind but I meant to tell you to come alone."

"Well, I didn't. This is my brother, Simon."

"Good evening, Mr Bradbury," Simon says cheerily. "Gloomy old place you've got here."

Victor Bradbury appears discomfited. "Well, it's the depression, innit," he says, "hard enough getting enough customers through the door, nothing to spare for decorating."

"Wouldn't cost much to slap on a coat of paint," says Simon, "a few bright colours would do wonders round here. I'll have a pint by the way."

Victor gathers himself together. "No, you won't have a pint. That's not why we're here."

"Look," I say, "you've just told us business is bad and here we are wanting to buy a couple of drinks. What's the problem?"

Victor straightens up and comes towards us. We brace ourselves but he stops just short and thrusts his face towards me.

"Look here, smart arse—"

"Arses, plural, actually," murmurs Simon but Victor pays no attention.

"— You might think you're real clever, going on about painting and drinks and that, but we both know why you're here."

I nod. "Yes, I'm here to try and track down an old school friend, Terry Baldwin. You said you had some documents to show me so can we get on with it?"

"You can scrap all that bollocks now. Terry bloody Baldwin and your book thing. Let's get on with the real business."

"Are you telling me we've had a wasted journey?"

Victor grins. "You've not been wasted yet, but unless you start talking I wouldn't bank on that continuing."

"What do you want to talk about?" Simon asks politely.

"You keep out of this. I'm talking to your big brother."

"Actually he's younger than me. I'm the big brother."

"I don't give a sod how old you are," yells Victor, "I want to know how much you know about the Hong Kong deal and who you're working for."

Simon and I look at each other. "We don't know anything about any Hong Kong deal," I say, "and we're not working for anyone. I just want to find Terry Baldwin."

"For God's sake shut up about this Terry Baldwin."

"Why should I? That's the only reason I'm here."

Victor is starting to look decidedly stressed. "You think we don't know what you're up to? You think we don't know you've talked to Rodney Montana?"

"Of course, I've talked to Rodney Montana. He's an old school friend too."

"Bollocks."

I sigh deeply. "You're beginning to irritate me, Mr Bradbury. Rodney and I were at Modbury Road primary school together back in the 1960s. So was Terry Baldwin. I found Rodney and I'd like to find Terry. Can you or can you not help?"

"No. Never heard of this Baldwin guy but I do know Rodney and you must be mad if you think we're buying that 'writing a novel' crap. Now I want to know who you're really working for and how much Rodney told you."

"Rodney told me nothing and if you can't help me find Terry then there's no point in staying. Goodnight."

Victor smiles and I have an irrelevant private thought that I ought to introduce him to Francesca at some time. His smile, like hers, makes you think of slimy things moving at the bottom of a cess pit.

"I don't think you're going anywhere, sunshine," he says.

We hear a movement behind us and when we turn round

we see a rather large man standing in the doorway. He's holding what looks remarkably like a baseball bat. As we turn back to Victor another man stands up from behind the bar with a similar weapon in his hand. I realise my feelings of unease about this place fell slightly below the mark.

This has the air of the sort of interrogation where the questioner has already decided what he expects to hear, and any other answer is just an excuse for action.

Victor is now all smiles. "Now, then," he says, "there's no need for anyone to get hurt. I just want some straight answers to my questions. First, who told you to ring Rodney Montana?"

"No one told me," I say, "I just wanted to talk to him about our old schooldays."

The two gentleman lift their baseball bats higher.

"I think you're being very stupid, Mr Kirkwood," says Victor. "We'll find out sooner or later and sooner is definitely more comfortable."

I'm finding it hard to believe how this is developing. Bradbury himself looks like a long streak of piss. I could almost certainly tackle him but I can't see how Simon and I can handle the two heavies and their baseball bats.

I glance sideways at Simon but he seems completely unperturbed. I decide to try and be conciliatory.

"Look, Mr Bradbury, I don't know what's going on with you and Rodney and I don't want to know. He told me that he'd called you and that you could help me find Terry Baldwin. If you can't help with that then we're going. Goodnight."

The veins on Victor's neck are standing out like a map of red arterial roads. "You're going nowhere," he says. "If you want to do it the hard way then we'll have to persuade you."

The two heavies start to move forward then Simon says, "Wait. I'll talk."

The tension relaxes and Victor smiles. "Your big brother has more sense than you, Mr Kirkwood." He turns to Simon. "Okay, talk. Or I'll get the lads to do your brother's legs."

He means it too. In spite of myself I feel the tension take hold in my stomach. Simon, however, just nods.

"Okay," he says, "now a few moments ago you said there's no need for anyone to get hurt."

"Not if you're going to be sensible."

"Oh, I'm very sensible," says Simon, "far too sensible to come to a dump like this," – Victor's mouth opens to protest but Simon goes straight on – "without a contingency plan. Now you were right. No one's going to get hurt. Gus will make sure of that."

"Gus? Who the hell's Gus?"

"I am," says a deep voice from the far end of the bar. All five us swivel round to see a tall, thin man in camouflage clothes and a black balaclava standing at the far end of the room, cradling what looks very much like an automatic rifle in his arms.

The two heavies tense but Gus continues, "Now the lads and I don't want any trouble" – I presume he means us but then a second man appears beside Gus, dressed the same and also carrying a weapon – "so if the gents in the cheap suits like to lay down their little sticks and move over here where I can see them ..."

The two heavies size up the odds and make a sensible decision.

"You too ..." Gus gestures at Victor. "That's lovely. Now I think we'd all feel more relaxed if you lay down on the floor and stretched out your arms."

The three of them do so and Gus's companion comes over and frisks them. Victor is clean but each of the heavies has a knife.

I look across at Simon. "So this is your insurance, is it?"

"Sure," says Simon easily. "You remember Gus."

Oh, yes. I remember Gus. Car mechanic and part-time soldier. I turn to face him. "Thank you, Gus. Good to see you again."

Gus gives a half nod.

"Right then," says Simon, taking charge. "We need to see where we go from here." He bends down and takes Victor's hand. "Upsadaisy, Mr Bradbury."

He heaves Victor to his feet. One of the heavies also stirs but Simon pokes him with his foot. "Not you, mate. Stay down there where we can see you."

He props Victor against the bar, leans forward, brushes some dust off his shirt.

"Doesn't seem to be your day, old son."

I'm still trying to come to terms with the fact that Simon's concept of 'insurance' and mine are poles apart. I've always known my brother looks out for me but this...

Simon goes on, "Now then. Why don't we have that beer and a little chat?"

Before Victor can respond a woman's voice says: "I'll get the drinks."

We look round to see a well-dressed woman in her fifties who's appeared behind the bar. She ignores the heavies, ignores Gus and his friends and addresses herself to Simon and me.

"Bitter or something stronger?"

Simon glances at Gus who shakes his head. "Two bitters please," he says.

She pulls the pints and pushes them across the bar then pours herself a scotch. She doesn't offer Victor anything.

My mind has finally caught up with the events of the last few minutes and suddenly everything is clear. I turn to Victor.

"This whole thing's been a con from the beginning, hasn't it? You don't know how to contact Terry Baldwin."

"Never heard of him."

"So the whole idea was for Rodney leave me that message to lure me over here, to do what?"

"What do you think?"

"What I think is that you and Rodney have got some little racket going and the pair of you thought I knew all about it. But why should you think that?"

"Oh come off it. Phoning Rodney like that out of the blue with some cock and bull story about wanting to find some kid from your schooldays. Give me a break."

I nod. "See what you mean. The only thing is it happens to be true. There is someone I'm looking for so when Rodney mentioned Terry Baldwin I decided to follow it up."

"Tough luck. I've told you, I don't know any Terry Baldwin."

"I do." The statement comes from behind me and I swing round to face the woman.

"You know Terry Baldwin?"

"Yes. Well, I did. He was in our class at school."

For a moment I'm speechless then suddenly everything falls into place.

"You're Linda Montgomery."

"I was. I've had a few other names since then. And you're

Richard Kirkwood. Nice to see you again, Richard, after all these years."

Simon intervenes again. "Touching though this reunion is, we need to get this sorted. What sort of racket are we talking about? Is it drugs?"

"What?" Victor is outraged and Linda is shaking her head. "You think we're running some kind of drugs racket? You must be nuts."

Simon is unfazed. "Has to be the first thought that comes to mind."

"Use your common sense, man". Victor is genuinely upset. "I wouldn't touch drugs. Dirty business. And anyway, d'you think I'd be running a place like this with protection from a couple of useless overweight morons if I had drug money behind me. You're crazy."

In spite of himself Simon laughs. "See what you mean," he says, "so if isn't drugs, what is it? Alcohol?"

"It's clothing," says Gus. We all turn and look at him and he jerks his head backwards. "Designer clothing, shirts, jeans, the full nine yards. There's boxes of them, back there. Fell over them as we came in the window."

I turn to Linda. "And how do you fit into all this?"

She shrugs. "Rodney and I were an item for a while. That didn't last but we stayed business partners."

"The fake designer clothing business?"

"All kinds of business. He's based in Hong Kong, Victor is here and I move between the two of them."

"Doing what?"

She looks at me coolly. "I don't really think that's any of your business."

"Not my business? When you went to all this trouble to

169

set me up."

Victor interrupts. The suggestion of drugs has clearly upset him. "We had to find out what you knew."

"Which is nothing."

"So you say. But now you do."

I turn back to Linda. "D'you know where Terry Baldwin is now?"

"No. Why do you want to find him?"

"Not him especially. Someone else."

"Ah, Julie Orford."

"How do you know that?"

"You asked Rodney about her and I remember you had a thing going for her when we were at school. Yeah?"

"Sort of."

"So why you looking for her now? After all these years?"

I look at her coolly. "I don't really think that's any of your business."

For a moment her eyes blaze with anger and then she laughs. "Touché."

Simon intervenes. "Look, this is all very well but we have to resolve this." He turns to Linda. "Let me get this straight. You have no idea where Richard can find Terry Baldwin."

"Absolutely none."

"And what about Julie Orford?"

"Same answer. We stayed friends for a while after Modbury Road but then we lost touch. It happens."

I nod, a little sadly. Another lead has fizzled out.

Simon is still intent on the current situation. "Okay, none of us has got what we hoped for out of this evening. The question now is what happens next?"

Victor and Linda exchange glances. "Well, you hold the

balance of power," says Linda with a sideways glance at Gus.

"For now," says Victor.

"For now," agrees Linda, "but if you choose to upset the applecart there'll be some very angry people in Hong Kong. People I personally wouldn't want to upset."

"But if we just walk away now then the balance of power, as you put it, reverts to you."

"So it's stalemate."

"Oh, for crying out loud." We all look round to see Gus shaking his head in despair. "What's wrong with you guys? Of course, it's stalemate but we can live with stalemate – all we need is some insurance."

We all look at him. I'm slightly nervous. The last time 'insurance' was mentioned its reality turned out to be two guys carrying automatic weapons. I really don't fancy a shootout with a group of Hong Kong hoodlums.

"It's quite simple," Gus explains patiently. "Ideally we'd all like to go back to the situation as it was before this evening began. Right?"

We all nod.

"Well, that's not possible because now we all know stuff we didn't know before and that's dangerous. So what we do is this. We, that is Simon, his brother and my friend, will forget we ever came here. I'm not interested in your clothing scam, though mind you, if it had been drugs it'd be different."

"How do we know we can trust you?" asks Victor.

"You don't. Not entirely, but now you know why we came here, you know we're not looking for trouble. Certainly we don't want to end up in a war with anyone from Hong Kong."

Linda seems completely unphased by all of this. "But they might still want a war with you."

"No," says Gus. "In a moment I'm going to photograph all those boxes, this club and all of you. Oh, and incidentally," he added, "I've been recording the whole of this conversation since we first arrived."

He holds up his hand, forestalling outbursts from Linda and Victor. "By this time tomorrow the photos and recordings will be in a safe place and there they'll stay, unless any harm comes to one of us in which case they'll go straight to the police. Stalemate, but with the status quo guaranteed."

So this is what we do. Under the watchful eye of Gus and his companion, Victor and Linda, plus the two heavies, have their photos taken. Then while Gus is taking the rest of the pictures Linda sidles up to me.

"Why d'you really want to find Julie again after all these years?"

I smile and shake my head.

"She really fancied you, you know. Pity you never followed it up. Missed your chance there, boy."

I don't find this helpful and she knows it. A tiny bit of spite as she adds, "You're having a mid-life crisis, aren't you? Much good may it do you, mate."

I don't feel this visit has been the most successful of school reunions.

40

GUS

It had been a good evening. He'd enjoyed it. When Simon had approached him and explained what he needed, he'd felt the familiar battle adrenalin rise up in him. Not the same as being in Afghanistan – that would always be a high spot in his life – but at least this was action. And it had all been so simple.

He'd recruited a friend and they had staked out the club before Simon and his brother had arrived. Done a recce. Prepared the back window for entry. After that it was just plain sailing. No significant opposition and the L7A2 General Purpose Machine Guns they carried were a guarantee they'd be in complete control.

He grinned to himself. He wondered what Simon would say if he'd known the guns were replicas. Simon had always been impressed with his range of guns and he'd always let him believe they were real. Not that it made any difference. It only needed the sight of a couple of blokes in combat gear cradling combat weapons to tip the balance. Anyway, judging from the look of the two guys with baseball bats, he and his mate could have taken them anyway, with or without guns.

And the end of the evening was very satisfactory. He had always admired Simon, the way he was good with people, his confidence, his way with words, his obvious ability. But tonight, when the chips were down, it was him, Gus, who'd known what to do and had done it. Now he just had to debrief Simon and his brother and they could be on their way.

41

Gus escorts us back to Simon's car. We shake his hand and say "thanks" though I'm still slightly overcome by the degree of planning that Simon thought constituted insurance.

Gus elaborates on what happens next. "I'll make copies of everything, photos, sound recording and so on. I'll also write a short sitrep on what happened here tonight."

"Including the guns?" Simon asks.

"Skipping over the guns," says Gus. "I'll send you each a set of copies. Lodge them in a safe place with appropriate instructions. I don't expect any comeback but you can't be too careful."

"Thanks for all your help, Gus," says Simon and I add my thanks too.

"No probs," says Gus, "we enjoyed it. Great fun. See you."

And he melts away into the night.

"Well, you kept that very quiet," I say to Simon.

He nods. "Thought it might be a bit over the top," he says, "but like you I wasn't entirely happy about the ten o'clock meet so I thought I'd take precautions."

I think for a moment. "You know, I'm really sorry about Rodney. We were good friends once. I wonder what led him into that particular game."

Simon says, "You realise we're withholding information about a crime?"

"Yes, but what choice do we have?"

"Not a lot."

There's a pause then Simon goes on rather more grimly, "I'd prefer it if Rita doesn't hear about all this."

"'Course not."

I'm still trying to come to terms with the events of the evening. Wherever I thought this quest would take me, I definitely did not factor in risking my brother's health and wellbeing.

Simon eyes me speculatively. "And you're a cool customer yourself, aren't you?"

"What do you mean?"

"I can see why you do the job you do – working out complicated business issues. Even when Victor was threatening to get rough, you never blinked."

"Oh," I say, taken aback. "Thank you."

"So, what next? Heard from Steve yet?"

"Yes. I got a message to ring him tomorrow. Maybe he's got a line on Heather. I hope it's simpler than this one. I'm starting to run out of options."

Simon wrinkles his nose. "When did you last talk to Lauren?"

"We've exchanged emails."

"I said 'talk'."

"Not lately. She's busy. Anyway there's the time difference ..."

He just looks at me, then we get in the car and go home.

42

On Monday morning I leave it until about ten then phone Steve Carling.

"I got your message. Have you found Heather Westcott?"

"Not actually found her, no, but we're making progress. She did do her nurses training at St Thomas's and stayed on there for about five years. Then she went north to Leeds Infirmary where she seems to have settled down. She may even have got married about then, just doing a final check. After that she seems to have moved on again, possibly to Wales. We need to confirm her married name before we can be certain but we're getting closer."

"Well, you're doing better than I am? Do I owe you anything yet?"

"Yes, please. As you're Simon's brother I didn't bother with a retainer but if I could send you an interim invoice ..."

"Of course, and you'll keep me posted."

"Sure thing," says Steve and rings off.

The next few days pass very slowly. I'm more shaken than I'd care to admit that Rodney set me up for such a nasty scene, and apart from Steve Carling's research, my quest seems to have reached a dead end. With nothing to occupy my mind, my thoughts keep turning back to the fraud investigation. I try and rationalise it. I'm innocent. I've done nothing to be ashamed of, so it's bound to all come right in the end. Isn't it?

But in the secret recesses of my mind I'm struggling

with the worry about the misplaced laptop and the police asking whether I'd foreseen the risk of someone adding files to my machine. I cannot escape the possibility that I'll never completely clear my name. And I know I cannot live with uncertainty. Most people see me as a success. Good job, comfortable lifestyle, lots of travel. Even Lauren thinks I am a high achiever. It's only me who knows it's all an illusion. Deep down I am always afraid. I camouflage it well, but I know that I don't deserve the respect that some people feel for me. I am a sham.

This garden leave is very painful, not just because it's forced me into places where I cannot bury the past but because it's also making me think about the future. The work I do, the pressure of the job, has always been my protection. But now, being forced to step back and take a look at myself, I realise that for a long time I have been running faster and faster just to stand still. Sooner or later I will trip and then everything will come tumbling down.

Perhaps it has already. For the first time I begin to understand what Simon has been trying to tell me for years. *You can't hide for ever,* he'd said.

I'm turning in on myself. I am in a very bad place but part of me wants to be there. I think I want to punish myself. I don't go out, I hardly eat a thing. I just sit and let the misery overwhelm me. Somewhere in the depths of my head a little voice whispers, "Don't be a fool. Call Simon. He'll get you out of this ..." but I know what happened the last time I did that. This is my problem, not Simon's, not Lauren's. If my world is going to implode I do not want to take anyone down with me.

Then on Wednesday afternoon my misery is interrupted

by a beep on my phone and I see I have another text.

This is a further warning. If you tell anyone what you know it will not be good for your health.

Suddenly, looking at this message, I find I'm angry. Who the hell is this person who's constantly tormenting me? Aren't things bad enough without these snide, unjustified accusations? If I knew who was sending me these things I'd break their bloody neck. And what the hell are the police doing about it? I grab my phone and call Sergeant Williams.

He listens to me in silence as I rant and rave at him. When I finally pause for breath he asks me what the text says. Then he tells me to forward it to him which I do.

"I understand your frustration, Mr Kirkwood," he says. "We are working on this but all these texts come from a prepaid phone which is virtually untraceable. The most we have is that it is using a UK network. But we're still trying."

"Then try harder," I snarl and cut him off.

Not a satisfactory call but, to my surprise, I find I am suddenly feeling better and hungry and I realise that, unlike self-pity, anger is not a passive emotion. Although, after spending two days feeling sorry for myself, I am unshaven and scruffy. I go down the pub and murder a seriously large steak. Then it's back home to the best night's sleep I've had in a long time. Perhaps I should get angry more often.

Then on Thursday morning Steve Carling phones again to say he's found Heather Westcott. She's living in a cottage in Mawgan, a village in Cornwall just outside Helston. That's all he knows at present.

"There are still a number of gaps, Richard. I don't have the full story yet. She vanished off the radar for a while which is a little unusual. I'm looking into that further."

"Last time we spoke you said you thought she was married."

"Yes, that's one of the loose ends we're following up. She's certainly calling herself 'Westcott' now and, as far as we can tell, she's living on her own."

"Divorced?"

"Possibly. I'll let you know when we have more."

"Okay, but you're sure this is her current address?"

"Well, she was certainly there a year ago. We haven't traced any movement since then."

"So Cornwall, eh? I like Cornwall, even at this time of year."

"Thinking of paying her a visit?"

"Well, yes, Maybe I will."

There's a brief pause then he says, "Actually I'm not sure that's the best plan, at least not yet."

"Why not?"

Another pause. "Don't know," he says finally. "Just an idea that something's not right. Or at least, there's something missing."

After my encounter with Rodney and Victor, I'd be a fool to overlook his warning. "Dangerous?"

He laughs. "No, I don't mean that. Just the trail is a bit odd. Irregular."

"But you're certain this is my Heather Westcott?"

"Oh, yes."

"Then where's the harm? She can only slam the door in my face."

"You could give her a ring."

"Maybe, but trying to explain to someone over the phone

why you want to talk to them after all these years isn't easy."

"No. Oh well, your call, but there's one thing you might want to think about."

"Yes?"

"How you going to explain how you found her? She might resent being investigated by private detectives."

"Good point. I don't know. Suppose I'll have to play it by ear."

When I hang up, Mrs Atkins is waiting to talk to me. Apparently our vacuum cleaner is on its last legs. We go online and I order a new one – the one she thinks is best. If only all my problems could be solved that easily.

The next morning I sit at my desk and update my strategic plan. It still looks quite impressive laid out on the screen but I can't help feeling I'm getting nowhere fast. Heather is now the only lead I have but will that move my quest forward or just be another mistake?

I know that if I just sit here brooding I will sink back into self-pity. Positive action, that's what's required so on the spur of the moment I decide to ignore Steve's advice and go to Cornwall today. Within half an hour I've packed a bag and I'm heading for the M3.

By the time I reach Exeter, it's starting to get dark and I'm feeling tired so I decide to stop for the night and continue my journey tomorrow. I don't fancy the bland sterility of a hotel chain but then I remember a pub on the edge of Dartmoor where Lauren and I once came for a long weekend. Somehow this seems very appropriate and half an hour later I'm pulling into the car park.

They have a room so I register, have a hot bath and then lie on the bed thinking back to the last time I was here. The few days that Lauren and I spent here were bittersweet. We'd been married for a couple of months by then. I had a flat in up-and-coming Battersea at that time and we'd settled in together comfortably, though we were both working long hours, of course. However, in those days we still had some free time and I'd thought it'd be nice to show her some other corners of England so I'd booked his long weekend on Dartmoor. Then, while we were here, a crisis suddenly erupted.

We'd been walking out by Haytor and had sat down on a rock to rest when Lauren suddenly said. "Something I've been meaning to mention."

"What's that?" I said idly.

"We've never talked about children, have we?"

It was so unexpected that I completely lost it. My response was instant and angry. "I'm sorry. That's out of the question."

She opened her mouth to speak but I leapt to my feet and began pacing around. "No children. Not now, not ever.

I absolutely refuse to even consider this. The idea's abhorrent, impossible, I'm not even prepared to discuss it, do you understand?"

I remember how stressed I felt as everything suddenly bubbled over. I remember shaking with the intensity of feeling. Lauren was clearly concerned. "Richard, whatever's the matter?"

I subsided onto the rock again but all I could do was mumble. "No children, no children. Never."

Hesitantly at first, then more surely, Lauren put her arm round my shoulders and held me as the shaking gradually subsided. Then she said, very gently. "Is there anything you want to tell me?"

I shook my head. "No."

She was silent for a moment and then she said. "Okay."

I was regaining control. "I'm sorry, I'm so sorry. That was uncalled for."

"On the contrary, it clearly was called for but we'll park it for the moment. I was about to say I'm not particularly interested in having children. I thought that might upset you and I was going to apologise for not raising it earlier but I guess it's kinda the other way round."

We walked back to the pub in silence. Looking back now after all these years I wonder how things might have been different if I'd been able to talk to her then, talk to her properly and unburden myself. I couldn't do it then and I'm not sure I could even do it now, though I have always been conscious of this no-go area between us. We never talk about it but I'm pretty sure she feels it too.

Back in the present I push these painful thoughts away and start getting ready for dinner.

As it turns out, the past hasn't finished with me today. Later that evening I'm sitting in the bar enjoying a single malt, when a man passing by suddenly stops and comes back.

"Excuse me," he says rather hesitantly. "It's Mr Kirkwood, isn't it? Richard Kirkwood?"

"Yes, that's me. Do I ...?"

"Oh, you won't remember me but you came to talk to the final year students on the Business Studies course at Exeter University about, oh, must be around seven or eight years ago."

I cast my mind back. That was around the time that *Swamplett, Benson and Dring* were trying to demonstrate that they were a 'caring corporate' and some of us were sent to fly the flag to a number of universities. Exeter could well have been one of them.

"I remember it very well", the man was saying, "in fact you could say it changed my life."

My heart sinks. Remembering Simon's words about action and reaction, I'm not sure I want to know how I changed anyone's life. Out loud I say, "I'm terribly sorry but I'm afraid I don't remember you ..."

"No reason why you should. Just another face in the crowd. Look, my name's Mark, Mark Trimble. If you're on your own can I buy you a drink?"

Why not, I think, I've nothing better to do and half an hour's chat is better than sitting in my room watching late night TV.

He buys me another malt, has a pint of beer himself and we settle ourselves down.

"I remember that day very well," he says, "it was our last term before graduating and we'd had a succession of visiting

184

speakers describing what life was like in the 'real world'." He makes quotation signs with his fingers. "Most of them were very dull. The virtue of hard work, the importance of results and all that stuff. But you were different."

I'm starting to wonder if he wants something but I put the ungracious thought from me.

"How do you mean, different?"

"Well, you told us about the reality. You helped bridge the gap between theory and the world outside. D'you remember the story you told about the graduate from Harvard Business School. The one where the guy leaves college, gets his first job, settles down at his desk the first day, buzzes his secretary and says 'Bring me my first case'." He roars with laughter. "That really touched a button with all of us."

In spite of myself I smile. "it wasn't a true story, you know, Mark. I invented it."

"Of course, we knew that, but you spelled it out. We'd spent all our time dealing with case studies then you come along and point out that real life isn't like that. Life isn't neat, you said, you start dealing with one thing and another crops up and while you're wondering which one to deal with first, yet another problem arises."

I smile ruefully. "That does sound like me. And I probably talked about prioritising and the skills needed to keep more than one ball in the air at a time."

"Yes, yes, you did. You spoke about stress too. You said stress was inevitable but it wasn't the stress that did for you, it was how you handled it." He pauses. "I've never forgotten that."

I had forgotten it. It's one thing to talk to a group of students, it's another to put all that good advice into practice.

I'm certainly not handling the current stress in my life very well. With an effort I bring myself back to the present. Mark is still in full flood.

"But that's not the main reason I remember your talk," he says, "it was later, when you were wrapping it up, that you said the most important thing."

I flinch slightly. "I'm almost afraid to ask what that was."

"You told us no matter where we went, who we worked for, whatever the business culture in a company might be, we should always be ourselves. 'Be true to yourself', you said. 'If you're comfortable in your own skin then you'll always work better'. I've never forgotten that."

I take a deep breath. "It sounds rather pretentious when you put it like that."

He laughs. "Yes, it does rather, doesn't it? But it made a huge impression on me at the time. Then a few years later I acted on it."

He sees the reaction on my face and hastens to reassure me. "No, no, it's fine," he says, "it's all worked out for the best."

"If we're into confessions I think it's time we had another drink." I go to the bar, replenish our glasses and then settle back by the fire again.

"Okay, Mark. Give me both barrels. How did I change your life?"

"Well, after I left college I went to work for a merchant bank in the City. Good money, quite interesting, at least at first, but then after a few years I realised I was bored."

"No promotion?"

"Oh, yes, I'd been promoted, they were pleased with my work. Long hours, of course, not much free time, but I was doing well."

"And then?"

"And then I just thought what's the point? I was earning all this money but I had no time to do anything with it. I had a flat in Docklands, I drove a series 7 BMW but I didn't have any friends, not outside work anyway. Life was just ... well ...work."

For a moment my mind flashes back to the house in Weybridge. Lauren and I, leaving early, getting back late, microwaved meals, working on papers most weekends, exhausted the rest of the time. Planes, airports, boardrooms, sensitive negotiations. Life is, or had been until recently, just work.

Mark is watching me intently. "You know how it is, don't you?"

"Oh, yes, I know how it is."

"I wasn't unhappy, you understand, I just felt sort of, well, empty. Then one day I remembered what you'd said. 'Be true to yourself. If you're comfortable in your own skin etc etc'. So that's what I did."

"What? What did you do?"

"I resigned. I bought a small workshop, just up the road from here actually, invested in a good set of tools and now I make furniture for people or anything else they want made out of wood. I'm good with my hands and I'd always dreamed of working for myself but I'd got obsessed with the whole career thing."

I am stunned. This is the last thing I expected to hear. "You've gone from merchant banking to woodworking?"

"Yes, it's brilliant. I've never had so much fun in all my life."

"And can you make a living?"

"Sure. Not as much as before, naturally, but quite enough for my needs. I meet a lot of people and they're always pleased with what I do for them. I can't tell you how refreshing that is after the culture at the bank."

"I can imagine."

Mark sits back in his chair. "Well, that's quite enough about me. How about you? Still with the same company?"

"Oh, yes. Still travelling the world. Still sorting out other people's cock-ups. If it's Tuesday it must be Finland, that sort of thing."

"Sounds very glamorous, but I bet it isn't. I can recognise the signs now. Are there days when you wonder if it's worth it?"

Suddenly a casual conversation has become serious. "I'm not sure how to answer that."

"Oh, I'm sorry, you don't have to. I don't want to intrude. I'm just curious. I wondered, you know, if you'd ever thought of doing what I've done?"

"I can't do woodwork."

He laughs. "You know I didn't mean that. I meant have you ever thought of hanging up the suit and doing something completely different?"

A good question. I never have, at least not until recently. Now though I'm starting to realise there may not be a way back, even if I emerge from this investigation squeaky clean. In the past few weeks I've been forced to face so many things I've always tried to keep hidden and I don't think I'll ever be able to force them back into the box. Will I ever be able to pick up where I left off? I don't know. But I'm afraid that if I can't, it means that whatever happens there cannot be any successful outcome for me.

Mark turned his dreams into reality. I fear that my dreams will stay dreams and that ultimately they are empty.

44

SAN JOSÉ

The sun was glinting off the sparkling white walls of the villa above San José, and spilling down the hillside to the village by the harbour. Richard was sitting on the balcony in shorts and sandals, bare from the waist up, his portable typewriter on the table in front of him. In the past few months he had turned a golden brown but as the day advanced he always moved under the shade of the awning. The midday sun on this part of the southern Spanish coast was too fierce, even for those who were used to it.

He had risen at six as usual, breakfasted off fresh orange juice, yoghurt and the honey from Manuel's hives. Then he brewed fresh coffee and took it with him to his seat on the balcony. Prompt at seven he booted up his laptop — the portable typewriter was so out of date — and opened the file of the latest novel at the point where he'd left it the previous afternoon.

He glanced back into the dimly lit room behind him to the grandfather clock that had belonged to his father's family. It had cost a lot of money to bring that to Spain with him but it was a link with his past that he did not want to break. Its presence here added to his sense of security.

The clock now said five minutes to twelve. Nearly time to stop work. At midday he would close the laptop, get his hat and walk slowly down the hill to the village. He would lunch in Pedro's bar on calamari and a glass of cold white wine. Then back to the villa for his siesta. At half past four he would wake again, by five he would be back on the balcony and would spend the next two hours revising the work he had done that morning.

Then perhaps he would drive into Mojacar for dinner or, if he didn't want the drive, he could go back down the hill and have whatever fish Pedro had bought off the boats that morning.

Today was slightly different though. Stella had flown out from London last night and was driving up from Almería to join him for lunch. She had the contract for the new film script with her and they were going to go through it together before he signed.

Or was this the day that Rosalie would come over from Nijar to share his lunch and his siesta, staying on till the cool of the evening?

Either way the chances of doing any more work that day were slim but it didn't really matter. In theory he was on a tight deadline, though no one was worrying. "Richard always delivers on time," they would say.

It didn't matter because neither Stella nor Rosalie existed and neither did the sun-drenched villa on the hillside above San José. Except in his dreams.

45

The following morning I indulge in a little nostalgia and take a wandering route across Dartmoor, re-visiting some of the places Lauren and I saw during that first visit. Widecombe, where I stood in the main street and treated my American wife to an uncertain rendering of '*Uncle Tom Cobley and All*' – to her embarrassment, and the amusement of other tourists. Dartmeet, where we jumped from rock to rock in the river and even caught a brief glimpse of an otter. By unspoken consent we set out to have fun that day and we did.

Thinking back though, perhaps there was a sense of forced gaiety to that weekend. I had expected Lauren to probe deeper about my outburst the previous evening but she never did. It was as though our conversation by Haytor had never happened. That was probably a mistake. We buried the whole topic, but it stayed there between us, an unwelcome elephant in the room which never went away.

I try to push the memories aside and drive on into Cornwall. I book into a hotel in Falmouth and get a room overlooking the estuary. It's very peaceful here and I sit for a while watching the dusk come down over the river.

The next day I set out to find Heather's cottage. I stop in Helston to buy some chocolate and suddenly my eye is caught by a display of three watercolours in a shop window. I recognise the subject immediately – they're pictures of the

Helford river, little boats, inlets, jetties, gulls.

Many years ago, long before I met Lauren, I'd come to Cornwall with my then girlfriend, Paula. I'd just started as a management trainee with an oil company but the initial salary was not generous so our holiday was definitely on a budget. We'd stayed in a guest house in Redruth which was so awful that we left it as soon as breakfast was over (sometimes even before it had started) and got back as late as we could at night. Each day we explored another bit of western Cornwall but time and again we came back to the Helford river, the peace, the tranquillity, the sense of being out of time.

I loved it there but I've never been back. The Paula thing ended soon after, not altogether amicably. She was a lovely person but she was getting too close. I knew the signs and was having none of it so I just walked away. I think I hurt her rather a lot. I hurt a lot of people over the years until I met Lauren.

But I never forgot those few days by the Helford river. I even bought a book about Cornwall with lots of photographs but somehow they never quite captured the true atmosphere in the way these pictures in front of me now manage to do. I'd like to look at them more closely but it's Sunday so the shop's closed.

That afternoon I drive out to Mawgan and find the address Steve has given me is a modern bungalow. I knock at the door, rehearsing my opening line, but there's no answer. I wait a few minutes and try again but there's an air of emptiness about the place and it's clear no one is in. In fact, it doesn't look as though anyone lives here at all.

I head back down the path and then, in that inevitable way in a small village, a neighbour pops her head up from behind the hedge.

"Hallo, m'dear. Was you looking for someone?"

"Well, yes, I was told Heather Westcott lives here."

"Was you now? Well, you was told wrong."

"Oh, I'm sorry. It's just that she's an old friend and ..."

"Her did live here. For a while."

This brings me up short. "She did live here but doesn't anymore?"

"That's right. This is a holiday place really. Mr and Mrs Travers up at Bristol own it and they let it out, mostly to friends, I think."

"And Heather came here for a holiday?"

"No, her lived here, but only temporary like, while her was looking for something permanent, if you take my meaning."

"Oh, I see. And when did she leave?"

The woman rubs her chin. "Well, now, must be well over a year, maybe longer. It would've been spring, I reckon, because the holiday season was starting. Let me think. Yes, must have been just after the dog broke its leg, 'cos her helped me get it to the vet. But I think her was gone before the plaster came off so that'd be sometime early April. Last year."

So much for Steve's timetable, I think. Aloud I say: "And do you know where she went?"

"Course I do, m'dear. I have to send on her letters." She pauses. "Not that there's been any, mind."

I ask for the address and at first she's a bit doubtful but when I explain that we were at school together she relents.

"Well, I daresay that'll be alright. Her be at Falcon Cottage, over by Helford."

"Oh, right. Do you have a postcode?"

"Oh, no, we don't bother with them fussy things. Everyone

194

know Falcon Cottage, m'dear."

I thank her and I'm just about to drive away when she taps on the window.

"Was you thinking of driving over to see Heather tonight?"

"Well, yes, I was."

"Well, I'd leave it till tomorrow, if you take my meaning. It'll be dark shortly and you don't want to be driving along all them rutty tracks at night. Anyway, it's right lonely out there and her might not want to answer the door in the dark."

She has a point. I thank her again and drive back to Falmouth.

The next morning I set off straight after breakfast and head for Helford. A sign at the edge of the village informs me that from May to September only residents are allowed to drive any further but, as it's November and anyway I'm a visitor not a tourist, I press on, down the hill, round the corner, cross the little bridge over the inlet and on alongside the water till I come to the pub. The road runs out here but I speak to a lady walking her dog and she sends me back the way I've come.

"Look out for the track on the right with three white stones on the corner."

I do this and soon find myself bouncing along over ruts and roots. I'm very glad I didn't attempt this in the dark last night.

The track does an abrupt right-hand turn, apparently straight through a hedge, and then suddenly I find myself out on a wide gravel space, the Helford River spread out below me and to one side an old granite cottage with a veranda which affords the most magnificent view over the water.

I have found Falcon Cottage.

46

HEATHER

Heather rose at 7:00 as she always did and had her breakfast sitting in the glassed-in section of the veranda looking down the river. She liked it here. The quietness and peace gave her the strength to get through another day.

When she'd had her fruit salad and toast there was just enough bread left for lunch so she made a note to bake that afternoon. However, today was one of her studio days, so when she'd cleared away the breakfast things she made her way round to the north side of the house.

Her studio was in an old outbuilding whose roof had been collapsing when she'd first arrived. The south gable had been rebuilt in traditional materials but the north facing one was now all glass. Her easel stood under this window and the light was perfect for her work.

She rationed her time in here, as she now rationed all of her time. A strict pattern with fixed starting and stopping points, a rigid framework that helped each day to pass. She wasn't sure this was a good way to spend the rest of her life but for the moment it seemed to be working.

She started at 8:30 and at 10:30 she stopped. This was the time she'd go back to the house, make some coffee and break for half an hour before resuming work at 11:00 and then working through to 1:00.

But this morning, as she was finishing her coffee, she suddenly heard the sound of tyres on the gravel and was immediately alert. No one ever came here except John, the local farmer who occasionally dropped off a box of eggs, but that wasn't a tractor engine. The only other person was the local handyman if she needed something building or mending but he only ever came by appointment.

She moved to the window and peered out cautiously. She saw a light blue BMW parked on the edge of her gravel space and a man she didn't recognise getting out of it. She had only a moment to make up her mind. She could retreat to the back of the cottage and pretend she wasn't here but then she'd always wonder who he was and what he wanted. Casual callers were unknown at Falcon Cottage.

He was coming towards the door now. She made her decision. She whipped off her paint covered smock, threw it over the back of a chair and moved to answer his knock.

47

There is an air of stillness about this place, an air that's not dispelled by the woman who opens the cottage door. There's no bustle about her, no expression, just a stillness. She stands there, not unwelcoming, but not smiling either. I don't recognise her at all but then I didn't expect to.

"Can I help you?" she asks and her voice has an edge of uncertainty to it as though she rarely speaks out loud.

I smile. "I don't know. I hope so. I'm looking for Heather Westcott."

There's a pause, almost as though she's wondering how to answer. Then she says: "I am Heather Westcott."

"Are you the Heather Westcott who went to Modbury Road primary school back in the 1960s?"

For a moment a look of complete amazement passes over her face but it's quickly suppressed. There's a slight pause, then she says cautiously: "Yes, I did go to Modbury Road but that's a very long time ago."

"It certainly is," I say, "I don't know if you remember me, Richard Kirkwood. We were in the same class."

Again there's a pause before she speaks and I'm expecting her to say "Who?" but instead she says: "Yes, I do remember you. You were involved in the school magazine."

"Yes, I was. That's amazing after all these years."

"What can I do for you, Mr Kirkwood?"

"Richard, please ..."

Again that faint smile. "You must want something to have tracked me down here."

"Well, I do in a way and it's going to sound very odd."

For a moment she hesitates and I wonder if she's going to close the door on me but then she steps back. "In that case you'd better come in. Would you like some coffee?"

The door leads straight into the living area of the cottage. A comfortable room, with a sofa and an armchair in front of a large open fireplace. A table and three chairs are off to one side and a curtained doorway that I guess leads to the kitchen. In one corner an open wooden staircase winds upwards.

A coffee percolator and a mug stand on the table as Heather gestures me towards the fire. "Have a seat. I'll get some more coffee on."

She vanishes through the curtain and I settle into the armchair and glance round the room. A low bookcase runs along one wall, there's a small portable television and a hi-fi set. Another rack holds a number of CDs.

A ginger and white cat pads down the stairs, starts to head for the kitchen but then sees me and comes over and sniffs my feet. I put my hand down and tickle its ears.

"Hallo, puss."

The cat purrs then leaps up onto my lap and settles itself down. I stroke it and suddenly feel very relaxed. This is a peaceful room. I notice a paint-splatted smock lying across the back of one of the chairs and my mind suddenly flicks back to the paintings in the shop in Helston.

Heather comes back carrying the refilled percolator and another mug. She almost does a double take when she sees the cat on my lap.

"You're honoured," she says, "Gladstone doesn't usually

199

tolerate strangers."

"Why Gladstone?"

"It's the name Florence Nightingale gave to one of her cats. It just appealed to me."

"I like cats," I say, "though I've never owned one."

"Nor have I," says Heather, "you don't own cats. You simply provide board and lodging. Black or white coffee?"

"Black please."

She pours it out and tops up her own mug. She sips for a moment and then, with what sounds like a little sigh, says: "All right, Mr Kirkwood, sorry, Richard. Let's have this odd story."

Now the moment has come I'm curiously reluctant to start so I take refuge in a diversion. I indicate the smock on the chair. "Are you an artist?"

She looks at me for a moment. "I paint pictures," she says, "I don't know whether I'm an artist."

"Were those your pictures I saw in a shop window in Helston yesterday?"

"That's quite possible."

"They were very good."

"Thank you." There's a pause, then she goes on. "I paint for pleasure Mr ... Um ... Richard, and today is one of my painting days so if we could ...?"

"Oh, yes, sorry." I try to gather my thoughts. "As I say, this is going to sound really weird but I've been trying to trace one of our classmates from our last year at Modbury Road."

I pause, but she says nothing so I plough on. "The trouble is, as you said, it's a long time ago and most people's memories don't go back that far. I was surprised when you said you remembered me, to be honest."

She smiles faintly.

"I've tracked down a few of them. Phillip Armstrong, Rodney Montana, Norman Huggett – well, sort of – Linda Montgomery. And I remembered some other names, Suzanne Duncan, Martin Green, Terry Baldwin ..."

"I remember Martin Green," says Heather, "He tried to kiss me once, in the cloakroom. He had very bad breath."

"Oh, right," I say, rather taken aback.

"And the name, Terry Baldwin. Wasn't he always getting into trouble?"

"Yes, I think so. I don't suppose you've kept in touch with any of them, have you?"

"Which one do you want to find?"

"Julie Orford." And I plunge into a brief explanation of my job, the current situation, time on my hands, needing a project and the more I talk, the more stupid the whole thing sounds. Finally I grind to a halt.

"Well, that's about it," I say. "You're welcome to laugh. Most people do. They think I'm nuts. Just another sad, middle-aged man longing after a lost part of childhood."

I'm getting used to her silences now. I can almost see her thinking.

"I don't think you're a sad, middle-aged man," she says finally. "I do think you're probably fooling yourself and I'd be surprised if finding Julie after all these years will help you at all."

I say nothing and after a moment she goes on. "But, on the other hand, the only way to make an itch go away is to scratch it." She pauses. "As it happens I did stay in touch with Julie and with Suzanne Duncan as well."

I am dumbfounded. "You mean ... you mean you know

where Julie is?"

"No," she says calmly, "I've no idea where she is now. But I do know where she was a few years ago."

"You do? Well, that's amazing."

"No, not amazing. Slightly surprising, maybe. If you'd asked about any of the others I wouldn't be able to help you."

"So how is it you stayed in touch with Julie?"

She gives a half smile. "Chance, like so many things. After we left Modbury Road we all went to different schools, Suzanne, Julie and me. That might have been it, but in my mid-teens I joined a local dance class and that's where I met them both again. We danced together, became friends in a way we'd never really done at school and then we just somehow stayed in contact."

"But you lost touch, a few years ago you said?"

There's a long pause and she turns her head away. She seems to be gazing through the window but somehow I sense she's looking way beyond that.

I say nothing, just wait, and eventually she takes a deep breath and turns back to me.

"I'm sorry," she says, "yes, we lost touch, or rather I lost touch with her and with Suzanne. There was a ... well ... sudden change in my life and I cut myself off rather."

And stayed cut off, I think, but I say nothing.

"My fault," she goes on, "I regret it sometimes. Not just Suzanne and Julie, other friends too. But it was my choice."

"Can you tell me where Julie was when you last heard from her?"

There's a pause while she considers this. "I'll have her last letter somewhere but I'll have to look for it and I don't want to do that now."

"No, of course, I understand."

"And also I need to think about whether I should tell you anyway. This is a rather unusual thing you're doing."

I laugh shortly. "So I've been told many times."

She nods. "All right, Richard. I'm going to ask you to go now. I have work I want to get on with and I need to think. Are you staying locally?"

"In Falmouth."

"Did you make a special journey to Cornwall just to see me?"

"Yes."

"And how long do you plan to stay?"

I shrug. "My time's my own."

She looks at me for a long moment and then she says, "I'm guessing you're married."

"Yes, I am."

"And is your wife with you?"

"No. She's away at present, working in New York. I'm on my own."

She gives a faint smile. "Even more time on your hands, I see."

For a moment she seems to drift away again then she says, "All right. Give me a couple of days." She pauses. "Do you know Porthleven, the other side of Helston?"

"Yes, I do. Not very well."

"There's a pub there. The Ship. On the far side of the harbour. Meet me there at midday on Wednesday and I'll tell you what I've decided."

"I'll be there."

She stands and I stand too, forgetting the cat who, caught by surprise, leaps for safety. We move to the door but as I step out onto the path I turn and hold out my hand.

"Thank you, Heather, not just for the coffee but for your courtesy. I have a strong feeling I've butted in where I shouldn't have done and I apologise for that."

She lifts her head and for the first time I really see her eyes. A kind of hazel with just a hint of green. I don't know how to describe her face. Calm certainly, possibly controlled.

"Thank you. You weren't to know, but I'd rather meet you on neutral territory next time."

"Of course. Until Wednesday."

As I drive away down the rutted track I'm not sure what to make of that meeting. There was an atmosphere there, not an unwelcoming one, but something was definitely amiss.

Later that day my mobile rings and I see it's Steve.

"Hi, Richard", he says, "look, we've learned a bit more about Heather Westcott and if I were you, I'd give her a miss."

My heart skips a beat. "Why?"

"Well, it's a bit of a sad story. She did get married when she was in Leeds to a guy called Robin Pearce. He was a pharmacist. They were there for some time and then they moved, but not to Wales as we first thought. They actually went to Gloucestershire."

"Okay, but now she's in Cornwall and calling herself Heather Westcott again. Divorced I presume."

"On the contrary. Her husband got cancer and she nursed him for a long time. He eventually died about two years ago."

"Oh, God."

"There's more. They had a daughter, Katherine. About a year before her father was diagnosed she went to live in New Zealand. She apparently got married out there but there was some kind of rift with her mother and I don't think they're in touch. Not sure what's going on but apparently Heather took it pretty hard. Once the funeral was over she sold up in Gloucestershire and buried herself in Cornwall. No idea what she's doing now."

"She's painting."

"She's what?"

"She's painting. And she's not at that address you gave me, she was only passing through there."

There's a pause. Then Steve says: "You're in Cornwall now, aren't you?"

"Yes, I've just been to see her."

"How was she?"

I think back to the room at Falcon Cottage. The sense of peace I'd felt but also the wariness of our conversation. "I think Cornwall's working for her but she's still a bit brittle. I'm seeing her again on Wednesday."

"Was she any help?"

"Maybe. She was actually in touch with Julie until a few years ago. When we next meet she's going to tell me if she'll let me have that address. If she does, then I'm gradually catching up with her."

"I don't know ... I'm cross we didn't pick up Heather had moved on again." Steve seems lost for words. "Well, in the circumstances I don't know there's much more I can do."

"No, you found Heather. That's what I asked you to do. Now it's down to me."

I spend Tuesday walking and thinking. The walking is good. The thinking is harder. Even if Heather decides to help, I wonder how much use it will be to discover where Julie was a few years ago. I suppose I could go there, wherever it is, and make some enquiries but, apart from the fact that the time gap is narrowing, it seems as though I always have to start again from scratch.

There's also the question of Heather herself. It's clear now that I'm intruding. She's obviously chosen isolation as a way of dealing with her loss and then I come crashing in. What am I going to say to her, now that I know what's happened, although she doesn't know I know? It's all getting very complicated.

I don't have any answers so I do what I always do when dealing with clients. Once you've made all the preparations you can, leave the rest to chance and instinct.

Wednesday, and I time my arrival at The Ship for just after midday. Heather is already there, sitting at a corner table with a glass of wine in front of her. We exchange greetings. She declines another drink but pushes the menu towards me.

There's the very faintest hint of a smile around her mouth as she says. "Well, I've made one decision. You can treat me to lunch."

We order, I buy myself a pint and settle down. For a moment neither of us say anything. I've decided not to rush her, let her set the pace.

Finally she shakes her head. "I should really be very cross with you, Richard. I didn't get any more painting done after you'd left on Monday."

"I am sorry. I didn't realise I'd be interrupting. Not until it was too late."

"Doesn't matter, not really. Like you, I've plenty of time." She looks down at her drink. "I lead a very structured life these days. Maybe a bit too structured."

"I'm the other way round. I did have a structure but then it fell apart. Now I'm floundering."

"Hence the search for Julie?"

"Yes."

"But you don't really want to find her, do you?"

"What? Of course I do."

She shakes her head. "I don't think so. I think she's an abstract idea. I don't know what it is you're really after. Maybe you really are just trying to recapture memories of a happy childhood."

"Oh, for God's sake." I bang my glass down on the table, surprising both of us. "Happy childhood? You've got to be joking."

She has no idea what I'm talking about and heads are turning from other corners of the pub. I get myself under control. "I'm sorry. I apologise."

"No need. I didn't mean to touch a raw nerve."

"You didn't. Well, yes, you did, sort of, but I over reacted."

There's a moment's silence then right out of the blue she says. "What's your wife's name?"

"Oh … er, Lauren. Why?"

"Is it difficult for you, her being that far away?"

I give the standard answer. "Not really. We both work very long hours. We don't get much time together anyway."

She nods, then says. "I only asked because I can see you're in pain and I'm wondering why. It's not just the problem with your job, is it?"

I don't know how to respond to this so, stupidly, without stopping to choose my words carefully I say. "You think I'm in pain?"

Perhaps I lay too much stress on the "I'm" because she suddenly looks wary.

"Oh, my ... You know about me, don't you?"

Rather shamefacedly I nod.

"How?"

I take a deep breath. All the half-formed ideas and excuses flash through my mind and then suddenly I realise the only option here is complete honesty.

"I hired a private detective. I couldn't do all the searching myself and I reasoned if anyone remembered Julie it was more likely to be another woman. You were the only one I knew anything about."

The food arrives in the middle of all this but now I've started I have to continue, so I explain about Phillip Armstrong and his sister who'd thought that Heather had become a nurse.

Heather listens to all this, her face expressionless and I eventually grind to a halt.

"I only found out the details on Monday night. I had no idea what you've been through when I pitched up at your cottage that morning. If I had known—"

"— You wouldn't have come." She smiles briefly. "I don't know whether to be outraged or flattered."

I take a forkful of my already cooling lasagne. "Why be

either? I didn't intend to intrude. Not in that way. Now that I know what happened I'm very sorry. Perhaps I should just finish my lunch and go away and leave you in peace."

"No, don't do that." She butters her roll and takes a spoonful of soup in the deliberate way I'm already finding familiar. "Look, Richard, it's possible we can help each other."

"Do you need help?"

"I may do." I wait, say nothing and after a moment she goes on. "It's been nearly two years since ... since ... Robin, my husband, died. The last few months were not easy, as I'm sure your private eye has told you. There was" – she hesitates – "there was some difficulty with our daughter. His death was not pleasant. She seemed to take it personally. I don't know ..."

Heather's eyes have taken on the faraway look that I saw in her cottage.

"After the funeral I cut myself off from everybody. Came down here. I wanted to be alone. I didn't think anyone knew where I was. I don't know how your man found me."

"He didn't. He only traced you as far as Mawgan. I went there first."

"Oh, you went to the bungalow. Yes, the Travers were very kind. Did you get my address from them?"

"No, I got that from the lady next door. She was a bit protective but when I said we were old school friends ..."

"Ah, Mrs Tregorran. She's a dear. Now I understand."

Suddenly, surprisingly, she grins. "Nice to think your detective couldn't complete the search but Mrs Tregorran did."

"And did it work? Coming down here?"

Again one of her thoughtful pauses. "Yes, it did. I think it did. The painting has helped and so has the solitude ..."

"Do I hear a 'but' coming?"

"Not a 'but' exactly. I don't know. It's hard to describe. You know I was a nurse ...?"

I nod.

"Yes, of course you do, that was silly. Well, sometimes a doctor will prescribe a course of antibiotics. These might well solve the problem, whatever it is, but if they go on being administered after their work's done, they can start causing problems of their own."

There's a pause while I digest this idea. "And you think this is happening to you?"

"In a manner of speaking. Grief is normal, of course it is, but there comes a time when you have to move on or you wallow in misery for misery's sake. I've been wondering lately if that's what's happening to me."

"And then suddenly I arrive out of the blue."

"Yes, a pebble dropped into a pond. Ripples everywhere."

Ripples, I think – can't get away from them. Aloud I say, "Are you saying you think it might be time to move on again?"

"Heavens, no. Not physically anyway. I love the cottage. I love my painting but maybe, just maybe, I'm starting to prolong the isolation unnecessarily."

I don't know what to say to this so I push my plate away and stand up.

"I'm going to the loo. Then would you like some coffee?"

"No thank you, but I will have a another glass of wine. It was the Pinot Grigio."

I visit the Gents which gives me time to collect my thoughts. The conversation isn't going the way I expected. I still don't know if she will tell me about Julie but I don't feel

I can rush her. I collect another wine and a coffee for myself and sit down again.

"This quest of yours," she says, then hesitates. "Is 'quest' the right word?"

"It's the one most people are using."

"Okay then, this quest of yours, tell me what you've done so far."

"You really want to know?" She nods. "Okay then."

I start at the beginning. I expand a little on the shock of suddenly finding myself with empty hours, nothing to do. I talk about the situation back in the office, the visit from the police. I tell her about Lauren's reaction, and Simon's. I describe the visit to Rodney's mum, the phone conversation with Rodney, meeting Philip Armstrong, failing to track down Norman Huggett and getting his wife instead. I give her an expurgated version of Polly and her own problems. I don't mention the Cerberus Club. I talk about my meeting with Steve. I recount how I was coerced into the talk at Modbury Road and my meeting with Januariusz Bronowski and all the time she sits there in her own circle of quiet, no expression, no reaction.

Finally I run out of words and stop. I feel drained. I meet her gaze for a moment then, rather embarrassed, I look away.

"It all sounds rather childish when I sum it up like that."

"I don't think it's childish. A little extreme possibly but we're all searching for something, it's just most of us don't know what it is and at the moment you do."

"Or think I do?"

"Or think you do, yes."

There's a pause and then I say tentatively. "About Julie ..."

"Yes. Julie."

"What have you decided?"

"Oh, yes, I'll give you the last address I had for her."

"Thank you. So is she married? Does she have a job? What's she been doing all these years?"

"No, I'm not going to tell you anything about her. I don't know a lot anyway but if you do find her she can choose what to tell you and what not."

"But you're happy to give me her address."

"The last address I had, yes. I can't see the harm in that and in any case I don't think it'll do you any good."

"Oh, thanks a lot."

She laughs. It's the first time I've heard her laugh and somehow it changes the atmosphere between us completely.

"Don't look so offended, Richard. It's at least five years old and that's a long time. She could be anywhere by now. I think she was going to move."

"But she might not have? She might still be there?"

"She might, but in a way I hope she isn't. I think, forgive me for saying something a little bit insensitive, but I think your journey is far more important to you than the destination."

This isn't a new idea and Heather's not the first person to suggest it but her direct approach is quite refreshing.

"It seems to me you've reached a crossroads in your life, Richard. And I think maybe I have too."

"Is that what you meant when you said you might need help."

She looks down at her plate. "I'm stuck. I know I'm stuck. I chose this way of life but I've known for a while now that I need a change. Perhaps your visit will be the impetus for that. Who knows, we'll have to see."

"You think there's something I can do …?"

She shakes her head. "No, that's not what I meant, but listening to you, just having this conversation might give me a nudge."

She pauses for a moment. "If I'm honest, no one else can help. I've got to find my own way through this, as have you. There's just one thing …"

She breaks off.

"Yes?"

"I'm being insensitive again, forgive me, but are you sure you're searching for the right woman?"

I stare at her, lost for words, but she goes on. "I really shouldn't be saying any of this. It's none of my business but I do know how easy it is to break bridges and how hard it can be to mend them again."

Now you're talking about your daughter, I think, but I say nothing and after a moment she says quietly, almost as if talking to herself.

"It's so easy to concentrate on one thing, ignoring other equally important things around you. Then the one thing goes and you're left with nothing."

Suddenly she reaches across the table and takes my hand.

"Richard, I cannot begin to tell you what I've been through the last few years. You apparently know the basic facts, but the rest … the struggle to come to terms with it, coping with the aftermath, trying to discover who I really am, what I'm doing and where I'm going, how to live with myself, you have no idea."

She laughs briefly, a rather harsh laugh. "But an essential part of the process for me has been the dumping of all illusions."

"And you think I have illusions that need dumping?"

She lets go my hand and sits back in her chair. "I don't know. We both know pain, don't we – and loss causes you to have a rough awakening to reality."

I'm becoming slightly uneasy with this conversation.

She says, more to herself than to me. "You can't repair everything but if you're going to live with yourself you have to try."

She suddenly snaps back to the present. "Sorry, I was miles away."

I smile. She picks up her glass, drains it and stands up. "I must be going. Thank you for lunch. I'm sorry if I was impertinent."

I also stand. "No, it was fine. I enjoyed our conversation. You've given me a lot to think about."

Again I see that faint smile. "Well, good. I've enjoyed it too. As you'll have gathered, I don't get out much."

I hesitate for a moment. "And Julie …?"

"Oh, yes, of course." She opens her bag and produces a piece of paper. "That's the last address I had for her. Good luck."

I take the piece of paper. It has an address in Scarborough but it's the name that strikes me. Julie Wigglesworth. So she did get married. I look up to say thank you but Heather has gone.

I glance down at the paper again and see that there's a phone number at the bottom and a scribbled note.

This is my number at the cottage. Let me know how you get on sometime. But don't call in the mornings. H.

MAY 1962

Monday morning. He is Gate Monitor. It's his turn to stand at the school gate and log anyone who arrives late while the rest of the school is in assembly.

This is normally a boring job. Most people arrive at school on time. However, this morning at five past nine he sees a figure in a school blazer running towards him. As it gets nearer he sees it is Julie.

Why does it have to be Julie?

She arrives at the gate, panting. She smiles at him.

"I'm glad it's you, Richard. I'm sorry I'm late. My mum's ill and I had to get breakfast for my dad and little brother. You don't have to report me, do you?"

Of course he does. That's what he's there for. But who will know? The rest of the school is singing hymns on the other side of the building.

She reaches out a hand and lays it on his arm. "Please, Richard."

He makes up his mind. "Go on. Be quick. Make sure no one sees you."

"Oh, thank you." She blows him a kiss. "Thank you."

He turns back to the road. Another compromise for young love.

The house feels bleak and unwelcoming when I get back the next day. I look round the rather bare living room, modern shaped chairs, mock coal fire running off electric, highly polished, seldom used dining room table, and I suddenly feel cold, nothing to do with temperature, just atmosphere, so I go down the pub for supper. I don't want to talk to other people but I need to know they're there.

Sitting in the pub I think back over the experience of meeting Heather. It hadn't exactly been what I'd expected. She has made me realise what Simon meant when he said that poking around in the past will cause ripples and who knows what those ripples might do.

I'd dismissed this idea at the time but now I'm starting to understand how easy it is to break the rhythm of someone else's life and not necessarily for the better. What ripples have I caused for Rodney ... for Polly... for Heather? For the first time I start to think seriously about what I'm going to say to Julie when I do find her.

And that's another thing. Heather thinks I don't really want to find her, but I do. The search for her has become compelling and I don't want to stop.

The next morning I turn on my laptop and google Julie's address in Scarborough. I print off the map and sit looking at it. Four hours or so in the car and I could be there, perhaps coming to the end of my search.

Then I think about Lauren. Heather's question, *"Are you sure you're searching for the right woman?"* really hit home. I realise she was relating my experiences to her own regrets about her daughter, but it has made me start wondering about the effect my search for Julie is really having on Lauren.

I'm sure Lauren doesn't seriously think I'm trying to recreate a forty year old childhood passion, but she might well see it as another example of the way we're drifting apart.

And that raises another question. Are we drifting apart? I don't know how to tell. We've spent so little time together over the last year or so, no days out at the coast or weekends away. Just work, snatched meals, floating tails of conversation.

Currently we're also physically apart. That puts a distance between us in a literal sense, but I'm beginning to think it's more than that. And that worries me. My increasing doubts about my future, whatever the outcome of the investigation, are frightening enough by themselves but if I were to lose Lauren as well, then I don't know what I'd do.

I realise that I am missing her. Without her this place is simply a house, not a home.

I've always assumed that my first priority is to survive this garden leave and make sure that no suggestion of malpractice ever sticks to my name, but maybe that's wrong. Maybe the first priority is to rebuild bridges with Lauren and that can't be done by text and email. I need to see her face to face.

I make a quick decision. Scarborough will keep, Lauren might not, so I go online and book an open return to New York. There's nothing available over the weekend so I settle for Monday. Remembering my conversation with Sergeant Williams I ring his number and leave a message saying I'm going to New York to see my wife and will be back in a few days. Must remember to send Lauren a text to say I'm coming.

I spend Saturday freezing cold, waiting for someone to come out to deal with a fault in the central heating boiler. Finding someone at all at a weekend calls for every bit of my persuasive power, but finally everything is working again. On Sunday I go to lunch with Simon and Rita.

Monday morning I look out some warm clothes, New York will be cold this time of year, grab a fistful of dollars from the supply I always keep handy, check my passport, recharge my laptop and I'm ready to go first thing in the morning.

LAUREN

Her days were very full and she was working a six day week, sometimes spilling over into Sundays. If she'd thought the pressure in London was great it seemed like nothing compared to New York. Occasionally she paused, blinked, wondered how she'd ever got onto such a rollercoaster but she got used to it and found she loved it. This Monday was a typical day. In the office by seven, meetings, phone calls, emails, a business lunch, a report to write, another meeting, briefing notes to prepare.

It was just before five when her phone buzzed and the reception desk said there was someone downstairs asking for her. She wasn't expecting anyone, didn't have the time to see anyone but asked who it was.

She was stunned by the answer.

With hindsight it's a pity I forgot to send a text telling Lauren I was coming. At the time I was so distracted by my plan and the hassle of the boiler and lunch with Simon and Rita that it slipped my mind. I take a cab to her office in Liberty Plaza and then have to wait in reception for nearly half an hour before she appears.

"Well, what a surprise," are her first words.

"That was the idea," I say, "I suspect you won't be home for Christmas so I thought it'd be nice to spend a couple of days together. Do a bit shopping, have an early Christmas dinner, you know."

"Just a couple of days?"

"Or three. Or four if you like. I've got an open ticket."

"Well, the thing is, Richard, this isn't really a very good time. I'm involved in a pretty complicated case at the moment with a very tight deadline so—"

"— My timing's lousy."

"Yeah, sorry, but it is. Now if I'd known you were coming ..."

"You'd still have been busy, wouldn't you?"

"Well, sure, I guess, but I could have suggested you left it until the new year."

Suddenly I feel very tired. I'd got up early – I was out of practice for that – driven to the airport, had the usual struggle through security, flown the Atlantic to see my wife, only to find I'm apparently just another complication in a busy day.

Some of this must show in my face because Lauren suddenly softens.

"Look, I'm sorry, Richard. I'm being ungracious. You've had a long journey. Hey, why not go down to the apartment, get a bit of rest. I'll get away as soon as I can and we'll go out to dinner somewhere."

Olive branches are always worth accepting, so I nod. "Good idea."

"Right, here are the keys. You've got the address. I'll book somewhere for dinner and aim to be back around seven-thirty. Okay?"

"Okay, see you later."

The apartment in Battery Park is surprisingly comfortable, not huge but more than adequate, especially as I suspect Lauren spends very little time here. It's strange to see all her bits and pieces, clothes, toiletries, night things, scattered round a different environment.

I kick off my shoes, lie down on the bed and fall asleep. I wake just before seven-thirty but there's no sign of Lauren. I wash and freshen up and am just wondering whether I should ring her when she arrives.

"Sorry, sorry, I know I'm late."

"No problem. I've only just woken up."

"Give me a minute and I'll be with you. I've booked a table at La Montana up on Chambers."

The meal is fine but the evening is not a success. Neither of us are relaxed, we're awkward with each other and we seem to have nothing to talk about. Lauren is obviously preoccupied with her case and all I've done since she left the UK is work at my quest to find Julie and I don't feel able to share that with her. Looking back on it later I think it's significant she doesn't ask.

She does ask after Simon and Rita and how I'm managing round the house. We touch briefly on the fraud case and I make a bit of conversational mileage by describing my meetings with Sergeant Williams. She seems happy that it was all routine and above board although as I predicted she suggests that if he wants to interview me again, I ought to have a lawyer present. I gloss over the anonymous texts as if they're just spam, or phishing or something generic and not at all personal, but I do at least tell her.

I don't tell her I miss her. It was always going to be difficult for me to put that into words and this slightly tense situation makes it impossible.

The next morning Lauren is up at 6:00 and gone by 6:30. Much the same routine as she has at home. Much the same routine I used to have myself before garden leave forced idleness upon me.

I have breakfast in a diner and then spend the morning shopping. In spite of what I said to Lauren yesterday there's nothing I really need but I wander round Bloomingdales anyway and manage to find a Christmas present for Rita. She'll like the fact that it comes from New York.

I'm expecting Tuesday evening to be a repeat of Monday – different restaurant, same forced conversation – but mid-afternoon I get a call from Lauren.

"Hi, look, d'you fancy joining us for drinks this evening?"

"Who's us?"

"Well, it's a client's do actually. Several of us from the office are going and when Justin, that's our senior partner, heard you were over he suggested you might like to come along."

"I don't have a DJ with me or anything."

"No problem. Smart casual's fine. It's five-thirty at Frisbees on West 55th."

"Okay, why not?"

It turns out to be an interesting evening. Lauren's colleagues seem very pleasant, driven of course, but that's the New York legal scene. I have quite a long chat with Justin during which he makes it clear that Lauren is one of their rising stars. I make all the right noises.

It's very interesting watching Lauren in this company. She sparkles. There's no other word for it. I'm glad she came to New York. She is clearly in her element.

Later a group of us go on to dinner and it's late when Lauren and I get back to the apartment. She's still on a high so we pour a drink and sit in the window looking out towards the Hudson river. We're more relaxed together than we were last night.

Lauren stretches out her legs and kicks off her shoes. "Oh, that's better. They were starting to pinch a little." She pauses. "Did you have a good evening? You seemed to be enjoying yourself."

"Yes, I did and I was. Justin seems a nice guy."

"Slave driver, but he's appreciative as well."

"He seems to think highly of you."

"Ye–es."

I take a deep breath and gear myself up to try and explain how much I am missing her but she gets in first.

"Richard, there's something I've been meaning to mention."

"Oh, yes."

"Early days, but Justin's talking about extending my time

here for another three months. How would you feel about that?"

This comes as a shock. Her current six months takes me to the end of my guaranteed paid garden leave. I have no idea what will happen after that, but if I'm still kicking my heels and Lauren is still in New York then what will that do to our marriage? It already seems stretched to breaking point. It's clear that my idea of trying to close the gap between us by making this spontaneous visit has not worked.

I glance up and see her watching me intently and I remember the way she looked earlier in the evening in her professional environment, and I know there's only one answer.

"I think if they offer an extension you should take it," I say. "It's too good an opportunity to miss."

She doesn't quite manage to control the expression of relief but she rushes on to make all the right noises. "I still feel guilty, leaving you all alone over there to face those arseholes by yourself."

"Thank you," I say, "I appreciate that, but you can give me your best legal advice when I need it, can't you? Even if it has to be unofficial. And this is what you've always wanted, after all."

"Yeah. Yeah, it is. Thank you for your understanding."

"However," I say, "I think I'll go home tomorrow if that's okay. You're obviously busy. This wasn't a well-timed visit and I should get out of your hair."

"Right. Look, I've been meaning to ask. What you going to do about Christmas? I mean I can't get back ..."

"No, no, of course not. Well, I hadn't really thought. Go to Simon and Rita's probably."

"Oh, that's great. I hate to think of you on your own."

"What about you?"

"Oh, Justin and his wife have invited me up to their place on Long Island. It's only for the day. They don't do Boxing Day over here."

"No, of course not."

There's a slight pause then she says. "Richard, was there any specific reason for this visit just now?"

How do I answer that? Part of me desperately wants to reach out to her, to tell her about my ever increasing fear about a not proven verdict but, as always, I find it difficult to express emotions and feelings. Anyway, I can see how much she is enjoying the challenge of New York so I just smile.

"No, no, not at all. I just thought it would be nice to see you. Sorry about the bad timing."

"Yes, so am I." There is a pause but neither of us say anything.

Finally she says: "So you'll be off tomorrow?"

"Yes. I think there's a flight around seven in the evening from Kennedy. I'll see if I can get on that. I'll call them in the morning."

And on that note we go to bed.

53

Heathrow at 6:30 in the morning, not exactly the stuff dreams are made of and with a long delay in the baggage hall bolted on it's hardly surprising I'm not feeling my best.

I eventually manage to extricate my car and head for Weybridge. I'd forgotten it was Thursday until I see Mrs Atkins' Toyota pull into the drive behind me. She follows me into the house, chattering gaily about the new vacuum cleaner. Nothing will do but that I look at it, admire it and assure her that I too think it is a magnificent specimen.

She makes coffee and I take mine through to the study. From force of habit I open the document with my strategic plan for finding Julie Orford. I've already added the information I got from Heather and there's nothing new since then. I read through it but it's all dead ends. The only lead that may be hopeful is the Scarborough address where Julie was, at least until five years ago. There are no emails waiting for me and no phone messages. I feel very alone. Somehow I battle through the day but I'm in bed by eight.

The next morning I feel more positive. There are things I can do and I will do them. I start by phoning the office. That achieves nothing. Hunky is unavailable and Francesca hangs up on me so I call Sally and leave a message. She gets back to me later in the morning but there's no news. The police are still poking around and seem to be spending a lot of time with Hunky. Francesca is more like a Rottweiler than ever, but no one really knows what's going on.

"Actually, Richard," says Sally, "the atmosphere round here is poison. I suppose something like this is bound to be unsettling but there's a nasty sense of suspicion hanging over everything."

She asks how Lauren is doing in New York and I tell her I've just got back from there. I'm very positive, I say all the right husband type things, but don't mention Lauren might be staying there longer.

In turn I ask how Mervyn Wilby is getting on and Sally gives a deep sigh. "Terrible. He's now lost us two major clients. He seems to put backs up wherever he goes."

Part of me feels a wicked satisfaction at this, the other part wonders if my future is already decided. If Mervyn is there much longer there might not be a job for me to go back to, even if the outcome of the investigation is in my favour. It's out of my hands though so I thank Sally and ring off.

The positive feelings of the morning are beginning to fade. I realise how easy it would be to just let go again and enter that downward spiral towards misery and despair. No, I have to fight this so what can I do to move forward?

I can't do anything about the situation at work so I put that to one side. I made a right mess of trying to bridge the emotional gap between Lauren and me – how to repair that damage is going to need a lot more thought. So that just leaves my hunt for Julie. I tell myself that the Scarborough address is probably just another dead end but, unless I give up completely, I ought to give it a try. I decide I'll go to Scarborough tomorrow.

Then the phone rings. It's a woman but I don't recognise

the voice.

"Is that Richard Kirkwood?"

"Yes, speaking."

"This is Polly Huggett. From Cromer."

Now that I wasn't expecting and I'm rather caught on the hop. "Oh, right. Hallo, Polly, how are you?"

"I'm fine. Well, sort off. The thing is I've had a letter from Norman."

"Oh, I see. Is he still in Thailand?"

"Yes." There's a pause. "I'm sorry to bother you, Richard, but I'm coming down to London this weekend to stay with my daughter and I wondered if there was any chance of seeing you. I'd quite like to talk to you about this letter if you wouldn't mind. I don't know what to do about it."

"You want to discuss Norman's letter with me?"

"Yes, if you wouldn't mind."

I don't know what to say. I hadn't expected to see Polly again and after last time I'm wary about any 'happy families' conversation. On the other hand she was very kind to me that night in Cromer and her voice definitely sounds strained. It occurs to me that it must have required a lot of courage to make this request to a virtual stranger and something in me responds to her obvious need. Anyway there's only two options. Say 'No' and hang up, or agree to meet her. A choice that is no choice.

"Well … yes, I suppose so. If you think I can help. When do you want to do this?"

"Whenever suits you really. I'm coming down by train tomorrow morning. I'm staying with Emily in Chiswick. Well, she calls it Kew but it's Chiswick really."

I think quickly. If she wants to meet this weekend I'll have to put off going to Scarborough but that's not a problem.

"Does Emily know about this letter?"

"No, not yet. Neither of the girls do. I want to sort it out in my mind first."

"Okay, well, let me think." I realise this meeting has to be on neutral territory so I reach the obvious conclusion. "Why don't we have dinner together tomorrow night."

"Oh, that would be wonderful. Are you sure?"

"I think that'd be the easiest, if Emily can spare you."

"I suspect she'll be relieved not to have to cook. She doesn't seem to do much of that."

"Okay, then, shall I pick you up at your door?"

"No, no, don't come to the flat. I'll meet you somewhere."

I think quickly. "Right, then. Why don't you get a train from Chiswick or Kew down to Richmond. I'll pick you up at Richmond station at – what time? – Seven suit you?"

"That's fine and thank you Richard. My treat this time, all right?"

"We'll worry about that tomorrow. See you then."

I hang up, slightly puzzled. Why does she want to talk to me about a letter from Norman?

54

POLLY

Polly had plenty of time on the journey down to London to worry about the impulse that led her to phone Richard Kirkwood. When she'd first opened Norman's letter she'd been shocked, then angry, then worried. She knew she had to discuss it with someone but her local friends were all firmly in the anti-Norman camp which was comforting but made an objective response impossible. Anyway the second page was not something she wanted to share with anyone. For the same reason she didn't want to tell Ruth and Emily until she'd made a decision. But who else was there?

She brooded over the situation for several days before she suddenly thought of Richard Kirkwood. She'd enjoyed the evening they'd spent together. She had felt relaxed in his company. He made no demands on her and he had the air of a man used to taking responsibility and making decisions, even though it was clear from the way the evening had ended that he was vulnerable too.

On the spur of the moment she picked up the phone and rang him. She lied – just a little – saying she was coming to London anyway and although he seemed a bit surprised, he did what she'd hoped he would do and asked her out to dinner again. Now she just had to fix it with Emily.

Emily was also a bit surprised to hear from her mother but was rather relieved when Polly explained that she just needed a bed for the night as she was going out to dinner with an old friend. Emily had planned to go to a party and for a moment she'd wondered if she might have to forego that to entertain her mother.

So everything was settled. Except for the actual discussion of course.

55

Richmond. Saturday evening. I'm a few minutes early so I hover by the ticket barrier wondering if I'll recognise her again.

I do and it's mutual. She comes straight up to me and says "Hallo" rather shyly. Instinctively we shake hands which is curiously formal but then the whole thing is rather curious really.

I take her to a Chinese restaurant and for a few moments it's awkward but then I fall back on my consultancy experience. The best way to put a client at their ease is to get them talking about themselves so I ask after her daughters and she describes Emily's flat in terms that make me laugh.

"Honestly, Richard, it could be a very nice flat but you get the feeling she's only camping there. Nothing's put away, no pictures or anything on the walls and do you know" – she leans forward confidentially – "she doesn't even have a cooker. Just a microwave. Can you imagine that?"

I can imagine it quite easily but clearly for Polly this is a contender for the eighth deadly sin.

The food arrives and the polite social chatter continues. I wait for her to raise the subject of Norman and his letter but she doesn't. Instead she talks about life in Cromer, her plans for Christmas, the book club she belongs to and what they've been reading. All very bland and innocuous.

There's a lull in the conversation and then, right out the

blue, Polly turns the tables.

"Thank you for meeting me tonight, Richard, and I'm sorry I upset you last time we met."

"Oh ... doesn't matter. Wasn't your fault."

"Even so." She pauses. "But there's something I don't quite understand."

"What's that?"

"When we first met you were looking for Norman in case he remembered this girl you are searching for. Then, when we were having dinner that night in the pub, you said you had time on your hands at the moment which is why you were looking for her."

"Yes," I say warily.

"But that doesn't seem to fit with the way you talked about your job, travelling all over the world and all that. You certainly didn't strike me as someone who just sits around with nothing to do so I just wondered why ..." She breaks off. "Sorry, am I intruding again?"

I think about this. "No–oo. Not really. But this is rather a strange conversation to be having with someone I've only met once before."

She looks at me expectantly and for the first time, I don't need to wrap up my request for information about Julie in half-truths.

"I'm in a rather strange place at present," I say and I give her a short résumé of the situation at work, my garden leave, how I feel at a loose end and how this hunt for Julie represents something positive.

When I finish she's silent for a moment, then says. "I'm sorry to hear about your trouble but I still don't understand how finding this old school friend will help."

I give a short laugh. "It probably won't, but it fills the time."

"Yes, I see." She thinks for a moment. "So, are you making progress?"

"Of a sort. I'm off to Scarborough next. In fact if you hadn't rung I was going there today."

"Why Scarborough?"

"I've tracked down an address for her, or at least, an address where she was five years ago."

There's an awkward silence and then Polly says: "I'm sorry if I spoilt your plans."

"No, you didn't. There's no rush. I'll go on Monday. As I say, I've got all the time in the world at the moment."

"You're going to a lot of trouble to find this girl. You must have very happy memories of her."

"Yes."

"And memories like that mean a lot, don't they. Much better than clinging onto the bad ones. They can be so destructive."

Something tells me that we're not speaking about me anymore so I make a noncommittal reply. "Things fester. Sometimes it can be hard to move on."

"Yes, and sometimes you don't even realise you have to move on. At least, not at first."

I sense an opening. "Are you moving on from Norman?"

There's a long silence then she says, quietly: "I don't think I have a choice."

"You wanted to talk about a letter you've had from him."

"Yes ... Yes, I did."

"And now you've changed your mind?"

There's a pause. "No ... no, I haven't, but it's a bit

embarrassing."

"You don't have to tell me about it. It doesn't matter."

"No, I want to ..." Then rather pathetically, "There's no one else I can ask anyway. It's just that" – she glances round the restaurant – "I wondered if perhaps there was somewhere a bit more private ..."

"Oh, I see." I think for a minute. "There's a pub over the other side of the river – a short drive away. Rather an old fashioned place, you know booths and seats with high backs and so on. Would that do?"

"Thank you."

I get the bill, which she insists on paying, and we walk back to my car. Once in the pub I get some drinks and we settle down in a corner seat well out the way of the other customers.

I wait. I say nothing.

After a moment she gives a sigh, reaches into her handbag and pulls out an envelope. She removes the contents, looks at them briefly and then hands the top page to me. I take it and glance across at her.

"You're sure you want me to read this?"

She nods. I unfold it and glance down the page.

Polly – it begins. Not even *Dear Polly* I notice.

Polly, as you have repeatedly ignored my emails I am forced to write to you and I have copied this letter to my legal representative. I did not want things to go this far but due to your unreasonable behaviour I am now making a formal application for a divorce. I will deal with all the details this end but I require you to sell the house and your car and send me half the money. I am sorry it has come to this but even you must realise that things cannot go on as they are …

I reach the end of the page and I pause and look across at Polly.

"This isn't very nice."

She shakes her head. There's a suspicion of tears in the corner of her eyes. "You see he wants me to sell the house. What do you think I should do?"

I hesitate. I'm always reluctant to give advice but she is waiting so I say gently: "Polly, if I'm going to help I need to know much more about all of this. Are you happy about that?"

She nods.

"Okay, then. So when you implied during my visit to your house that emailing him was a problem, you didn't mean that he didn't reply. You meant that he's been sending you harassing messages?"

"Yes."

"And when he says *'your unreasonable behaviour'* what does he mean?"

She drops her gaze. "This is so embarrassing."

"Of course it is, and we don't have to do it."

"No, we must. That is, I must. I've got to move on." She takes a deep breath. "A few months ago, Norman sent me an email. He said he'd made a new life for himself in Thailand but he still missed England. He suggested we could have the best of both worlds. He'd spend three months with this woman in Thailand, then come back here for three months, then go back there and so on."

I'm a bit taken aback. "You mean, he was suggesting that

you and this other woman effectively share him."

"Yes."

"And what did you say?"

She looks outraged. "I said 'no way', of course. It's disgusting."

"And that refusal is what he means by 'unreasonable behaviour'?"

"I presume so."

"And has his solicitor been in touch?"

"I don't think he has a solicitor. I mean we had a solicitor we used for our wills and so on but Norman hasn't contacted him."

"How do you know?"

"Because *I* did. I've changed my will, left everything I legally can to the girls. While I was doing that I asked him if he'd heard from Norman and he said no."

"Okay, let's come back to that. Now, the house, is it in both names?"

"Yes."

"Good, so he can't sell it over your head. That's why he needs your co-operation, unless it forms part of a divorce settlement. Do you want a divorce?"

She hesitates. "I don't know."

"When did he go, remind me?"

"Last February."

"So the best part of a year. Does he still pay any of the household bills?"

"Not a penny."

"Good." I see the look on her face and grin. "I only say 'good', because that means he's already abandoned the home. Makes your case stronger."

"Oh, I see."

"What about this car he seems to want you to sell? I thought he went off in his car and left it somewhere."

"Oh, he did. That was the Rover. He's talking about the Peugeot, my car."

"Your car? Then he can't force you to sell that."

"We call it my car but it's registered in his name?"

"Why's that?"

"He always insisted on both cars being registered to him. He had very strong views about who was earning the most out of either of us, and therefore whose money was being spent on things."

Norman is sounding more and more like a controlling bastard to me but all I say is: "Well in the overall scheme of things the car's replaceable at least."

"So you don't think he can force me to sell the house?"

"I very much doubt it, but I think we need to know what he means by his legal representative. Does he mention it again in the rest of the letter?"

"Well, I think it must be someone in Thailand. There's a phone number at the end of the letter see …" She takes another sheet out of the envelope and hands it to me. "There at the end. That's not a UK phone number is it?"

I look at the page she hands me. There's no name just a line saying:

Phone this number to arrange the details …

The number begins +66. I imagine that's the code for Thailand.

I ask, "Have you rung it?"

"No, I've been trying to think what to do. I don't want to

sell the house."

"Would you want Norman back, on a permanent basis I mean, not as part of a wife share?"

She thinks for a moment then shakes her head. "Do you know, I don't think I would. He's a bit of a bully really. I was devastated when he went but now I've kind of got used to making my own decisions. It's just ... well ... things can't just go on drifting, can they?"

"It's not ideal." I look at the phone number again. "You know my instinct's saying this isn't a qualified legal person or you'd have his name and professional details. My guess would be that Norman's bluffing."

"Well, what should I do then?"

I'm wondering how to answer her when I realise she's handed me another two sheets rather than just one. I glance down at the other one and suddenly realise what I'm reading. She sees my expression change and says: "Oh, no, I didn't mean to give you that one. Please don't read that, please."

But it's too late. I look across at her and now she is crying.

"He wrote this? To you?"

She nods through her tears as I look at the words in front of me.

I know you'll agree to this as you're too weak to say no but I'm telling you now, you can't win this divorce as you're the one in the wrong. They'll give me everything. You're a frigid cow, you refused to obey me, you refused me sex the way I like it, you refused to wear the things I told you to. I've learned a lot out here about how nice girls behave and now I realise just how unattractive and selfish you've always been.

I thought I'd seen everything but this shocks me. The idea that anyone could write such stuff, especially to someone they presumably once loved, is beyond my comprehension.

I look across at Polly but she will not meet my gaze. She just sits there crying softly. I reach across the table and take her hand.

"Polly, listen to me. This is a disgusting thing to write to anyone …"

"It's not true, it really isn't true …"

"I'm sure it isn't, but that's neither here nor there. I'm appalled. I don't know what to say. But I'll certainly help you in any way I can."

She sniffs. "Thank you but—"

"No buts. I don't think you should reply to this letter. I think it needs a formal response."

"You mean a solicitor?"

"Yes. He's threatening you and you don't have to take abuse like this. Plus it's wildly incorrect in terms of how divorce actually works."

Her brow furrows. "Well, I suppose I could talk to Mr Darrow, he's the one who did our wills, but I wouldn't like to show him that letter."

"I am sure Mr Darrow is a perfectly good solicitor but I think this needs some heavier guns. My wife's a lawyer – I can't ask her to help because she's in New York, but thanks to her, I do have a lawyer friend in one of the big City firms. He could deal with Norman for you and, although he'd have to see this letter, you don't know him so it'd be less embarrassing. Would you like me to try and arrange that for you?"

She really is crying now. "A city lawyer … I couldn't afford …"

"Don't worry about that, not for now. We'll sort something out. But this has to be nipped in the bud. It's disgusting."

"This is so kind. I don't know what to say."

"Don't say anything. Not now. Why don't we wrap up things here then I'll drive you back to Chiswick, Kew, wherever. Okay?"

"All right."

And that's what we do. I drop her off at Emily's flat, say I'll ring her the next day to see how she is and I head for home.

On the way it occurs to me I've now spent two evenings with Polly and both have ended in tears.

56

Sunday morning. I sleep in and it's nearly nine before I wake. As so often these days I feel sluggish and unrefreshed. Mechanically I go through the showering, shaving, breakfast motions.

I think back to last night and remember I promised to phone Polly. She sounds subdued, perhaps a bit distraught, so I take a positive tone with her. As I've discovered before, talking to someone else helps lift me out of my lethargy.

Polly tries to apologise for breaking down the previous evening but I'm having none of it. "Of course, it was distressing, it had to be. I'm just flattered you trusted me enough to share it with me."

"Well, it's like we were saying. It's easier to talk about these things with someone you don't know very well."

"I suppose. Anyway, if you haven't changed your mind overnight, I'll give my friend a call in the morning and set things in train."

"Thank you, Richard."

I relax. "So, are you heading back to Cromer today?"

"On Sunday trains? No thank you. I'm staying another night with Emily. I gather she's going to microwave us something tonight."

In spite of myself I laugh. "It won't kill you. I'm sure she just wants to be hospitable."

"Ye–es. We're going to Kew Gardens together after lunch.

If it doesn't rain."

"Will you tell her about Norman's letter?"

"No, not yet. I want to be absolutely clear in my own mind what I'm going to do before I tell the girls and then I'll want to tell them together."

There's a pause, then she says, in a rush as though she's been holding it back, "Richard, I've been thinking. Are you still going to Scarborough tomorrow?"

"Yes, I think so. Why?"

"Why don't I come with you?"

"What?"

"I'm in no rush to get home. It'd be company for you and if you do find Julie then having another woman with you might make it easier."

"Polly, thank you for the offer but I don't think—"

"No, listen, listen. Please say yes. It would make me feel useful. Even be a bit of an adventure. And you've been so kind, I'd like to help you if I can."

This is a crazy idea and I'm about to refuse, firmly but politely, but then I pause for a moment. She might have a point. If Julie is still in Scarborough and I roll up and knock at her door with this tale of how I found her she might feel threatened, might even see me as a stalker. But if there were two of us …

I prevaricate. "But, I don't know how long this trip's going to take."

"Doesn't matter. If necessary you can always drop me off somewhere and I'll get a train home."

"Well, I don't know." I cast around for another objection. "What would Emily think of you going away with a strange man?"

She makes a little tutting noise. "I'm not suggesting that sort of trip but anyway it's none of her business. Please Richard, I'd really like to come." Then, when I don't respond immediately she adds, "I think you're spending too much time alone at the moment. This could be good for both of us."

I give in. "Well, okay then, if you're sure."

I arrange to pick her up at Emily's the next day then she rings off and I'm left wondering what I've agreed to.

First thing Monday morning I ring Max Cortini in his city law firm and explain about Polly and Norman.

"Sounds like a right bastard," is his only comment. "No problem, Richard, let me have the details and I'll whack off a letter to him and we'll see what happens."

"Thanks, Max. I have to go away for a couple of days so I'll give you a call later in the week."

"Okay." There's a brief pause then he says, "How's Lauren doing? Enjoying New York?"

"What do you think? She's having a ball."

He laughs then says: "Word on the grapevine is you're in a bit of trouble yourself. Is it serious?"

"More irritating than serious. I'm just kicking my heels till they sort it all out."

"Well, don't forget I'm here for you as well if things get nasty."

I'm touched by this because I know he means it. "Thanks, Max."

"Don't take anything for granted, Richard. Justice has nothing to do with right and wrong. Trust me, I'm a lawyer."

I know he means well but this is not a message I want to hear. The possibility that this investigation may not have a definitive end still haunts my dreams.

I try and put all such thoughts out of my mind as I collect Polly from Emily's flat and we head for the M1. It's one of those wet and windy December mornings and I wonder if the rain down here could become snow by the time we reach Yorkshire.

I tell Polly I've spoken to Max and we'll set things in train later in the week and she's grateful all over again.

"I'll need a copy of the letter," I say, "we can do that in the hotel this evening."

"Have you booked anywhere?"

"No, we'll sort something when we get there. I doubt there'll be a run on hotels in mid-December."

We reach Scarborough just after five and find a hotel on the edge of town. I book two rooms and let Polly have the one with the sea view. We arrange to meet in the bar around six-thirty and I go to my room. After all the time I spend in hotels I've got my routine down to a fine art so I'm quickly sorted with time to spare. On a whim I leave the hotel, cross the road and stand looking out over the dark sea. The tang of salt on the wind makes me think of those early days with Lauren, striding along cliff tops, hair blown everywhere, revelling in the scenery and thinking of the fish and chips we'll soon be enjoying on whichever prom we're headed for.

But now Lauren is far away. I'm alone, it's cold and there's the occasional flurry of rain which is almost, but not quite, snow.

What the hell am I doing here? In fact what have the last few weeks been about? Should I have resisted the garden leave, stayed and argued my corner? Gone in with legal guns blazing? Why did I just walk away and leave others to decide my future? In spite of myself I wonder again if I have a future.

I've never believed there is any risk of my being convicted but even if I'm completely cleared of all the unspoken charges, can I really contemplate going back to the same old round with the same old people?

And then there's Lauren and our life together. I am always at my happiest when she is around, but there is still that area of my life I have never shared. I know it's there and I suspect she knows it's there as well. If there is any glitch in our relationship I know it is my fault, but in the last few days I have begun to wonder if she has been completely open with me. There was a reserve about her in New York that I found vaguely unsettling.

Over the years we've developed a way of living together, taking strength from each other, often physically apart but always knowing the other one was there when needed, but is that still true?

Her life is changing. Mine is changing. Will those changes stay in sync, or is our connection about to close off completely? If this were a work situation I'd evaluate it and deal with it. I'd be in control and I wouldn't be personally involved. And that's the problem. At the moment I'm not in control and I am involved. It's the uncertainty of what lies ahead – it's constantly dragging me down.

My mood is beginning to match the weather. Then, while I'm standing there being philosophical in the cold, my phone beeps and a text arrives.

You are safe so far. The others have kept quiet. Say nothing to the police.

Again I feel the anger rising in me. I haven't got the faintest idea what this means. Who the hell is sending these things?

And why can't the police get their bloody finger out?

I suddenly realise I'm freezing cold. I look at my watch and see it's twenty to seven so I cross the road back to the hotel.

Polly is waiting for me in the bar with a glass of white wine in front of her. "I didn't get you anything. I didn't know what you'd want."

I order a large single malt and we settle back in our chairs. There's a moment's silence then she says. "I saw you, from my window, looking out to sea."

"Yes."

"Are you all right?"

"I don't know."

"Are you worried about actually meeting Julie after all this time?"

"Well, yes, suppose so, but that's not it. Not really."

She says nothing. I take a drink. "I know this sounds dramatic, but at the moment I can't see any way out of this mess."

She doesn't respond and after a moment I go on.

"Trouble is I've never had time to stop and think about stuff before, but now I have and there's just so much of it to deal with, and I'm not sure I can cope."

"Are you worried about being prosecuted for this fraud thing?"

"No, that's not it. I haven't done anything they could prosecute me for. But 'not proven' is not the same as 'innocent'. Mud sticks."

"But it doesn't stick everywhere. You could have a complete change, do something completely different."

I give a wry grin. "And is that what you're going to do?"

For a moment she looks confused. "That's not fair. It's what I should do, I know that, but it's much easier to sort out other people than yourself."

"It certainly is, which reminds me I need a copy of Norman's letter to send to Max."

She takes it out of her bag and gives it to me, I use the hotel's photocopier then return the original to her.

"I suggest you keep it safe," I say, "but don't read it again. Let Max deal with it."

Over dinner we discuss our plans for the next day. Not that there's much to plan. We'll go to the address Heather gave me, knock on the door and see who answers.

"She might be out," says Polly, "she could easily be at work."

"We'll play it by ear," I say, "that's all we can do."

The following morning, not knowing how the day's going to pan out, we check out of the hotel and take all our stuff with us. We set off soon after ten and after a bit of hunting around we find the address. I don't know why I'd assumed it was a private house, but it isn't. It's a small café-restaurant and it's closed. The sign on the door says it opens at eleven. Not knowing what else to do we drive back to the seafront and sit there, looking at the sea.

We don't talk. Polly seems lost in her own thoughts and I find myself thinking of Lauren again. She certainly wasn't relaxed in New York, she seems to have erected a barrier of her own between us and that saddens me. It suddenly occurs to me that I may have helped build that barrier but I don't know what to do about it and just at the moment I don't have the emotional energy to try.

We return to the café just after eleven and are greeted by a very pleasant woman but I'm pretty sure this isn't Julie.

"Good morning," she says, "table for two?"

"Well, yes," I say, "we'd certainly like a coffee but actually I'm looking for someone. Do you know Julie Orford?"

She looks blank so I add. "Or she might be called Julie Wigglesworth."

Her face clears. "Oh, Julie, of course. No, I'm sorry, they're not here anymore."

It's no more than I was expecting but it's still a disappointment. "Do you happen to know where she went?" I ask.

"Well, my husband might know but may I ask why …?" She tails off.

I'm getting better at answering this, I think. Aloud I say, "Well, we're actually old school friends … I was told she was here and, as we were in the area, we thought we'd look her up."

"Oh, I see, well, I'll go and ask Pete."

"Thank you and could we have a couple of coffees as well please."

"Of course. Won't be a tick." And she disappears.

I join Polly at a table in the window and a few minutes later a man appears with the coffees. He pulls out a chair and sits down.

"Angie says you're looking for Julie."

"Yes, we had this address for her but it's obviously out of date."

"It certainly is. She and Brian left here couple of years ago."

"Oh."

"We bought this place off them. We used to come in

here a lot, Julie was a great cook, simple meals, you know, but always good. Business was booming and not just in the summer either."

"So why did they sell up?"

"Julie said they wanted a bigger place but Brian told me she just wanted to be nearer her mother. Whatever, I don't really know. Anyway we'd become sort of casual friends, you know how it is, and one day they mentioned they were thinking of selling. I'd just been made redundant so we thought it'd be a good business opportunity."

"And were you right?"

Pete smiles. "I was. Business is great. We've never been happier."

Polly says, "Hope you don't mind my asking but what did you do before you were made redundant?"

"I was an accountant".

"He was Finance Director for Hammerfest Haulage," says Angela from behind the counter. "They're based down in Bridlington."

"Golly," says Polly, "that's a bit of a contrast."

Angela laughs. "It certainly is. But at least I get to see him these days."

For a moment I have a flash memory of Mark Trimble in the Devon pub, giving up merchant banking for woodwork. Clearly, for some people at least, there is life after a high-flying career.

"Do you know where Julie and ... er ... Brian went?" I ask.

"I don't. Not exactly," says Pete. "We used to send their mail on to her mother. But that was only temporary until they got their own place."

"Do you still have that address?"

He shakes his head. "Not a hope. Too long ago."

Angela comes across and says. "They were talking about looking for somewhere in Harrogate or Knaresborough. Somewhere over that way."

"But you don't know for certain they did go there?"

"No, I don't. 'Fraid we can't help you."

"Oh, well, it doesn't really matter, it was just a thought."

We finish our coffee and stand up to go. Then Angela suddenly says. "There was one thing. What they really wanted to do was to open a proper restaurant, you know without the café bit. They had a name for it too. They were going to call it 'Wiggles'."

Polly stifles a giggle and I try and keep a straight face.

"Now, now," says Angela, "don't be like that. It's just the kind of off-beat name that could catch on. It's a play on their surname, see. They were called Wigglesworth and they had this draft advert 'It's Worth coming to Wiggles'. I thought it was quite funny."

We say thank you, pay our bill and go out into the cold.

"What now?" says Polly.

"Don't know. Another dead end. I'm getting used to them."

"Not necessarily a dead end. What if they did get a restaurant and called it 'Wiggles'?"

I see what she's driving at. There can't be that many restaurants called 'Wiggles' so we go back down into the town, find the tourist office and make some enquiries. After a bit of searching we discover a restaurant called 'Wiggles' in Knaresborough. Bingo.

"Wow." I say and Polly looks pleased.

"So, we going to give it a try?"

"Might as well. Let's think, Knaresborough must be, what, about sixty, seventy miles. If we drive over there now we can stay there tonight—"

"— And have dinner in their restaurant?" suggests Polly.

"My thought exactly. Let's give it a go."

57

BRIAN

It was not a good day. Another not good day but at least the physical work tired him out and helped him sleep and he was nearly finished. The kitchen had been the worst. They had kept it spotless when it was in use, of course, that went without saying, but since then he'd rather let things go and now there were lots of nooks and crannies that needed attention.

The staff were all long gone. Most of the outstanding bills had been paid apart from a couple and he still had two or three weeks before they were due. The storerooms had been cleaned out, the flat upstairs tidied but not re-decorated. The bar stock had gone back to the wholesaler apart from half a dozen bottles of vodka that he kept for himself.

He was putting the final coat of magnolia on the walls of the restaurant, covering up the faded patches where the pictures had once hung. There were parts of the floor that could do with attention too but he was running out of energy, both physical and emotional. He finished the final wall and stood back to see what it looked like. Not bad. One more coat should do it.

He was just cleaning his brushes when he heard a knocking on the door. For heaven's sake, he thought, we're closed. Isn't it obvious. He carried on with his cleaning but the knocking continued. Clearly whoever it was could see there was a light on and it didn't sound like they were going away. Irritated, he laid the brush down and stalked to the door. Through the glass he could see a man and a woman standing there. He flung the door open.

"Yes? What d'you want?"

58

From the moment we arrive it's clear there'll be no meal for us in Wiggles Restaurant this evening. We see through the window that the place has been stripped, dust sheets are covering everything and there's an abandoned feel about it.

"Doesn't look hopeful," says Polly with remarkable understatement.

I agree, but I can see a light on in a back room so I knock tentatively on the door. Nothing happens so I knock again and this produces a result. A man in overalls erupts from the back room, strides across to the door and flings it open.

"Yes? What d'you want?" he barks. He does not seem friendly.

I take a deep breath. "Sorry to disturb you but I'm looking for Mr and Mrs Wigglesworth."

"Why?"

Polly chips in. "Well, it's rather a long story. Do you know where we can find them?"

The man transfers his gaze to her and when he speaks he sounds rather less hostile.

"I'm Brian Wigglesworth. But I don't know you, do I?"

"No, we've never met," I say, "but I used to know your wife many years ago."

"Did you indeed?"

I can see the thought that's passing through his mind but the presence of Polly by my side rather rules out the obvious conclusion.

"Yes, but a very long time ago. We were given this address for her and thought it might be nice to look her up."

"Well, you're out of luck then, aren't you?"

I give a little laugh. "Yes, I am. That seems to be the story of my life just lately."

He looks at me for a moment then sighs. "I don't know what the hell is going on, who you are or what you want, but to be honest I'm past caring. Do you want a cup of tea?"

The change of attitude is so abrupt that we're taken aback for a moment then Polly says meekly, "Thank you, that'd be very nice."

He steps aside and we go into the restaurant. As he leads the way through to the kitchen Polly continues the bland conversation.

"I see you're re-decorating. Giving the restaurant a face lift?"

"In a manner of speaking. I'm tidying it up to sell it."

He shifts a couple of dust sheets and we sit on stools while he fills the kettle and rummages for some mugs.

"It's only tea bags. It's all I've got left. Unless you'd like something stronger. I've got some vodka."

"Tea's fine, thank you."

He hands us two mugs. "Sorry, don't have any sugar."

The tea is strong. We sip in silence for a moment then he says: "How d'you come to know Julie, then?"

"We were at school together," I say.

"School?"

"Yes," and I launch into a very brief summary of why I started on this search. As usual it sounds more and more implausible as I go on and I finally trail off into silence.

He shakes his head in disbelief but then Polly says: "It's

true. I know it all sounds very unlikely, maybe even silly, but it's true. That's how he found me."

"How d'you mean, found you?"

"I'm married to another of their school friends, Norman. He would have known Julie as well."

"And is Norman looking for her too?"

She hesitates. "No. Norman's abroad at present so I said I'd help Richard."

"That you?" He looks at me.

"Yes, sorry, I'm Richard Kirkwood. This is Polly Huggett and you must be Brian."

"Yeah, that's right." And we all solemnly shake hands.

I think to myself that this is just another surreal moment in a very strange few months. Polly is more practical and cuts to the chase.

"So Julie's not here at the moment?" she asks.

"Julie's not here, period," says Brian. "She's left me."

"Oh," says Polly, "I'm so sorry."

She so clearly means it that suddenly the dam bursts and it all comes tumbling out.

"It was after her mum died. She said she'd had enough. We came here to be near her mum, see, we had a nice little business going over in Scarborough."

"I know. We were there this morning. We saw Pete and Angie."

"Oh, did you? How they doing?"

"They seem fine."

"Good for them. They got more out of that deal than I did. I'd've stayed but Julie, she wanted to be nearer her mum over in Arkendale so we sold up and bought this place. It was fine at first. Steady turnover of customers. Lots of repeat business – you need that you know."

"Sure."

"Then her mum became ill and Julie spent more and more time over there. I understood why but it didn't help the business. I had to keep getting standby chefs in and it's not the same. I'll be the first to say it – Julie's the main reason we were successful. She's a damn good cook."

"So I heard."

"Standards started slipping. Business dropped off. Julie and I had a few rows." He clutched his mug firmly in both hands. "You know how it is."

We both nod.

"It wasn't serious. At least, I didn't think it was. Then about three months back her mum died. Well, we shut the restaurant for a week, sorted everything out. Opened it again for the do after the funeral and then I thought things would get back to normal."

"But they didn't?"

"No. We struggled on for a while but business wasn't good, then one day, right out of the blue, she announced she was leaving. Said she hadn't been happy for some time and it was best we called it a day. I didn't see it like that. I thought we could work through it, but she was having none of it. She packed a bag and left six weeks and three days ago today. Haven't heard from her since."

"Did you try to find her?" I ask.

"Of course I tried. I don't want to run a bloody restaurant on my own. I've been in touch with some of our friends but she hasn't. Tried a few places she might have gone, but she hasn't. She has a brother but he lives abroad somewhere. Think it's Australia but that's a big place. Don't know what else I can do."

He looks at me, a wry grin on his face. "If I can't find her after six weeks, mate, you stand bugger all chance after all these years."

"So you're selling up?"

"Yup. Can't run this place on my own. Anyway, don't have the heart for it."

There's not much else to say so we finish our tea and leave. We walk down the road not looking at each other.

"Poor man," says Polly at last. "It's such a shame."

"Yes," I say.

"And poor you too. I think this really is a dead end."

"Yes."

"I suppose you got quite close though."

"What?"

"Well, you started forty odd years behind her. Now you're only six weeks adrift."

I just look at her and she gives an embarrassed giggle. "Suppose that's not much help really."

"Not really," I agree dryly.

We get to the car but pause before getting in. I'm feeling very down and from the look of her Polly is not much better.

"It's so sad," she says. "Everyone's splitting up. Norman's left me, Julie's left Brian. What's gone wrong with us all?"

I think of Lauren and wonder.

We get into the car but I don't start the engine. I don't know what to do next.

"Where we going now?" asks Polly.

I shake my head. I really don't know.

"Well, I have a suggestion," she says, "I think it's too late to set off back to London today. Why don't we find a hotel, have dinner, get a good night's sleep and go home tomorrow." She adds hopefully, "Things often seem better in the morning."

So that's what we do. We find a pub that does bed and breakfast, book in and have dinner in the bar. Our conversation is stilted. Polly seems lost in her own little world and the relentless Christmas carols playing over the pub's speakers are depressing. I'm finding it impossible to think clearly. It seems my search for Julie Orford really has come to an end.

It turns out I wasn't ready for that.

Up in my room I find I can't sleep. I lie there in the dark wondering what I'm going to do, fighting the sense of despair that is hovering round me. Now I have nothing to distract me from all the other unwanted thoughts. Lauren, my future. All the unvisited parts of my childhood ...

Slightly desperately, I wrench myself out of bed. Anything to escape that train of thought. Then suddenly there's a gentle knock at my door. Disorientated, I pull on my dressing gown and open the door. Polly is standing there, also in her dressing gown.

"I'm sorry to disturb you, Richard. Can I come in?"

I step back, she comes into the room and I close the door. I see she's been crying.

"What's wrong, Polly?"

"Everything. Norman, the horrid letter, that Brian – so unhappy – your disappointment. I can't sleep. Everything is shit."

I'm a little taken aback. I've never heard her swear before.

"And I'm cold. The radiator in my room isn't working."

"Well, we can soon do something about that."

"No." She stops me as I move towards the door. "It doesn't matter."

"But if you're cold …"

"Inside as well as out. Richard, please, would you just hold me for a moment?"

I hesitate. "Polly, I'm not sure that's a good idea."

"Only for a moment. Don't worry, Richard, I'm not going to add to your problems. I'm just feeling very low tonight."

I know what she means. I'm feeling low too. I open my arms and she comes into them and nestles her face into my shoulder.

"Oh, that's nice. Warmer."

We stand like that for a few moments then she stirs.

"Let me try and get them to sort out the heating in your room," I say, "then you'll be able to sleep."

"No." She pauses. "Richard, could I stay with you tonight? I'm so lonely."

I take a deep breath. "Polly, I really don't think we should be doing this …"

"No, I thought you'd say that, but it's not what you think. I don't want to have sex with you Richard. I'm not falling in love with you or anything like that. All I want is to be held. For someone to be there with me tonight."

We stand in silence for a moment then I feel her shiver. I don't know if it's cold or nervousness but suddenly I make up my mind.

"Yes, all right. I'm lonely too and cold inside."

"Then let's do this."

She slides out of my grip and slips off her dressing gown and gets into the bed. I take off mine and join her. For a moment we lie stiffly side by side then she turns towards me.

"Cuddle, please," she says as a command.

I put my arms around her and she nestles close. I can feel

the warmth of her body but interestingly I don't feel aroused, just protective. The soft smell of her hair is in my face and suddenly I pull her closer.

"Does the definition of a cuddle include a kiss?" I ask.

"Of course." She lifts her head and kisses me. I kiss her back and I start to feel the tension draining away. She puts up her hand and strokes my face.

"So kind," she says. "Now we must sleep."

She turns to face away from me but keeps my arms round her and nestles back into my lap. Within moments I hear her breath become even.

And so we keep each other warm.

JUNE 1962

A warm summer's day. Richard is feeling restless so after school instead of going home he turns the other way and makes his way to the park. They call it a park but in reality it's a wide open space surrounded on all sides by narrow woods.

He likes walking in these woods. He likes the canopy of trees about him and the way the light filters down. He feels relaxed here. And safe. The band of trees is so narrow, he can see the open park on one side and the backs of houses on the other. Controlled isolation.

He is all alone here or so he thinks until he hears footsteps behind him and, turning, sees another figure coming down the path. As she gets nearer he sees it's Julie and she's on her own.

"Hallo."

"Hallo."

"I was just going for a walk."

"So was I."

He hesitates but then desire beats shyness. "Shall we ... um ... would you like to walk together? Just for a bit."

She smiles. "Yes."

They walk side by side, close but not touching, arms self-consciously by their sides. By chance, and it really is by chance, his hand brushes against hers. It feels like an electric shock.

Then suddenly she seems to stumble and instinctively he catches her arm to stop her falling.

"You okay?"

"Yes, I just tripped."

He is still holding her arm. He looks round and sees part of an old tree trunk buried in the bushes.

"Would you like to sit down for a minute?"

She nods and they push their way through the bushes towards the log and sit. They're not hidden but they're certainly out of sight of any casual passer-by.

He has let go her arm but now they're looking at each other. He doesn't know what to say and takes refuge in banalities.

"Won't be long now and we'll be leaving Modbury Road."

"Yes. Things will change, won't they?"

"I suppose they will." He's not looking forward to it. An all-boys grammar school, homework, no Julie to gaze at across the classroom. He wishes time could be frozen.

It is shady under the trees and the sun has gone behind a cloud. Julie shivers slightly.

"Are you cold?"

"A little."

He hesitates for a moment then puts his arm round her shoulders. "Is that better?"

"Much."

She leans against him and they sit for a while. Then he says. "I wish this moment would never end."

She turns her face to look at him. "So do I?"

Her beautiful oval face framed in gentle brown hair is close to him. Ten years, perhaps only five years, later faced with the same situation he would lean forward and kiss the lips in front of him. But it's the 1960s. He is 11 years old so he does nothing. The best he can manage is: "I do like you, Julie."

"I know, Richard," she says, "I like you too."

This moment sitting on that log is burned into his memory. It's a purely innocent moment and yet one that is full of importance. It's a memory that will never entirely leave him. Almost certainly enhanced and polished as the years go by, probably embellished as well, yet it becomes something he clings to in the dark hours of dark days.

But here and now the moment must end. Their respective tea-times are drawing near. They have to go home.

They stand. She takes his hand and they walk back towards the entrance to the park. He is in heaven. He never believed an object so ordinary as a hand could mean so much.

"Can we ... can we, do this again?" he manages to say.

"Yes, please," she says, but as they approach the end of the woods she lets go his hand. He understands and holds back to let her go ahead. At the gate of the park, she stops, turns round, blows him a kiss and is gone.

He is left alone, in the gloom despite the blazing sun, to make his back home to a familiar darkness, but a darkness which now has a new light.

Neither of them have used the word but he feels loved. It's a novel feeling.

60

I wake and for a moment I don't know where I am. Then I feel a warm body stir against me and the memory of the previous night returns. Sometime in the night we must have turned over as I'm now facing into the room with Polly cuddled up behind me, one arm draped across my chest.

I ease myself out from under her arm but in so doing she wakes, blinks for a moment, then smiles.

"Hallo."

"And good morning to you too. Would you like a cup of tea?"

"Oh, yes, please."

I get out of bed and busy myself with the kettle and bits and pieces on the other side of the room. While the kettle is boiling I nip into the bathroom. When I come out I make the tea and take hers over to her. She's sitting up in bed and pats the place beside her.

"Come back for a few minutes, Richard. I want to talk to you."

Rather doubtfully I take my tea and get back into the bed.

For a moment she says nothing, just sips her tea, then she turns and smiles at me: "Thank you for last night, Richard. For the first time in a long while I feel loved."

This isn't really what I want to hear but she senses my tension.

"No, don't worry, please. I said last night I don't want

anything from you and I don't."

"Polly, I don't want to hurt you ..."

"You haven't and you won't. I'm not in love with you, Richard, and you're certainly not in love with me. What you did last night was unbelievably kind and that's why I feel loved this morning. Not specifically loved, but generally loved and it's wonderful."

I'm silent. I don't know what to say.

"I felt desperate last night," she goes on, "and when I knocked at your door I'd have done anything not to be alone. I told myself if you let me stay I would do whatever you wanted."

"Oh, Polly ..."

"No." She stops me with a finger on my lips – a surprising and intimate gesture. "But all I actually wanted was not to be alone and" – her voice breaks a little – "you understood that and I'm so grateful."

"I felt very lonely last night too."

"Yes, I know you did. But you're often lonely, aren't you? That's a real puzzle. You're a lovely man, I don't understand why you're lonely."

Of course you don't understand, I think, no one does. Because I never tell them. Not even Simon, fully.

Polly finishes her tea and puts down the cup. "Now then, we have to move on. You have a wife to go back to and I have to create a life without Norman. I've decided I won't let him bully me any longer."

I look at her. "I think you're amazing."

She blushes slightly. "You're not so bad yourself." She reaches across and takes my hand. "Oh, Richard, I really do like you. We're good together but we're friends, that's all. You know that, don't you?"

"I do, but I'm very glad I met you."

"It's mutual, but now we'd better see about breakfast and heading back home."

She starts to get up but I stop her. "One last kiss?"

"Of course." She leans across, my arms go round her shoulders and our lips meet. This is the moment that all our good intentions could go wrong, but they don't. After a moment she pulls away, gets out of bed, and grabs her dressing gown.

"See you downstairs in half an hour," she says and slips out through the door.

After breakfast I insist on taking her home to Cromer – she would have happily caught the train from Peterborough but I feel it's the least I can do. We pull up at her door just before three. She asks if I'd like to stay for a cup of tea but I say I'd rather get going.

"I'll give you a ring in a couple of days," I say. "I'll have another chat with Max then put the two of you in touch and you can deal with him direct."

"Thank you, Richard. Not just for Max but for everything. Please stay in touch. I want to know how you get on."

She leans in the driver's window, gives me a quick kiss, then picking up her case heads up the garden path, pausing by the door to wave.

I go back to the emptiness of Weybridge and a takeaway curry.

61

The following morning I'm woken by Mrs Atkins still having a wonderful time with her new vacuum cleaner. She apologises for waking me but I don't mind. It's time to do some re-evaluation.

Work habits die hard so I sit at my desk and draw up a list of action points. Simon – need to talk to him, especially if I want to spend Christmas there. Sally – to see what's going on at the office, though I'm sure she'd have called if there'd been any developments. Sergeant Williams – to tell him about the latest text. Max – to get him started on Polly's problem. And Lauren – just to see how she is, a call which I realise is long overdue.

And then there's Julie but I don't see where I go from here. I know where she was six weeks ago, but now she could be anywhere. I wonder briefly whether I should have left my phone number with Brian in case she got in touch but on reflection that would've been both difficult and insensitive.

I know your wife's walked out on you, old chap, but in case she has second thoughts and comes back, would you tell her that her 11 year old admirer has resurfaced and would like to see her again.

No. that doesn't play. It looks as though my search for Julie Orford really is over.

I can see long empty hours looming up ahead of me but for the moment I have my Action List. Where to start? Simon?

Do I really want to spend Christmas with him and Rita? Not sure, but I need to decide, Christmas is only eight days away?

Eight days. I suddenly realise I've done nothing about a Christmas present for Lauren and I've left it too late to post anything to New York in time. Well, that's not going to help anything, is it? I should have got something while I was actually there. But I didn't.

I put that problem on hold and move on. Sally. I ring her mobile and leave a message then I do the same for Sergeant Williams. Then I try Max's number and get straight through to him.

"I've spoken to Polly Huggett again," I say, "and I've got a copy of the letter Norman sent her. Shall I scan it and email it over?"

"Yes, please. Then I'd better deal with the lady direct."

"Of course." And I give him her address and phone number.

"Do you know what she wants to achieve?" he asks.

"You'll need to talk to her about that," I say, "but she doesn't want to lose the house and she certainly doesn't want any threats hanging over her."

"Unless he's got a really smart lawyer there won't be any more threats," says Max.

"That's great," I say. "Now about the cost. I don't know how much she can afford ..."

"Let that go for the moment, Richard," he says. "I'll see how it goes but I won't let it run up too much."

"Thanks. If push comes to shove I'm willing to help out."

I can almost hear his eyebrows go up. "Oh, like that, is it?"

"No, it isn't like that. She's a friend and she's been very kind to me. She needs to do what she can for herself but I

270

don't want to see her lose out to that bastard for the sake of a few quid."

I can almost hear him smiling as he rings off but so what. A few minutes later the phone rings again. It's Sally but, as I suspected, there's no news. Mervyn doesn't seem to have lost any more of my clients but she makes it clear the atmosphere in the office is pretty toxic.

Sergeant Williams doesn't call back.

I lunch off bread and some cheese that looks somewhat the worse for wear and decide a supermarket visit this afternoon is a good idea. Back home, as I'm unloading the car, the phone rings. It's Simon.

We chat for a while, then he says: "Is Lauren coming home for Christmas?"

"No, she can't get away."

"Thought that might be the case. Do you want to come over here?"

I'm in two minds. I wonder if the jollity of Christmas, even with Simon and Rita, is something I can face this year. On the other hand I've got to face it somewhere unless I just hide myself away and brood. That sounds an even worse idea. And if I'm to be with anyone, then my brother is the person I'd choose.

"That'll be great," I say, "thanks a lot."

The next day I try Sergeant Williams again but still can't get through to him. The paranoid side of me begins to think he is deliberately avoiding me. My logical side says this is nonsense, it is simply that there's no news worth passing on but the silence doesn't bode well for a rapid conclusion to this whole situation.

I reason myself into a relatively calm state of mind but

then another one of these damn texts arrives.

*We suggest you keep your passport handy in case you have
to go abroad in a hurry. Things are hotting up.*

That does it. I cannot tolerate this any longer. Someone's
trying to wind me up. I'm not involved in anything illegal
and I deeply resent the implication that I am. I can't see the
point in ringing Sergeant Williams yet again so I decide to
follow my own instincts and see if I can sort this out.

I check the number for the Cerberus Club and dial it.

LINDA

Linda was sitting in the office at the Cerberus Club thinking about her future. Ever since the confrontation between Victor and Richard Kirkwood she'd felt unsettled. She hadn't undergone any crisis of conscience, she wasn't floundering in a sea of regrets, but she was starting to feel that it was probably time to move on. She suspected that Rodney had plans of his own that didn't include her but that was fine. They hadn't been an item for a while now and she was quite capable of looking out for herself.

The question was where would she go? She couldn't just stop. That would be too dangerous. She'd have to disappear. Well, she could do that. She currently had four passports – two Rodney and the group knew about, and two they didn't. Vanishing wasn't the problem; it was where to vanish to and how much money she could take with her.

Her thoughts were interrupted by the barman poking his head round the door. "Linda, there's a call on the bar phone. Some bloke wanting Victor but he's not around this afternoon."

"Who is it?"

"Says his name's Kirkwood. Wouldn't say what it was about."

Linda went very still. Then she said. "Put it through here. I'll speak to him."

When I get through to the Cerberus Club I ask for Victor and I'm told to wait. There's a pause, a click and then I hear Linda's voice, slightly mocking.

"Well, well, Richard. We can't go on meeting like this."

"Ah, Linda, I was hoping to talk to Victor."

"Were you now. Why? I didn't expect to hear from you again."

"I didn't expect to either but I'm getting seriously pissed off with these texts and I want them to stop."

There's a silence on the other end of the phone. When she speaks again the soft mocking edge has gone from her voice.

"What texts?"

"The threatening texts I keep receiving. '*Don't talk to the police*', '*Be very careful, they're watching you*', all this sort of bollocks."

"And you think Victor sent them?"

"Who else? Unless it was you."

"No, it wasn't me." There's another silence and I can almost hear her thinking.

"Are you still there?"

"Yes, I'm here. Look, Richard, I don't like the sound of this. Can I see these texts?"

"Why?"

"Because I didn't send them and I can't believe Rodney did either which means if they're coming from here we may have a problem."

"Your problem or my problem?"

"I don't know. Maybe both."

I think for a moment. "I'm not handing this over to you. If you want to see them we'll have to meet."

"Fair enough." She pauses, then I hear a hint of mischief back in her voice. "I don't suppose you want to come to the club, do you?"

"Too right, I don't. Why don't we make it somewhere nice and public and in the middle of the day."

"All right. How about ... um ... I know, the Holiday Inn on the Guildford bypass, up near the hospital? Say midday tomorrow."

"Okay, you're on. See you then."

The following morning it's tipping down with rain and I get pretty wet scurrying from the car into the hotel. Linda is already there and we exchange brief greetings. We settle down at a table in the bar, I order a coffee, Linda orders a G &T. For a moment we just look at each other then she says, "You've changed, you know."

"Hardly surprising," I say, "Modbury Road's a long time ago."

"Yes, sure, but it's more than that. I remember you as being a bit shy. More into books than people. You never really joined in the playground games and stuff, did you?"

I shrug. "We grow up."

"Some of us maybe."

"How did you get into all this, Linda? Have you and Rodney always been—?"

She cuts me off with a gesture. "Why does anybody do anything? It doesn't matter now. I could ask why you're suddenly hell bent on finding Julie Orford."

"It's a long story."

"Most of them are. And they don't always make sense." She takes a long drink. "Right then. To business. Let's see these texts."

I move my chair round to sit beside her. I have no intention of letting go of my phone. I scroll through the messages to the first one.

We strongly suggest you say nothing. To anyone. You have been warned.

She reads it. Stays silent. I open the second one.

You are being warned. So far you are safe. Say nothing to the police.

Still no response, so I go on and open the third, fourth, fifth and finally the one I received yesterday.

We suggest you keep your passport handy in case you have to go abroad in a hurry. Things are hotting up.

Linda still says nothing so I say, "What would you call those if they're not threats? And you've got to admit that you and your crowd have a pretty solid motive."

She shakes her head. "There's something odd about all of them. They don't ring true."

"Are you still saying you didn't send them?"

"Me, personally? Certainly not, and neither did Rodney or Victor."

"How can you be so sure?"

"Two things. Well three, actually. To start with look at the time you received that message. 10pm. That would make it

5am in Hong Kong. Do you seriously think that Rodney'd get up at that time just to send you a weird text?"

I hadn't noticed that.

"And then the first three messages were sent before your visit to the club."

"True. But after my first call to Rodney. He could have passed this on."

"Yeah, okay, that call did ring alarm bells. Your reason for getting in touch out of the blue like that just sounded so … well, artificial, I suppose. But what would have been the point in threatening you then? Messages like these are more likely to make you curious, not put you off."

"Okay, point taken. What's your other reason?"

"The language. I'd never send a text like that, nor would Rodney."

"How do you mean?"

"Look, let me see them again."

I go back to the text messages and scroll through them. She stops me at the second one.

"There. See that." She puts on a prim voice. *"We strongly suggest you say nothing'.* That's very correct isn't it? So formal."

She has a point.

Linda goes on. "And as for the last one. This *'We suggest you keep your passport handy'* stuff. Well, you can't take this seriously, can you?"

"Why not?"

"Oh, Richard, be your age. This is straight out of Agatha Christie or James Bond. No one says stuff like that."

"I see what you're saying but the fact is someone's sending them. If it's not you guys, then who is it?"

"No idea. But it's definitely not us. Victor can't spell that well anyway." She pauses. "You say you've shown these to the police?"

"Yes."

"In spite of the messages telling you not to?"

"Yes. I've got nothing to hide."

"No, but as you didn't obey their instructions you'd expect some kind of comeback. Has there been any?"

"No, don't think so."

"No action, no increased threats, no reference to your calls to the police?"

"Perhaps they don't know."

"Then they're not very well organised, are they? No, there's something else going on here."

"Like what?"

"Don't know." She pauses again. "What do the police say?"

"Not a lot. The texts come from a prepaid phone – no contract, no address. And they originated in the UK."

"Which rules out Rodney ..."

"Well, that's all they've told me."

She thinks for a moment. "This search for Julie, have you trodden on anyone else's toes?"

"Not that I'm aware of and I didn't know I was treading on yours until that night in the club."

"No. Okay, it's just I don't think these are threats. I think someone's trying to set you up."

I feel my jaw set. I'd been afraid of this.

Linda doesn't know about the fraud case of course, so she goes on enthusiastically, "Yes, throw suspicion on you. Make the police think something's going on even if it isn't."

"Well, it isn't?"

"No, okay, keep your fur on. This language, it's too polite.

278

It's as though it's a means to an end."

"How do you mean?"

"Apart from the fact that it repeats itself, it's too neat. It's bland. Tells you nothing about the sender."

"Texts never do."

"Oh, yes, they do. References to the kind of danger they're afraid of, increasing panic as time goes on, that sort of thing. There are all sorts of identifying things that creep in if you don't keep your cool. But these, well, it's as though all emotion has been drained out of them. They aren't real."

"They're real enough for me."

Linda is watching me closely. "I'd say someone's trying to point a finger at you, Richard. Forget Julie, is there anyone out there in this big bad world who's got it in for you?"

I say nothing and her gaze narrows. "There is, isn't there?"

Reluctantly, I admit the truth. "Yes. I have a bit of a situation at work at the moment. I haven't done anything but I suppose it's just possible that someone is trying to make out that I have. The police suggested as much, but I thought they were joking ... No, surely not, it's all too farfetched."

"Maybe, maybe not. But that wouldn't be anything to do with Rodney and me?"

"No."

"For what it's worth, Richard, I can promise you we've got nothing to do with this but I can see why you thought we might have."

I look across at her and for a moment I glimpse the vivacious, irrepressible Linda Montgomery of old.

"Thanks, Linda," I say, "you've been a great help."

For a moment she looks a bit shy then quickly recovers herself. "Glad to be of assistance and even more glad we're not involved. That could've been bad news for me."

"How?"

"Stuff going on I don't know about. Always dangerous."

"Linda, how did you and Rodney get into—?"

But she holds up her hand to stop me.

"Don't go there, Richard. We all make choices. I made mine. Anyway," she grins, "you made yours too, didn't you? Why are you really looking for Julie Orford after all these years? You don't strike me as a man going through a mid-life crisis."

"I'm not, or not in the traditional sense anyway. Oh, I suppose I might as well tell you …" I give her a brief summary of the fraud accusation, the quest and its various outcomes which, slightly to my annoyance, she finds funny.

"Crazy old world, isn't it?" she says, "here's me, up to my neck in dodgy dealings walking free as a bird and there's you, whiter than white, stumbling into things and looking over your shoulder the whole time."

"It'll all get sorted," I say rather tetchily. "I'm not involved in the scam and time will prove that."

"Maybe."

I am starting to get cross. "I am not involved. No way."

"I didn't mean that sort of 'maybe'. I meant maybe time will prove it, maybe it won't. Be careful, Richard, inexperienced these people may be but whoever is behind these texts means this mud to stick. The white hats don't always win in the real world."

I am silent. At the beginning everyone was utterly upbeat about my innocence, but a lot more people seem to be warning me about this lately. I find myself wondering what Sergeant Williams really believes.

Linda goes on. "So in the meantime, while you wait for absolution, you fill the empty hours by searching for your long lost love."

"Now you're laughing at me."

"No, I'm not, but all I can say is I hope you don't find her."

"Oh, thanks a bundle."

"I'm serious. Keep the dream. It's almost certainly better than the reality. In fact, that's another option for you too, Richard."

"What is?"

"Disappear. Vanish. Start again. If you can't solve your problem, abandon it."

"It's not as easy as that."

"Actually, it is. I could probably fix you up with a new passport, wouldn't cost much. Not for you."

I am rather taken aback. "Thanks for the offer, Linda, but no thanks. I'm going to fight this out to the end."

"Suit yourself." She stands up ready to go. "I don't suppose we'll meet again, Richard. But if we do—"

"—If we do, you won't be happy to see me?"

She just grins. "Who knows? Thanks for the drink."

I watch her go, the last tangible link to my dreams of Julie.

64

SYDNEY

The sun sparkled off the water in Sydney harbour as Richard sat on the deck of his waterside mansion in Vaucluse, a glass of cold, dry white wine in his hand. In front of him a path ran past the swimming pool down to his private jetty where his boat was moored. Life was good. Filming of his latest script had just finished, and now he could relax, safe and secure in his new home.

Inside, on his desk – a Victorian writing desk he'd imported from England – lay a letter from his agent outlining a new project he might like to consider. On the surface it was just another thriller about the links between a Hong Kong gang and a British gambling club but the interest lay in the central characters who'd been friends at school, had a brief fling in their teens before losing touch with each other until they met years later in a bar in Hong Kong. Was their new relationship a rekindling of the love they had once had or simply a business arrangement? Or possibly a bit of each?

It was the kind of complex relationship he enjoyed exploring but he would make no decisions now. Lucy would be arriving soon. Her flight from Santiago would get into Kingsford Smith airport around eight tomorrow morning. He'd meet her in the Aston Martin, then bring her back here and show her his new home. He thought she would appreciate the modern house, a temple to chrome and glass. He wondered what name she would be travelling under — it wouldn't be Lucy Merryweather that's for sure. Not after that business in San Francisco.

Or maybe it wouldn't be Lucy. It could be his old friend Marcus, tired and dusty after the four days drive from Perth. Richard kept telling him to fly but he would seldom be parted from his beloved 4x4. Marcus would have a quick shower and then they'd go out to eat, talk, catch up, as they had done every time he'd visited Australia since he had saved Marcus from drowning.

On the other hand maybe he would take his boat across to Circular Quay in the morning and meet Diana as she came off her cruise ship. They would take it for a trip around the harbour and then would walk out towards the Opera House, have coffee in one of the bars and talk about ...

Yes, what would they talk about? He had no idea but it didn't matter as Diana didn't actually exist any more than Lucy or Marcus did.

And neither did the house with its harbour view.

65

In spite of my earlier suspicions I'm inclined to believe Linda when she said she had nothing to do with the texts. And then, when she asked if I'd trodden on any other toes, another thought came to me. I know I'm not involved in this fraud but I'm the one they've put on garden leave. I'm the one whose laptop was apparently interfered with. Is that significant? Am I being set up?

And if so, is there actually a danger they'll succeed?

During the week a handful of Christmas cards arrive and I stick them on the mantelpiece. Lauren and I have never bothered much with cards and this year I forgot about them completely but I must remember to get some chocolates and flowers for Mrs Atkins before she comes on Thursday.

Then on Wednesday there's a surprise in the post. Another card arrives, unsigned but obviously homemade. The picture is a light colour-wash drawing of a cottage that I recognise. The message inside is simple.

Good hunting.

It's clearly from Heather and it gives me a warm feeling. My first instinct is to ring and thank her but on reflection I decide to respond in kind so when I go to the shops I buy a card for her. I eschew the appalling robins, snow and stagecoaches and instead choose a picture of Weybridge High Street which, on reflection, might not be much better. I scribble a line inside

"*The hunt may be over*" and put the card in the post. It's only much later I realise my reply is somewhat ambiguous.

As the week goes on I am very glad that I accepted Simon's invitation to spend Christmas with him and Rita. The hours hang heavily, the house is oppressive and in spite of myself I cannot shake off the possibility that things are happening behind the scenes that might affect my future.

On Thursday I decide I can't let it lie so I ring Sergeant Williams again and voice my growing suspicion that someone is setting me up.

"That is certainly one possibility, Mr Kirkwood," he says.

"One possibility?"

There's a pause and I can almost hear him working to frame his words. Finally he says, "You might like to know that our technical guys recovered the deleted items from your laptop."

"Did they? And what did they find?"

"Nothing, or nothing unexpected. All the correspondence, notes etc between you and the contracting company, just as you said."

"So why did someone go to all the trouble of deleting them? Was it to try and make you think that there was something on there I didn't want you to see?"

"Quite possibly." Another pause then he says, "I think it only fair to tell you that we're now fairly certain that there has been some involvement in this fraud from within your company."

"Has there indeed. So who is it?"

He leaves one of those telling silences which I've observed him use before – the sort where the main suspect rushes to fill the gap.

I rush to fill the gap. "But you know it's not me?"

There's another long pause. "I wish I could say that for certain, Mr. Kirkwood, but unfortunately I can't."

"What do you mean, you can't? I haven't done anything. Doesn't my laptop show that?"

Sergeant Williams is clearly uncomfortable. "We are still investigating. Until we've put together the pieces of this whole matter, until we have some firm evidence, then we have to keep an open mind."

"Well, thanks very much," I say rather bitterly.

"I'm sorry, Mr Kirkwood, I know it's not what you want to hear …"

"Too right, it's not," I say angrily and cut him off before he can invite himself round for another informal interview.

Christmas passes. It's not unpleasant, but I'm glad not to be alone. On Christmas Day Rita cooks a turkey with all the trimmings, a wonderful meal that leaves all three of us flat out in armchairs in front of the fire. When the time difference is right I ring Lauren and we exchange Christmas greetings. I apologise for not sending her a present but she points out she didn't send me one either, a fact that had somehow passed me by.

On Boxing Day Simon, Rita and I go for a long walk over the downs and the fresh air and exercise manage to drive all other thoughts from my mind. That night, after Rita has gone to bed, Simon and I sit by the fire and talk. He asks me how my quest is going.

"Actually I think it's over." And I bring him up to date on my trip to Yorkshire, though I don't mention Polly.

"So what will you do now?"

"Not much I can do. The trail's gone cold. Frankly, looking back on the past couple of months I think I was lucky to get as close as I did. It was always a hell of a long shot, wasn't it?"

Simon looks at me speculatively. "So, a complete waste of time then."

I think for a moment before answering. "No, I wouldn't say that."

"But you set out to find her and you didn't."

"No, but it was interesting to give it a go. Stopped me

brooding, at least for a while. I don't regret a moment of it. Well, except …"

"Nothing like a bit of adrenaline for reminding you that you're alive." He makes light of our trip to the Cerberus Club. "Now what's happening about work?"

"That's not looking good." I tell him about my growing suspicions and about my conversation with Sergeant Williams.

"Don't like the sound of that," he says. "What can you do about it?"

"That's the frustrating thing. Nothing. I can't refute an allegation that hasn't been made."

"What does Lauren say?"

"I haven't told her the latest development. She can't do anything so what's the point?"

"The point is she's your wife. You have heard about sharing, haven't you?"

I am silent. I have heard about sharing but I've seldom practised it.

"Richard?"

"She can't help me, not legally, vested interest and all that. If I find I do need legal advice I'll turn to Max."

Simon thinks for a moment. "We have to try and stay positive, Richard. I'm confident this will get sorted, but then what? Will you just go back to the same old same old?"

"Don't know. It won't be easy. Even if I'm cleared completely it will be hard picking up the pieces. And if I'm not, if there is still uncertainty … well, that would be bad, but maybe even that isn't the worst option."

"What do you mean?"

"What if I actually end up being convicted of something?"

"I can't believe that's possible." Simon thinks for a

moment. "Look, this isn't helping. Don't think about that. Stay positive, okay?"

"I'll try but that's not easy either. Oh, and I told you Lauren's New York stint's been extended by three months, didn't I?"

"Yes. How do you feel about that?"

"It's what she wants and she's good at it. I can't stand in her way."

Simon looks at me for a moment. Then he raises the scotch bottle and lifts an eyebrow. I nod and he tops up our glasses.

"Richard, we've always been close, haven't we? You and I."

"Ye–es …"

He smiles. "I could say I love you like a brother but then you are my brother."

"Spit it out, Simon?"

"You don't get close to many people, do you?"

"Nonsense, I know a lot of people."

"Know, yes, but how many of those are really close? People you'd trust with anything, people you'd turn to in times of trouble."

I'm silent. He's right, of course. I know that.

"I know why, of course, and I understand …"

"For heaven's sake, Simon, not that again."

"Yes, that again, well not entirely that again."

"Now you're talking in riddles."

"Richard, the only other person I've ever seen you get really close to is Lauren. I can't tell you how happy I was when you two got married.

"What are you trying to say?"

"Don't bugger it up, that's what I'm trying to say. Don't just let yourselves drift apart."

"I think we've been drifting apart for some time but I've only just recognised it. I'll be honest with you – I've started to wonder if she'll ever come back."

His eyebrows shoot up. "That would be a great pity."

"Maybe"

Since my visit to New York I've realised how distant Lauren and I have become from each other. I've tried telling myself that my timing was bad, she was just busy, it doesn't matter, it's inevitable when you turn up unannounced. But the last couple of months on my own have shown me that loneliness exists in our relationship. And the fact I don't quite know what she thinks of me anymore hurts. It matters very much. At least to me. I am no longer sure about her.

Aloud I say, "Anyway, what can I do about it? She deserves this chance in New York."

"Of course she does. And I don't have any easy answers. All I know is that if you value her, and I think you do, then your marriage is worth fighting for. I've no idea how you can sort it out, only the two of you can do that, just don't let it all slip away by default. Please."

If I were having this conversation with anyone else I'd be resenting it deeply but Simon is the one person I trust completely. I know he's right about Lauren. At one time I was determined never to let anyone get close to me, far too dangerous, but somehow Lauren managed it and I am so glad she did. She brought love and light into my life, and I'm grateful for that, but even so I've never been able to give myself entirely and the bit I held back, still hold back, has always lain there between us. Unacknowledged but festering. Why, oh why can't I do something about it?

I look up and meet Simon's eyes and suddenly the tears

start to come, my emotions are very near the surface at the moment. Then Simon is holding me in his arms, just as he did when we were children.

"Let it go, Richard, let it go."

"I just don't know what to do."

"Of course you don't, and now's not the time to be making serious decisions. But, problems don't go away, you know that. Sooner or later they have to be faced. You can put them all on hold, Richard, but don't bury them. Okay?"

Gradually I calm down. "Sensible old Simon."

He grins. "Maybe, but then I don't have the baggage you do. Just don't do anything in a hurry."

"Don't worry," I say, "I won't."

And I mean it. But then three days later, the day before New Year's Eve, all my good intentions are put to the test.

LAUREN

The meeting with the senior partner on Christmas Eve came right out of the blue. She knew she'd been doing good work, her three month extension was proof of that, but the offer he now made came as a total surprise.

Justin made it clear he didn't expect an instant answer. "Go away and think about it," he said.

She gathered her thoughts. "I'll need to discuss this with Richard too."

"Sure you will. Look, why not take a break across new year. Go back to London for a few days. Talk to the guy."

She left the office in a daze. When she spoke to Richard on Christmas Day she made no mention of the meeting with Justin, but back in the office the day after Christmas she knew a decision had to be made so she picked up the phone and booked a flight to London in three days' time.

I've always found the days between Christmas and New Year rather flat but this year they're worse than ever. The morning after my emotional breakdown, as I was leaving to come home, Rita gave me a big hug. Whether Simon had told her anything or whether she just sensed I was disturbed I don't know. But the hug was welcome. I always feel safe in their home.

Tuesday and Wednesday drag by but then on Thursday I suddenly remember Heather. I wait until mid-afternoon then give her a ring. Her voice is cool and calm on the phone.

"Hallo," she says, "thank you for the card."

"Thank you for yours," I say, "it's a beautiful picture. D'you make all your own Christmas cards?"

"Yes, I do."

"Must take you hours."

"Not really, though this year I did double my output."

"Wow," I say, "how many did you make?"

"Two," she says.

"Oh." I don't know what to say to this. I imagine the other one must be for her daughter and I suddenly realise I've been paid a huge compliment.

She obviously senses my confusion because she quickly changes the subject.

"I didn't know what to make of your message," she says. "Does '*hunt may be over*' mean you found Julie or that you've given up?"

"No, I haven't found her and I don't think I'm going to."

"Did you go to Scarborough?"

"I certainly did."

"And?"

"Another dead end."

"Oh." There's a pause and then she says, "So what now?"

"I don't know. I can't seem to think straight. The work situation is still not resolved but ..." Suddenly I stop speaking. I hear a sound I'm not expecting. The sound of a key in the front door.

"Hang on a minute."

I walk into the hall to be greeted by the sight of Lauren holding a small case and closing the door behind her.

"Lauren?" I say in surprise.

"The very same," she says.

I turn back to the phone. "Heather, I need to go. I'll call you back."

I hang up and turn to Lauren. "Well, this is a surprise."

Even as I speak I realise I sound as though I've been caught out in something.

Lauren raises an eyebrow. "Heather?"

"Just someone who's been helping me with my search."

"Oh, that."

We seem to have got off to a bad start so I take her bag and help her off with her coat.

"I wasn't expecting you. Have you just come from New York?"

"Yeah. Had to come via Amsterdam. Couldn't get a direct flight."

"You should have let me know. I'd've picked you up."

"Sure, but I didn't really know about the last leg out of Schiphol until I got there. Ended up in Gatwick so I just grabbed a cab."

"Okay, but …" I'm about to say why are you here when I realise this might not be very tactful. "But how long you here for?"

"Why? D'you have anyone coming?"

So much for tact. "No, of course not. I was just wondering."

She relents slightly. "I'm booked on a flight back on Sunday so I'm here for New Year. But right now what I need's a shower and a change of clothes."

She seems brittle but she may just be tired. I'm puzzled by this flying visit but now's not the time to probe deeper.

"Okay, well, why don't you go upstairs and sort yourself out. I'll nip down to the shops and get something for supper."

"What were you going to have?"

"To be honest, I hadn't thought. Beans on toast, maybe, or fish and chips."

Laurens grins. "Been living it up while I've been away, I see. Why don't we just settle on some good old British fish and chips."

"If you're sure."

"I'm sure, but now I really must have that shower."

Later that evening, fish and chips consumed and the remains of a bottle of white wine on the table between us, Lauren asks me about the situation at work.

For a moment I hesitate. Do I tell her about my suspicions, my fears, my last conversation with Sergeant Williams? But what's the point? I know Simon talked about sharing and, if there were something definite to report, I would… I think. But why talk about a vague possibility, especially as talking about it might make it seem more real and that's the last thing I want.

"Unchanged," I say finally, "the investigation is still going on."

"So you don't know when you'll be going back to work?"

"No idea."

"How are you managing alone?"

I shrug. "Some days are better than others. I try and find things to do but it's not always easy."

"What about the search for Miss Wonderful."

I open my mouth to respond but she beats me to it. "Sorry, sorry, that was unfair."

"It's been an interesting search. Helped pass the time."

"And this Heather's been helping you?"

"Her and many others, yes."

"But I guess you haven't found her, what's her name, Julie?"

"No. And I won't."

"Given up?"

"Come to a dead end."

"I see. Are you sorry?"

"Partly. But as people keep telling me, maybe the journey was the interesting bit, not the destination."

Lauren nods. Then there's a silence. In the end I lean across the table and take her hand.

"Come on Lauren, spit it out. What's going on?"

"What d'you mean?"

"Oh, come on. You couldn't get away at Christmas but suddenly you're here for New Year. There has to be a reason."

"Yeah, there is."

She gently withdraws her hand and I have a sudden

foreboding.

"Is there someone else?"

Her jerk of surprise is obviously quite genuine. "No … no! Well, no, there's not someone else, but there is *something* else."

I take a deep breath. "Okay, can we just get on with it?"

"Sure." A brief pause. "You remember Justin was thinking of extending my attachment by three months?"

"Yes…"

"Well, now he's gone one better. He's offered me a permanent senior partner's position."

"Wow. That's wonderful … Isn't it?"

"Yeah, it is, but the position's in New York. I'd be living there permanently."

"Oh. I see."

Silence as we look at each other over the congealing remains of our fish and chip supper. Neither of us look away.

Eventually I say. "When would this start?"

"In the spring, April. In effect it means I'd stay out there when my original six months comes to an end."

I think about this for a moment. It's a lot to take in. "This is a wonderful opportunity for you, isn't it?"

She says nothing, just nods. She should be happy but I can see she isn't.

I take her hand again. "What are you going to do?"

She snatches her hand away. "No, what are WE going to do? This isn't just about me."

"No, I suppose not."

She bites her lip." I'm really torn, I want it but then there's us. I guess I'm trying to have my cake and eat it too."

I manage a smile. "Always a tricky one that."

"Oh, Richard, what are we going to do?"

I fall back on my professional consultant's skills. Never make a hasty decision. "Do? Well, tonight, nothing. Let's sleep on it. We'll talk more tomorrow."

The next day it's very cold but the sun is shining so on the spur of the moment we decide to go out. By mutual consent we go to Bosham Quay. Days out like this have become a rarity in our marriage and it's many years since we last walked by the sea together.

We sit on the harbour wall looking out across the water and to my surprise, I notice that the little boat with a different name each side of its bow, is still bobbing gently at its mooring just as it was back in October. I'm struck by a sense of timelessness in a place like this.

Although the sun is bright the wind is quite keen and I see Lauren shivering. I put my arm round her shoulders and she leans against me.

"What's going to happen to us, Richard?"

"Nothing bad," I say.

"But maybe something sad?"

"Only sad if we let it be so."

"It's decision time, isn't it?"

"Yes. I suppose it is."

We watch the boats for a while and the gulls skimming the water. Then Lauren says. "Okay, let's do some sandbox profiles here."

"Do some what?"

She giggles. "Sorry. That's one of Justin's pet phrases when he wants to explore various options. Bit geeky, isn't it?"

"Well, at least you didn't say 'Let's run some ideas up the flagpole and see who salutes'. That's one blessing."

We both dissolve into laughter and for a moment we have a glimpse of the early days of our relationship when life was fun and we laughed a lot before work began to seal us off from each other.

"Okay, let's start with the givens," I say. "You've been offered this chance, a wonderful chance, one that you've worked for and earned, I might say…"

"Well, thank you."

"And you want to take it, don't you?"

"I don't have to."

"No, but I think you'd always regret it if you turned it down. And you can't build a happy life on regret. Believe me, I do know that."

Perhaps the last bit comes out more bitterly than I'd intended. Lauren looks at me strangely. Then, after a moment she says.

"Okay, so where does that leave us?"

I suddenly realise that she is looking for some kind of reassurance, reassurance I don't know how to give. I wonder why she has really made this flying visit, to tell me about the job offer? Or to see whether we still have a future together?

Time to be honest.

"Lauren, I've not mentioned this before but it may not be possible for me to continue with Swamplett, even after this investigation is over."

"How come, not possible?"

"If I'm not cleared completely – your 'not proven' theory – I don't think I could face going back."

"Are you serious? Is that a risk? Really?"

"Yes, as it happens I think it is."

She is silent for a moment and then says, "I guess I'd always assumed that once all this is over you'd be back to work full time again."

"So did I, at the beginning."

A little flotilla of ducks appear below us and gaze up at us expectantly. After a moment they give up and paddle away. I glance sideways at Lauren but she's gazing out across the water.

"This is getting to be kinda difficult, isn't it?" she says.

"It is."

"Part of me really wants to say 'yes' to Justin."

"I know."

"But if those bastards are going to sell you down the river I can't just leave you to face them alone."

That statement warms me but deep down I know there can only be one answer.

"Thank you. I appreciate that, but we need to think long term."

"What kind of long term?"

"Let's look at this objectively. If you say 'No' to Justin and come back here, the chances are you'll never get such an opportunity again. We'll both know that you made a sacrifice for me. Maybe fine for now, but sometime in the future that could rebound on us and you could end up resenting the fact that I spoilt your career."

"Maybe." She thinks for a moment. "Suppose it does all go belly up for you here, you could always come and live in New York."

I shake my head. "I'd thought of that, but I don't think it would work. I don't know what I'd do over there."

She hesitates. "We don't have to be close with a dollar. I'll be earning more than enough for us both to live on."

I laugh and after a moment she joins in uncertainly. "Money's not the point, is it?"

"No, it isn't. I'm fifty-five. I could probably take early retirement from Swamplett and still get a reasonable pension."

"You just don't want to live in New York."

"No. I can't just 'live' anywhere. I need a purpose and I think I'm more likely to find that in England than America."

Lauren is silent for a moment then, still staring straight ahead, she reaches sideways and takes my hand.

"So, are we saying we've reached the end of the road, you and I?"

Suddenly the chill wind coming off the sea has an extra bite.

"I don't know," I say.

Behind us the church clock strikes twelve, long ponderous notes that echo in the cold air. The sadness between us is almost tangible.

"So this is how a marriage ends," says Lauren and I can hear a slight break in her voice, "not with a bang, but with a church clock striking?"

I force a smile. "Not only a lawyer. A poet too?"

For a while we sit there in silence, holding hands and gazing out across the harbour.

After a while Lauren says. "So what happens now?"

Her direct question crystallises the thought that's been running through my mind. "Nothing," I say.

"Nothing? What do you mean, nothing?"

"I mean nothing. Nothing we've said today has changed the current situation, you in New York, me here. There's no reason to force an instant decision. By doing nothing for the moment all our options are still open. If we take a hard and fast decision now we might regret it later."

She thinks about this for a moment. "And when your investigation is over and you know the outcome, what happens then?"

"No idea. We'll have to wait and see."

"So you think I should say 'Yes' to Justin?"

"I think you should."

She hesitates and for a moment I wonder if she is expecting me to say something else. Part of me wants to. I want to say "I'll miss you" but the words won't come and anyway it wouldn't be fair. I can't put that sort of pressure on her.

"Will you be all right, Richard?"

"I'll be fine," I say with more confidence than I actually feel. Then I have another thought. "There is one thing. If you're living permanently in New York then how would you feel about selling the Weybridge house?"

She is silent for a moment then she says, "We bought that house together. The first real home of our own."

"Yes, but we've never really spent much time in it, have we?"

"Suppose not and I guess it is a bit big for one person."

"Yes. I don't really want to rattle around in it on my own."

"But you've got to live somewhere."

"So have you and New York isn't cheap."

"That's not a problem. That apartment's big enough for me. I can just go on renting it. But what would you do?"

"Find something smaller, I suppose."

"You mean get an apartment in London or something."

"Maybe, depends what I end up doing."

We're still holding hands but we're not looking at each other.

"So the decision is not to make a decision?"

"Apart from you saying 'Yes' to Justin."

"And you selling the house."

"Yes."

As I speak I realise that, given complete freedom of choice, I would not choose to live in a London flat. I glance round me at the small headland jutting out into Chichester harbour, the church standing in the small graveyard, the pub on the edge of the beach.

"If it all goes belly up at Swamplett, maybe I'll buy a house in a place like this. Peaceful. Look out at the sea all day."

Lauren looks at me sceptically. "And how would you pass the time? Take up painting?"

A flash picture comes into my mind of Heather in Cornwall and her pictures of the Helford River. "I don't think that's likely. If it does happen I'll sort something out but that would be my problem, wouldn't it?"

She looks at me for a moment, then says. "Well, I guess that's that. Okay, I'll accept Justin's offer, you put the house on the market and wait and see if you still have a job to go back to. We'll put the rest on hold for a while." She lets go my hand and stands up. "Now let's get some lunch. I'm frozen."

As we walk along the sea wall towards the pub, I run through our conversation again in my head. On the surface we've agreed not to make any hasty final decision, but deep down I'm wondering if we're just fooling ourselves. I'm also wondering whether the significant things are the things neither of us have actually put into words.

70

HEATHER

Heather had thought long and hard before deciding to send Richard a Christmas card. She still wasn't sure why she'd done so except she hadn't been able to get his visit out of her mind. At first she'd been slightly resentful of his intrusion but after a while she realised that it hadn't been entirely unwelcome. For the first time since Robin's death she'd put her thoughts about her husband to one side. The questions Richard seemed to be asking about himself also applied to her.

For a long time now she'd existed pretty much in isolation though she acknowledged that had been her own choice. Although she'd only had two conversations with him, Richard had been easy to talk to and, unusual for a man, he listened. On their second meeting in the pub she'd even found herself on the verge of telling him about Katherine but the words wouldn't come. Katherine was a pain buried deep inside her. She constantly told herself she'd dealt with it, but she knew she hadn't.

She'd thought a lot about that lunch with Richard. His quest was certainly strange but she sensed something else in him, something deeper. All through Robin's illness and finally his death, she had tried not to be irritated when friends said things like, *"I'm so sorry"*, *"It must be terrible for you,"* and, worst of all, *"I do know how you feel."* They were trying to be kind, she knew that, but she also knew that they had no idea what she was going through.

But when she met Richard there was something about him that made her think he did know.

She knew she'd like to talk to him again. Because of him, she was starting to feel the need for company once more, to have a conversation that wasn't centred round the price of groceries, roof repairs or having the car serviced. She was also genuinely curious about his search for Julie and so she had sent the card.

Then he had rung and she'd been pleased to hear his voice but the call was abruptly ended as his wife, apparently unexpectedly, had arrived home. She wondered about that, even felt slightly guilty, though she didn't know why.

She suspected she should steer well clear but found she couldn't, so a few days later she phoned him.

71

New Years' Day, the last day Lauren and I have together before she goes back to the States, is a little awkward. We're polite with each other but hanging over everything is a sense of sadness. We act as if we haven't made any final decision, but there is somehow a sense that at best our marriage has been put on hold. We spend the day on practical matters, mainly about what to do with all our bits and pieces so I can sell this house.

On our last night we share a bed, something we haven't done for a long time, but whether this is an indication that love, real love, still exists between us or whether it's saying 'farewell', I am not sure.

I take her to the airport on Sunday and our goodbyes are rather muted. As before we don't linger, Lauren heads off through security and I drive back to the Weybridge box.

I don't like to use the word 'depressed' but I'm certainly feeling increasingly like I've failed. At everything.

I take refuge in mindless activity and spend the afternoon continuing to sort out the house. Some things can be sold, lots can be thrown away. It's a long, lonely day and I'm feeling emotionally drained when the phone rings. It's Heather and I'm caught by surprise.

At first she is very tentative. "Am I intruding?" she says.

"No, it's fine."

"Only when we last spoke ..."

I cut her short. "Lauren came home for New Year and I wasn't expecting her. Only a flying visit though. She went back to New York this morning."

There's a silence on the other end of the phone for a moment then Heather says. "So everything's all right?"

I don't have the energy to lie. "Well, no, actually everything's anything but all right."

"Oh."

"Look, I'm sorry I had to hang up on you last week. It's just that Lauren arriving like that caught me by surprise."

"Yes, I understand." There's a pause then she says. "It was just ... well ... I don't mean to pry, but ... you said Scarborough was a dead end. Does that mean you've giving up looking for Julie?"

"I think so. I can't see where to go from here."

"How do you feel about that?"

"I'm not sure. Defeated probably, if I'm being honest. I wonder why I ever bothered. It was a stupid idea, complete waste of time."

"Maybe. Maybe not."

"Well, I haven't achieved anything. I'm still under suspicion at work, I haven't got a clue what I'm going to do next and I've ruffled a lot of feathers, yours included."

"Maybe you have. Maybe some of them needed ruffling. I'm starting to think mine did."

"Well, it's kind of you to say so but basically I think I've made a right balls up of everything."

There's a short silence but I can hear her breathing. Then she says, "You sound very low. Has something else happened?"

"Yes, you could say that."

"Do you want to talk about it?"

A good question. Do I? Normally Simon's the only person I can talk to intimately but after our recent discussion about Lauren, I'm not ready to share this with him yet. I look round at the litter of boxes and suddenly the bare walls seem to close in on me. I realise I have to get away from here, away from Weybridge, away from impersonal possessions, away from policemen, away from what might be the shattered relics of my marriage.

"Yes," I say, "I think I do."

"Then why not come down here," she says, "give yourself some space and we can talk if you want to or not if you don't."

For a fleeting moment I wonder what she's suggesting but then she goes on. "The pub in the village doesn't have rooms but there are plenty of holiday cottages around and this time of year you can rent them by the night. I could fix one of those for you."

I picture the Helford river in my mind, the steep banked trees running down to the water, the chuckle of the stream as it flows through the village. The silence. The light. The calm peace of Heather's cottage. The cat on my knee.

"That's a wonderful idea," I say. "I'll be there by tomorrow night. If there's no cottage free I'll find a hotel somewhere but I'm coming."

Twenty-four hours later I'm installed in a small stone cottage looking out onto Helford creek, getting ready to walk down to the pub for a meal with Heather. I know it's early January but the silence is immense.

Initially we're slightly awkward with each other. It is only our third meeting after all and I'm exhausted, the long drive adding physical tiredness to the whole emotional upset of the past few days. I'm already wondering if this was a good idea or

309

just more procrastination. Heather senses my mood.

"Just try and let go," she says. "No need to talk about anything tonight. There's plenty of time."

We eat fresh fish with potatoes and salad and after a while, to my surprise, I find I am starting to relax a little. We don't talk much, a bit about Cornwall, a bit about painting, a bit about the other items on the pub menu. There are long silences but they are comfortable silences.

When it's time to go we stand beside her car for a few moments looking out over the dark river. Then, surprisingly, she holds out her hand and I shake it.

"Thank you for this evening, Richard. I've enjoyed it."

"Will I see you tomorrow?"

"Of course. I've got some things to do in the morning so why don't you come up to the cottage, say early afternoon. Then I'll cook something for us in the evening."

The sound of her car's engine fades into the night as I walk back beside the creek. I sleep well. The silence of a Cornish village in January wraps me round like a blanket.

The following afternoon is bright but cold. We sit, well muffled up, on the terrace outside Heather's cottage, drinking tea and eating cake, looking down the silver curve of the river.

We chat casually for a while and then, thoughtlessly perhaps, I ask her why she chose to come and live in Cornwall.

Her face goes blank. "I wanted to be alone."

I say nothing and after a moment she goes on. "I chose Cornwall because I knew I could borrow the Travers' cottage with a minimum of fuss. I didn't know anyone down here and I also knew I wanted to paint and Cornwall seemed a good place for that."

"I thought St. Ives was where all the painters went."

"I didn't want to be with other painters. I wanted to be alone."

I leave it a moment and then say gently. "Was it that bad?"

"Yes." A pause then … "It all got so complicated. Not just Robin … there was Katherine too, living so far away. She's in New Zealand, a place called Paihia. I think that's north of Auckland somewhere. She breaks off. "No, enough about me. Tell me about Scarborough."

So I tell her about Scarborough. I don't mention Polly but I tell her about the café, meeting Pete and Angie, learning that Julie and Brian had moved on, the encounter with Brian in Knaresborough, the realisation that Julie had vanished and probably didn't want to be found.

The last statement brings a wry smile from Heather. "Funny, isn't it?" she says, "there we all were, just another group of 11 year olds. Who could have guessed back then what would happen to us all?"

We couldn't have guessed, of course we couldn't. We all went our separate ways and if I hadn't had this mad idea of trying to find Julie none of this would ever have emerged. I think of the dry barrister, Philip Armstrong. I think of Norman Huggett abandoning a wife and children for a Thai teenager. I think of Rodney wheeling and dealing in Hong Kong, of Linda living a courier's life on the move. I think of Heather nursing others for years before nursing her own husband to his death. I think of Julie running a Scarborough café and I think of myself, constantly on the move, burying the past under endless work.

Out of the blue a remark Simon made a few months ago comes into my mind: "*If you go back into the past you're bound to cause ripples and who knows what those ripples might do.*"

I've certainly caused some ripples over the past few weeks but then I remember Mark Trimble in the Devon pub and realise that the ripples began long before my quest for Julie. Perhaps we all cause ripples every day, mostly without knowing it.

I suddenly realise Heather is looking at me and I bring myself back to the present. "Sorry," I say, "I was miles away."

"You certainly were." A pause. "So the Julie quest is over?"

"Yes. It was all pretty silly, wasn't it? The past is best left alone."

"Not always. And sometimes it isn't our choice."

"How do you mean?"

"Well, you might want to move on but the past might not let you."

I suspect she's talking about herself now but I still find this uncomfortable and Heather notices.

"Something's changed, hasn't it?" she asks. "When we first met you were so determined to find Julie."

"Yes, I was."

"But no longer. I'm wondering if the memories of her have led you somewhere else, wakened other memories. Maybe stuff you thought you'd buried deep enough not to be touched."

I am silent and after a moment she goes on.

"I don't want to pry, Richard. I'll only say this once and then I'll shut up. I know about pain. Physical pain, internal pain. I know what it is to bury pain and pretend it's not there. As far as I'm concerned I've tried hiding from it. It worked for a while but it's not working now and somehow I'm going to have to deal with that. I don't know what it is you've buried but I'm certain there's something and I'd guess this search for Julie has brought it closer to the surface. All I want to say is, if you want to let it go, I'll listen. That's all – listen. And if you don't want to do that, then fine. We'll have supper and pretend this conversation never happened."

There is a long silence. Neither of us are looking at each other. I watch the boats on the river, the gulls flying above them, the wind in the trees on the opposite shore.

I can't let it go. I never have. I've never shared it with Lauren, I don't even talk about it to Simon anymore, or at least only obliquely. Why should it be talked about? It's gone. It's over. Forget it.

Except I can't. And never have been able to, which is why the memory, probably the completely false memory, of Julie is so important. The one bright light in those terrible years. A time which I can't forget, much as I'd like to. Simon knows that and I've always known deep down that he's right. I have to deal with this but I don't know how.

The silence continues and once again I'm struck how silences with Heather are not awkward or embarrassing. They're natural.

I glance sideways at her. She too is gazing down the river, her hands in her lap, apparently completely at ease. I envy her that ease but I suddenly have a glimpse of how hard won it has been.

A herring gull, bolder than the rest, swoops low over the terrace, probably with his eye on the remains of the cake, but doesn't quite have the bottle to take it from under our noses.

Heather. Her perception, the knowledge that she is facing her own demons. The sense of calm that surrounds her and this place. She is alone but I am lonely and I realise they are not the same thing.

Suddenly, sitting there, it all gets too much and, almost

involuntarily, I find myself finally, finally letting go.

I half turn away from her and gaze down the river. "I had a sister, no one knows that apart from Simon. Anne was the youngest of us. She was knocked down and killed by a car. She was three years old."

For a moment I falter. The picture of that moment, so long suppressed, suddenly fresh in my mind again.

"I was six, Simon was eight. He wasn't at home. I was playing in the garden with Anne. The ball bounced out into the road. Anne went after it. I couldn't stop her. The car hit her."

My stomach is churning. I feel sick. Heather is silent.

"Our mother was devastated. Anne was the apple of her eye. Dad was distraught too but somehow mother edged him out. It was her tragedy, her daughter who'd been killed. She went into a kind of mourning and never came out of it. I suppose she was depressed but that wasn't always recognised back then, certainly not in the kind of background I came from. Then a few years later Dad died. Nothing related. He had a bad attack of bronchitis, he'd always been a smoker. I don't think he fought it though. I think he was in mourning too, not just for Anne, but for my mother and their marriage, both of which he'd also lost."

I'm beginning to shake. "My mother never put it into words but I knew, deep down, that she blamed me for Anne's death. Not logical, of course, I was yards away. There was nothing I could've done, but somehow the unspoken accusation stuck. Our childhood, Simon's and mine, was bleak. We weren't abused in any way. We were fed, clothed, physically looked after, but it was a silent household. Simon played the part of the older brother, took responsibility for everything. My mother rarely spoke. The house might have been warm but the atmosphere was always cold. Nothing bad. Just – nothing."

I feel Heather stir and hear the slight scrape of her chair on the flagstones.

"Anne was never mentioned again. Her photos all vanished. It was as though she'd never existed. After that I'd find reasons to stay out of the house, anything to escape that corroding atmosphere. School was the one bright spot. I could talk there, play games, be natural. And then there was Julie. I remember Julie, the first day she smiled at me. It was like coming in from the cold and finding a warm fire. I can't begin to tell you what that smile meant. There weren't many smiles in my life. It was all so innocent and yet it became the subject of dreams. A glimpse of warmth to be had out there in the world if only I could find it. Probably most of it was fantasy but I've never forgotten her."

I fall silent. Heather doesn't move. After a moment I go on.

"I left home as soon as I was old enough. Simon had already gone. A few months later our mother died. I felt nothing. Not even relief. In fact I was glad she was dead. Glad."

The short winter afternoon is coming to a close. The sun is going down throwing the trees along the east bank of the river into silhouette. I shiver but not just from the cold. This is the first time I've said aloud what I've always thought and as the words hang in the air I realise how harsh and unforgiving they sound. And yet they are true.

There is another long silence then Heather says very softly.

"Death is always significant. It can give you freedom but it also freezes a situation so it can never be changed."

And there is so much guilt in that.

I say nothing, and after a moment I hear her get up and go into the cottage.

I go on sitting there, motionless as the dusk gives way to dark and the banks of the river disappear into the night leaving just the silver gleam of water winding towards the sea.

72

Later, I don't know how much later, Heather comes out and gently takes me by the arm.

"Come inside, Richard, it's getting cold."

I follow her into the cottage and suddenly realise I'm freezing. The fire is burning and she sits me down in front of it. The cat arrives, jumps on my lap and settles down. Wrapped around by warmth and purring I gradually bring myself back to the present.

We open the bottle of wine I've brought, Heather cooks a Spanish omelette for supper, then we sit by the fire again. We say very little but soon I know it's time to go.

I start to get up but Heather puts out her hand and stops me. "Before you go, Richard, I want to thank you."

"What for?"

"For trusting me. For telling me about Anne. Tell me, when did you last speak to anyone about her?"

"I never have."

"Ah."

"What was the point? Talking about it doesn't change anything. I just buried the memories and tried to forget them."

"But you failed."

I wince but acknowledge the truth. "Yes, I failed."

For a moment she is silent, then out of the blue she says. "Robin always said that failing wasn't a problem, it was how you recovered from failure that mattered."

Suddenly and unexpectedly she puts an arm round my shoulders. "Richard, listen to me. This afternoon was very painful for you, wasn't it?"

"Very."

"And you think your search for Julie failed too, don't you? But I think it succeeded beyond all expectations."

"But I didn't find her."

"You didn't need to. But I think you found something more important."

"What?"

"Specifically, I don't know. But think of it like this. If you'd come on holiday to Cornwall and we'd bumped into each other…"

"I wouldn't have recognised you."

"Probably not, but leave that aside. If we'd just met casually, two old school friends after 40 odd years, we might have had a drink together, yes?"

"I guess."

"But over that drink would you have told me about Anne?"

"No way."

"Exactly. Without your search, without going back into the past, meeting and talking to all those people, you'd never have reached this stage."

I give a half smile. "A pebble dropped into a pond. Ripples everywhere."

"Ripples everywhere, some flowing away from you, some towards."

"You're very perceptive."

She frowns. "About others, maybe."

Abruptly, she takes her arm away and stands up. "Come

on, Richard. You're tired, you need to sleep. It's been a bit of an emotional roller coaster, hasn't it?"

"Yes, it has."

I get up and put on my coat. At the door Heather suddenly says, "And tomorrow – what are your plans? Do you like walking?"

"Er ... yes, yes, I do."

"Right then. Let's get some physical exercise. I'll pick you up in the morning and we'll try a stretch of cliff path from Kynance Cove."

I make my way back down the hill to another night of silence. I am tired but it's hours before I finally fall asleep.

The next day is bright and cold. The cliff path is narrow, muddy in places, and you have to watch where you put your feet. There's also a lot of up and down which is good for the heart but not so good for conversation.

When we reach the Lizard we sit down on a bench looking out to sea and Heather produces a flask and some biscuits from her bag.

"I thought we might be ready for this."

The hot coffee is very welcome. The exercise is doing me good but I'm still feeling vulnerable after letting my long suppressed memories out into the open. I still can't quite believe I did it but now I have, I realise what a relief it is.

Rather shyly I try and express this to Heather, but then I realise she isn't really listening. She's clearly following a train of thought of her own as she suddenly says. "I suppose you've been all over the world in your business."

This catches me on the hop but I quickly recover. "Well, yes ... when I'm working I'm constantly on the move."

"Must be exciting."

319

"Not really. Hotel rooms, company offices, meeting rooms, they're the same the world over. You go to a lot of places but you never relax in them. You're there to solve a problem, you solve it – hopefully – then back you come before winging off to the next one."

"So you never get much time at home?"

"No, but I'm not sure what 'home' is. I have a house but I'm starting to realise that's not the same thing."

Heather is gazing out to sea. "Have you ever been to New Zealand?"

"Two or three times, yes."

"And is it as beautiful as they say?"

"I don't know it very well. I've really only been to Auckland. I did once spend a long weekend with a client in his home in Whitianga, that's on the Coromandel peninsula in the northeast. That was beautiful. I don't know the South Island at all."

She's silent for a moment then she says, "You paid me a huge compliment yesterday, Richard."

"Compliment?"

"Yes. For trusting me enough to talk about Anne."

"It wasn't… sorry…" I swallow. "It wasn't easy."

"Of course it wasn't, but it made me realise that trust works both ways."

"How do you mean?"

There's a pause and then she says, "Can I tell you about Katherine?"

There's only one answer to that.

"Yes, of course. If you want to."

"I do want to. I think it's time."

"I gather there's some sort of problem."

Heather nods. "You could say that. Katherine no longer speaks to me."

Her voice is tense and I suddenly realise the ease I saw in her yesterday is not ease at all. It is rigid control.

I decide to take her lead and go for the direct approach.

"Why doesn't she?"

"She blames me for her father's death."

"He had cancer, didn't he?"

"Yes."

"But that's not your fault."

"No."

I open my mouth to say, "then why does she think it is?" but stop myself in time.

There's a long silence then Heather says, "Katherine was already living in New Zealand when Robin was diagnosed. She worked for a bank, in Auckland. She came home on a brief trip to see Robin but at that stage the prognosis was quite hopeful so she went back."

"You were caring for him, weren't you, nursing him?"

"Oh, yes, I was caring for him. I thought it would never end." She catches my surprised glance and goes on. "I know that sounds callous but you have no idea. I loved Robin. Very much. That was the problem. Watching him go downhill, helping where I could but knowing the end was inevitable. Day after day after day."

"It must have been very difficult."

"Yes. Initially it was all very gradual, but then it began to speed up. I'd promised Katherine I'd let her know when things got really bad. Which I did. She made the journey again, the bank was very kind, but by the time she arrived he'd rallied. I suspect she thought I'd just panicked. She knew

I hadn't wanted her to go to New Zealand in the first place so maybe she thought I was just making a point."

"And were you?"

Heather looks shocked. "No, of course not." She pauses a moment. "At least I don't think so. Not intentionally. It's just that it's such a very long way and her father was dying."

"So what happened finally?"

"He got worse, of course he did. There was always only going to be one ending but then it all happened so fast."

There's a pause as she gazes into some distant place where I can't follow. "The last week was dreadful. Robin was in such pain but he wouldn't die. Yes, I know how that sounds but it's no fun watching someone you love suffer like that. I phoned Katherine but I think she thought I was just panicking again. He'd seemed so good when she'd last seen him."

Some other people appear on the path, a man and two women with a little yappy dog at their heels. I nod and smile as they go past but wait until they're out of sight before turning back to Heather.

She hasn't moved. I don't think she was even aware of the other people.

I ask, "Was he in hospital?"

"No, he wouldn't go. He wanted to die at home and of course I was there to look after him. The doctor came regularly but there was nothing any of us could do. I couldn't bear it. And then …"

"He died."

"Yes." She pauses. "He died. It was a blessed relief but … but…"

I suddenly realise. "Katherine didn't make it in time."

"I didn't know if she would come or not but she arrived

the next day. She couldn't believe he'd died the night before. She was very angry. She barely spoke to me and the minute the funeral was over she flew back to New Zealand. The next thing is I get an email to say she's married. I wasn't even invited to the wedding."

"Have you had any contact since?"

"One way only. I write to her. I never get a reply."

I am silent. There's nothing I can say. The waves crash on the rocks below us, the screams of the gulls echo above us, but we're enveloped in our own cocoon of silence.

Faced with Heather's pain I let my thoughts drift back to my own life. Yesterday, for the first time, I finally managed to speak about Anne. I was able to say aloud what I had felt deep down for so long. It was painful, very painful, but sitting here on this cliff top I finally accept that Simon is right, he's always been right, it's time to stop wallowing, time to turn and fight. And then I realise I've already begun that process. Yesterday, at last, I let the pain out into the open and I was only able to do that thanks to the woman sitting beside me now, wrapped in her own pain.

All these years, feeling the anguish but never acknowledging it. The hidden anger. The sense of bitterness against my mother long since dead. A wholly unrealistic desire for redemption from guilt. What redemption? What guilt?

I've let that childhood tragedy affect my whole life. Simon moved on, I never did. But why not? I realise I have taken an important step forward. I thought I had to learn how to talk about Anne. But perhaps I also had to sit here and listen to Heather talk about Katherine.

I give a short laugh. "Couple of wounded soldiers, aren't we?"

"Suppose so." She suddenly turns and looks at me. "I don't know why I'm telling you all this."

"Because you need to tell someone. And I'm here."

She smiles, a grim tight smile. "Because I made you come. No reason why you should be lumbered with it, though."

"There's every reason."

"Why?"

"Well, perhaps because I want nothing from you, and perhaps because you let me talk yesterday."

"When you didn't really want to."

I nod. "When I didn't really want to."

"But you did. Have you ever told anyone before?"

Now it's my turn to look away. "No. Never."

"Not even Lauren?"

"I don't even talk to Simon about ... about ... Anne."

"But at least Simon knows about her. Lauren doesn't."

"She doesn't need to."

"Oh, I think she does. I'd be willing to bet she's always known there's something you've never told her."

An uncomfortable thought but I know it is true.

"These things fester if they're not dealt with. I should know."

"Am I the first person you've told about Katherine?"

"Yes."

"So we're agreed. There comes a time when you have to let go?"

She smiles faintly. "Yes, I think so, but you have to feel safe first."

I realise I've just been paid a compliment, but thinking back to yesterday on her terrace I think that 'safe' was also a good word for what I'd felt.

I say something like this to Heather and she manages a wry smile.

"It was you, yesterday, trusting me enough to tell me about Anne. Made me realise it was possible to break the silence."

"It's not easy, is it?"

"No. At first, after Robin died, I had to be alone. I didn't want to talk about it. I never thought I'd tell anyone about Katherine. I shut myself away down here to try and forget. Forget Robin's last days and, perhaps forget Katherine altogether, but I can't."

"Forget her altogether? Your daughter?"

"I thought it would be best. She made it clear she wanted no more to do with me."

"Anger of the moment. Anger at not arriving in time."

"Maybe. Maybe more than that. Maybe it's like you and your mother and she can see things I can't about how I treated her." Abruptly Heather stands up. "But it's got to be talked about if I'm ever going to move on. And on that note, come on, time to go. It's a fair step back to the car."

The return walk is accomplished in virtual silence but it's not an embarrassed silence. When she drops me off in the village she says tentatively. "Would you mind if we don't meet again tonight, Richard? I think I need some time to myself."

"Of course."

."Come up to the cottage in the morning and thank you for being such a good listener."

"Thank you too. I need to do some thinking as well. I'll see you tomorrow."

But the next day my world is turned upside down.

325

73

Thursday morning, cold, frosty, clean. While I'm in the shower it suddenly occurs to me that I haven't heard from Sally lately, or Simon come to that. I take my mobile out of my jacket pocket to see if there have been any missed calls only to find it isn't even turned on. Of course, I turned it off when I was with Lauren and, unusually for me, forgot to turn it on again. I do so now and suddenly messages come flooding in, voicemails and texts. Two from Simon, three from Lauren, several from Sally and one from Polly.

I start by calling Simon whose response is what you'd expect from a brother. "Where the hell are you? Your office has been trying to contact you since Monday. No answer at home, no response to emails, mobile switched off. So they email Lauren who rings me. We were about to report you missing."

"I'm in Cornwall. I forgot to turn the phone on."

"Cornwall? Why Cornwall? No, that doesn't matter. Just ring the office will you. Sort it out."

"Yes, yes. I'll do that now." There's a pause, then before I can stop myself I say. "Oh, and by the way, Lauren's accepted a full time job in New York. She won't be coming back to the UK."

"*What?*"

A screech from Simon. Maybe this wasn't the moment to share that bit of information.

"One thing at a time, Richard. Now get off the bloody phone and call your office. Let me know what happens."

He rings off and I call Sally. She is also frantic. "Thank goodness, Richard, I've been trying to get hold of you since Monday."

"I know. Sorry about that but I'm here now. What's going on?"

"We need you here. Now. How soon can you get here?"

I glance at my watch. It's already nine-thirty. "Does it have to be today?"

"Yes, yes, yes. It should have been yesterday, the day before yesterday. Just come. We've had the police all over us like a rash. Gaynor Wiles is champing at the bit and Kenneth Bannerman's here too. It must be serious if the National Director's involved."

"Where's Hunky?"

"No idea. He seems to have gone to ground. Richard, I can't tell you. This place is bedlam. Everyone's screaming for you. When can you get here?"

"Well, not till later this afternoon. I'm in Cornwall."

"Cornwall?" Her voice goes up an octave then she gets control of herself. "Okay. Cornwall. So give me an ETA and I'll see what I can fix."

I think rapidly. I can't leave without seeing Heather and the car needs petrol. Then something else occurs to me, I'll have to call in at Weybridge on the way. I suspect this meeting is going to be difficult enough without me arriving in a pair of grass stained jeans and an open neck shirt.

"Tell you what, Sally. Let's play safe. How about we say around six?"

"Six this evening? Here at the office?"

"Yes. That should be fine."

"I'll try and fix it for then, but please, Richard, please, please, don't turn your mobile off again."

She rings off and I spurt into action. While I'm packing I think about the other messages. It's far too early to ring Lauren in New York and Polly will have to wait. The priority now is to get on the road.

I sling my bag in the car and drive up the hill to Heather's cottage. I explain the situation as briefly as possible and she nods.

"Will you let me know what happens, Richard?"

"'Course I will but now I need to get going."

I set off down the track. In the mirror I can see here standing there, watching me go. She doesn't wave.

SIMON

Simon was sitting at his desk trying to concentrate on the paperwork in front of him and failing. Rather to his surprise he found he was uncharacteristically cross with his brother.

He had sensed all was not entirely right between Richard and Lauren but he was sorry to hear she was staying in New York permanently. He supposed that probably meant the end of their marriage and that was sad. He liked Lauren. She was not a restful person but then, if he was being honest, neither was Richard. Two driven people leading stressful lives.

Just lately though he'd sensed Richard was letting his pace of life slow down. Partly inevitable given the circumstances, of course, but he'd begun to wonder if at last Richard was coming to terms with a less frenetic lifestyle. In Simon's view that would be a very good thing but before anything else could happen Richard had to get the situation at work sorted which was why, Simon finally realised, he was cross with him. Simon had very few rules in business but one of the most important was, when there's trouble brewing – be there.

Now there clearly was trouble and Richard had not been there. Simon just hoped he hadn't left it too late.

LAUREN

S he woke at six and the first thing she did, as she'd done every morning since she'd had the email from Richard's PA, was to try his cell phone. This time, to her relief, he answered. Their conversation was brief, he was on the hands-free in the car, but she managed to ascertain he'd spoken to Simon and to Sally and was on his way to London to face whatever was happening there.

She asked where he'd been and was not reassured when she heard it was Cornwall. She wondered about this Heather who was helping Richard with his search. She wasn't jealous. She didn't believe for one moment that Richard was being unfaithful, not in any sexual sense, but it hurt that he seemed to be sharing things with Heather that he didn't seem willing to share with her.

Lauren had never found it easy to express emotion but she desperately wanted to support Richard at this difficult time. The physical distance between them made that hard but the emotional distance was even worse. They were both matter-of-fact people and rarely talked about personal feelings. Deep down she knew he loved her but she wished he would occasionally say so. However, she was well aware that this worked – or didn't work – both ways. She found it difficult to put her feelings for him into words especially as she had always sensed that there was part of Richard that was hidden from her. Openly sharing personal feelings had never been part of their marriage. Perhaps it should have been but they never seemed to have the space to try

She wondered if their relationship would have been different if she'd ever managed to find that space.

And had the courage to use it.

She didn't say any of this to Richard but made him promise to let her know the outcome of the meeting, no matter what time it finished. She was relieved he was all right but life carried on and within minutes Lauren was fully back in work-concentration mode, although her day was beginning with a lighter heart.

76

SALLY

She was so relieved when Richard finally rang that she almost burst into tears. The last few days had been really difficult. First was the arrival of Gaynor Wiles who took over Hunky Dory's office and started issuing instructions. No one knew where Hunky was but Francesca had been moved down the corridor and Gaynor's PA had taken over her desk.

Then the police arrived and were closeted with Kenneth Bannerman and later with Gaynor and after they had gone she was told to set up a meeting with Richard for Monday afternoon. Fine, except Richard wasn't answering his phone. She tried his home and his mobile but all she got was his voicemail.

This was not well received but there was nothing to be done so the meeting was re-arranged for Tuesday. Except by late Tuesday morning there was still no response from Richard. This didn't go down well either. Sally said she'd been trying his numbers regularly, even throughout the previous evening, but there was simply no reply.

On Wednesday afternoon she was summoned to Hunky's office where Gaynor was uncompromising.

"Why have you failed to find Richard Kirkwood?"

"I keep ringing his numbers and leaving messages. What else can I do?"

"You must know where he is. You work for him. Are you always this incompetent?"

But Sally had had enough. "I don't work for him, not anymore. I did work for him before you slung him out to grass for something everyone knows he didn't do. I have no idea where he is but if you're going to treat him the way you're treating me I hope he stays away for a bloody long time."

"I think that's quite enough, Mrs Mountford."

"No it isn't quite enough. You've kept him dangling for months, telling him bugger all and then you go ballistic just because he's not at your beck and call the second you want him."

Gaynor's voice was icy. "Are you asking for a formal warning, young lady?"

"No, she isn't." Sally turned round to see a man she didn't recognise seated at the back of the office.

"I think we need to calm things down a bit, Gaynor, don't you? I'm sure Sally's done all she can and if she spoke hastily it's probably because she's as worried as the rest of us."

There was a pause. Gaynor Wiles was clearly controlling her emotions, then she said: "Of course, Mr Bannerman. We're all worried. Makes us a bit tetchy."

So that was Kenneth Bannerman, the National Director. Now he said: "Doesn't seem to be anything more we can do until Richard gets in touch." And then to Sally, "I assume you've contacted his family."

"Oh, yes. I've spoken to his brother and emailed his wife—"

"— Who is currently in New York, I believe."

"Yes, but neither she nor his brother have heard from him either."

"We've had the police check his house," said Gaynor, "but they say he's not there and there's nothing to suggest anything is wrong."

"Then we wait," said Kenneth Bannerman, "not much else we can do."

And that was that for Wednesday. Then finally on Thursday morning Richard rang. Once she knew he was on his way she went to see Gaynor and set up the meeting for six that evening. She rang Richard, confirmed the meeting was on, then went out for a long walk to calm down.

77

I take Sally's call as I'm approaching Bristol. She sounds very relieved but warns me that Gaynor is in a filthy mood, although Kenneth Bannerman seems calmer. Regional Manager, National Director, plus head of HR. Sounds like I'm in for a jolly evening.

I swing onto the M4 and settle down for the final haul into London. Then the phone rings again and this time it's Polly and she's bubbling over.

"Richard, I just had to let you know. I've been talking to that solicitor friend of yours ..."

"Oh, Max."

"Yes, Mr Cortini. He's ever so nice, isn't he?"

I suppose 'nice' is as good a word as any. Ruthless is another one that comes to mind, but I guess it depends on the context of your conversation with him. Max and I have always got on very well and I've done him a couple of favours over the years which is why I thought of him to help Polly. He's certainly very loyal which, in Polly's case, could easily translate into 'nice'.

"Yes," I say, "he's very nice."

"He's getting it all sorted. He's already written to Norman and he says there's no way I'm going to lose the house and I don't have to sell my car."

"That's great news."

"Yes, it is, isn't it. And it's all thanks to you. I'm very

grateful, Richard."

"Glad to help," I say.

"You sound rather odd. Where are you?"

"In the car, on hands-free, heading for London."

"Oh, I see. Has anything happened? With your fraud thingy."

Fraud thingy just about sums it up. "No idea," I say, "all I know is that I've been summoned to meet the bosses so I suspect things are coming to a head."

"Oh, well, perhaps they've come to their senses. I'm sure it will all work out for you, Richard."

"Thank you," I say, thinking for all I know I'm about to be arrested. "And I'm very glad about Max."

I reach the Weybridge house just after four, grab a quick shower, change my clothes and I'm ready to face the fray. For once the traffic driving into London isn't too bad and I'm parked in our underground car park at a quarter to six. I sit in the car for a few moments, gathering my thoughts. I feel strangely calm and I realise it's because I now feel in control. I have no idea what's going to happen in this meeting but I'm tired of living with anxiety and uncertainty. If this is a precursor to being charged with a crime, I'll call Lauren and then Max. If they opt for the not-proven route and decide to sack me I'll pre-empt them and resign. From now on I'll make the decisions.

But then, sitting there, in this subterranean place with the aroma of petrol and diesel all around me, I realise I've already made one.

Whatever happens I do not want to go back.

The space, the lack of constant pressure, that so scared me when I began this garden leave has started to seem attractive.

I have no idea what I want to do, but at least now I know what I don't want to do.

With that realisation firmly fixed in my mind I lock the car and head for the lifts.

78

Sally is waiting for me as I get out of the lift on the third floor. To my surprise she gives me a big hug.

"Oh, it's good to see you, Richard. I've been so worried."

I hug her back. "Thanks, Sally. Don't worry. It's going to be okay now."

"They're all in there, waiting for you."

"Who's 'they'?"

"Well, Gaynor Wiles, of course, and her PA, Marcie. She's there to take minutes of the meeting. Then there's that woman from HR, I can never remember her name."

"The one with the frizzy red hair?"

"That's her and there's also Kenneth Bannerman, but he keeps insisting he's only there to observe. It's Gaynor who's chairing the meeting."

"Hence her PA taking the minutes. Okay. Let's go."

"Oh, I'm not coming. I'm not invited. I just wanted to brief you."

"Thank you, Sally, but you are coming. Got your notebook?"

"No, but I can get it."

"Do that. I want you there taking notes for me, just in case."

Sally grins. "Be right with you."

As we enter the meeting room all eyes turn towards me and I launch straight in.

"I'm sorry I wasn't available earlier this week. I had some urgent personal business to attend to and unfortunately my phone was inadvertently left switched off."

"That's not the sort of behaviour we expect from an employee, Richard."

That's Gaynor firing from the hip but I'm in no mood to be bullied.

"Oh, I'm still an employee, am I, Gaynor? Having been virtually ignored for the last three months I wasn't certain."

That earns me a scowl and she switches her attention to Sally.

"Thank you, Mrs Mountford, that will be all."

I smile sweetly. "I asked Sally to be here with me to take notes of this meeting."

Gaynor meets my gaze, unsmiling. "There's no need for that. Marcie will keep notes."

"Marcie will keep your notes. Sally will keep mine."

Gaynor doesn't like that but out of the corner of my eye I see Kenneth Bannerman smothering a grin. The HR woman with red hair sniffs audibly.

"Very well. If you insist. Let's get down to business." I move forward and take a seat at the table. There's no chair for Sally but Kenneth Bannerman fetches one from the other side of the room and places it next to mine.

I turn towards him. "Thank you, Mr Bannerman."

He nods, and Gaynor makes an impatient noise. "Can we get on please? Now then, Richard, although this unfortunate fraud investigation is by no means completed, we've had an interim report from the police which is why we have convened this meeting."

She pauses and looks at me but I say nothing so after a

moment she continues. "This report deals with many aspects of the on-going fraud investigation as it impinges on this company but for this meeting we're specifically concerned with the section that relates to you."

She picks up a sheet of paper from the pile in front of her. "The relevant section reads. *After a detailed and thorough investigation we have no evidence, firm or circumstantial, to suggest that Mr Kirkwood had anything to do with this fraud or had any knowledge that it was going on. He is therefore completely exonerated'."*

"Ye–es." There's a clenched fist shout from Sally, who immediately goes bright red and mutters, "Sorry."

Gaynor glares at her. "We're all glad about the outcome, Mrs Mountford."

Sally looks down and Gaynor switches her gaze back to me. For a moment I am numb. It really is all over. No suspicion. No uncertainty. I've been cleared. I realise the room has gone quiet. I take a deep breath and look up to see Gaynor watching me. She manages a smile.

"Good news, then, Richard. For you and for the company." But even then she can't resist a little dig. "Would have been nice to have told you on Monday though, wouldn't it?"

I let her have that one and Gaynor goes on. "Right then, to business. We will need a couple of weeks to re-organise things here but basically we're happy to tell you that your garden leave is over and …"

"Just a moment."

Gaynor looks startled but I press on. "It's not as easy as that. I've just had three months or so under suspicion—"

"You weren't under suspicion. Your garden leave was a temporary arrangement, merely to make sure the police investigation could proceed without prejudice."

"Well, that's not what it felt like."

"Well, I can assure you—"

"And I would like to know more details about that police report."

"The rest of the report is not relevant to this meeting. You've been cleared of all suspicion. That is enough."

I decide to attack. "With all due respect it is not enough. And there's another thing. I would like to know why my line manager, Mr Dory, is not present at this meeting."

There is a silence round the table then Kenneth Bannerman steps in. "Mr Dory is, unfortunately, currently unavailable."

"Unavailable. I see." On the spur of the moment I decide to follow a hunch. "And while we're about it, what does that report say about the threatening texts I've been receiving from someone within this company?"

Gaynor's face is a picture. The HR woman's face is bright red. Sally's mouth is open wide in amazement.

I guess my hunch is correct as they don't deny it so I seize my advantage. "I am very pleased to be cleared of these charges, whether they were formally made or not. However, before deciding what I do next I need to know more about the ongoing investigation and who else is mentioned in that police report."

"There is no need for you to know that."

"Oh, I think there is. I've just had several months out of the loop. My stand-in has, to put it mildly, upset a lot of my clients, I've been harassed by one of my colleagues and just patting me on the head and saying 'good boy, now you can come back to work' isn't enough."

"Are you asking for compensation?"

"I don't know. Maybe. Maybe not, but I resent being treated like an office junior."

"That is certainly not our intention." Kenneth Bannerman has decided to take control. "And I hear what you're saying, Richard, but there's nothing further we can tell you at this stage. The rest of that report has to remain confidential for the time being."

As he says that he looks me straight in the eye. For a moment I hold his gaze, then I nod slightly and he goes on.

"However, listening to what's been said, I think all that needs to be done now in this meeting is to formally record the fact that Richard Kirkwood has been cleared of all suspicion – and I mean suspicion, not charges – and therefore his status in the company remains unchanged."

Gaynor opens her mouth to speak but Kenneth Bannerman shakes his head and she subsides again.

"So that's our decision, yes? Good." He looks at Marcie and Sally in turn. "And that's duly recorded I hope, ladies."

They both nod.

"Right then. Now, there are clearly a lot of details still to be sorted but I think that completes the formal part of this meeting. Gaynor, can you and I have a little chat, please. Shall we say your office in about five minutes," and he gives her a beaming smile.

For a moment I think Gaynor is going to protest but maybe she also senses the sub-text so, together with Marcie, who is looking bemused and clutching her notebook, she sweeps out, followed by the nameless woman from HR who refuses to meet my eye. Bannerman turns to me.

"Right then, Richard. I need to talk to you too, once I've spoken to Gaynor. You okay with that?"

"Sure."

"Good." He turns to Sally. "Well, Mrs Mountford, Sally, I can see you're dying to cart Richard off somewhere and probably buy him a drink."

Sally blushes and nods.

"And would, say an hour, be long enough for you?"

"Oh, er … yes, I should think so."

"Fine. Well, In that case Richard why don't you and I get together in about an hour from now? We can use the board room."

"Okay."

He nods to us both and heads towards the door. Before he gets there Sally calls after him.

"Mr Bannerman …"

"Yes?"

She gives him a big smile. "You be nice to Richard. You owe him that."

I open my mouth to protest but Kenneth simply laughs. "Don't worry, Sally. I'll be nice to him. I promise."

He goes out of the room leaving Sally and I gazing at each other.

"What the hell is he playing at?" I ask.

"What the hell was all that about threatening texts?" counters Sally.

"Long story."

She shakes her head. "Tell me in the pub. He was right. I do want to buy you a drink. Come on."

79

JULY 1962

The last day of term and his time at Modbury Road school is finally over. The long summer holidays stretch out ahead of him. Weeks of emptiness before the grammar school system with its new challenges sucks him in.

The last day. At lunchtime a spontaneous group of those leaving gathers in the playground. There is much swearing of undying friendship and then someone, he thinks it was Rodney but his memory is uncertain, gathers them into a huge dancing circle, twirling and laughing and singing.

And suddenly everyone's hugging and giggling, and then in the crowd Richard finds himself next to Julie and is instantly shy. For a moment they look at each other and then she leans forward and gently kisses him on the lips. For one glorious, symphonic, never-to-be-forgotten moment he responds and then the crowd sweeps them apart.

Later after the final assembly, the speeches from the platform, the anti-climax that the first stage of school life is now over, Richard wanders towards the main gate, satchel clutched in one hand. As he turns the corner of the main building he sees Julie just ahead of him and quickens his pace to catch her up.

"Hallo."

"Hallo."

"Though I suppose it's really goodbye, isn't it?"

"Yes."

There's a pause then, fighting down his shyness, he says. "Julie, I don't suppose we could meet, could we? Go for a walk, perhaps one day next week."

Her eyes are grey which he has always loved but now the greyness signals the message.

"I'm sorry, Richard, but we go on holiday tomorrow. Bournemouth. We go every year."

"How long?"

"Two weeks."

Two weeks. A lifetime. He makes one last attempt. "Perhaps when you get back."

"That would be nice."

He desperately wants to kiss her again but they are exposed, no longer lost in the safety of the crowd, so he doesn't.

"I have to go, Richard. My tea will be ready."

"Yes, of course. Bye."

"Goodbye." She gently reaches out and brushes his fringe from his forehead with her fingers then turns and heads down the road.

He feels bereft. He senses that it's all over. In fact, although he doesn't know it at this moment, he will never see her again.

KENNETH

He was cross with himself as much as with anyone else. As National Director he believed in accepting responsibility for what went on in his territory. So ultimately it was his fault. Yes, of course Gaynor should have picked up on it earlier. Yes, perhaps he had been too quick to authorise the garden leave for Richard Kirkwood without asking more questions. But all that was past history. It was his responsibility and now it was down to him to see what could be salvaged from the wreckage.

He sat in the board room, alone, thinking how to achieve the best result for the company. He knew he would have to tread carefully. Richard was an independent spirit which was, of course, what made him so good at what he did, but it also meant that he couldn't be manipulated or coerced. He had to be persuaded. He admired that and he admired the loyalty Richard engendered in people around him. He'd been impressed by the way Sally Mountford had stood up for him, in a way that Gaynor clearly disapproved of.

There was a knock on the door. It opened and Richard came in.

It's a large room with a large table that will comfortably seat twenty people. Kenneth Bannerman is sitting on one side at the far end so I move across and take a seat opposite him.

There's a brief silence then Kenneth says. "I wanted to meet you like this so we can have an off the record conversation. Are you happy with that?"

"Yes, though I reserve the right to withdraw that approval at any time."

Kenneth grins. "You're a canny bugger, aren't you?" he says.

I blink. This is not the sort of language you normally expect from your National Director. He sees my reaction.

"Oh, don't worry. I'm all for it." He hesitates for a moment as if trying to decide whether to go on but then does. "That Sergeant Williams told me how you returned your laptop to Francesca Thompson."

I feel rather embarrassed. "Oh."

"I like someone who thinks of all the angles." He pauses. "I gather from what you said in the meeting just now that you've got a pretty good idea what's going on."

"I think so, yes. Those texts came from someone in this department, didn't they?" He nods and I hazard a guess. "Was it Hunky – sorry – Mr. Dory?"

"Hunky will do and no it wasn't but you're close."

I suddenly realise. "Oh, my God, it was Francesca."

"Apparently so, but that's not something we want to share publicly until the investigation is completely over. That's why I stopped the meeting when I did. The record will show that you were cleared and reinstated. That's all that needs to go in writing at this stage."

"Maybe."

He eyes me keenly. "Would it ease your mind to know that Mrs Thompson is about to be charged? Not sure what the police have decided, wasting police time, perverting the course of justice. That's down to them but she's not getting off scot-free."

"Good. But why would she of all people start sending me harassing texts? To go so far as to get hold of a prepaid phone just for the task. It seems crazy. I mean, she doesn't like me and I don't like her but even so …"

Kenneth gives a wry smile. "The police believe she was trying to protect someone."

"Oh, I see." My mind goes back to the last conversation with Sergeant Williams when he said they suspected there was some inside involvement in this fraud and suddenly the second penny drops.

"You mean … oh, don't tell me … are we talking about Hunky? Do the police think he's part of this fraud?"

"It appears to be a strong possibility."

"How strong?"

"Well, at the moment we can't prove anything but speaking personally I'd say that at the very least there must have been the occasional blind eye."

"And Francesca knew?"

"I'm pretty sure she didn't, or not for certain, but once he suspended you she thought it was a possibility so she tried to throw suspicion elsewhere."

"But why would she want to protect him?"

Kenneth grins and leans back in his chair. "Still off the record, and I'm still guessing of course, but I think she fancies him."

My response is instinctive. "Oh, my God."

He laughs. "Love conquers all, eh?"

There's a short silence while I gather my thoughts. "Okay, so I was the fall guy. And it was Hunky who set me up, wasn't it?"

Kenneth has the grace to look embarrassed. "Possibly. The problem was that Dory wasn't under suspicion at that time and they were your contractors. We sent you on garden leave to make sure there was clear daylight between you and the investigation."

"What changed?"

He looks me straight in the eye. "The investigation proceeded. Other stuff emerged – I really can't talk about that. Then those texts started arriving and it seemed obvious that someone was trying to implicate you. So then the question was 'why'?"

"Did you ever think I really was involved?"

He shakes his head. "No. In fact those texts suggested the contrary, the police were always convinced you were being set up. I'm sorry we couldn't let you off the hook earlier but when our other suspicions were aroused, we needed to see what would develop."

"Thanks a bundle."

"I'm sorry. Must have been very difficult for you."

"Yes."

"Which is why I wanted to talk to you personally. First

to apologise on behalf of the company for what you've been through the last few months."

"Thank you. I understand why – objectively, but it's not always easy to be objective."

"I'm sure it isn't, but now we need to talk about your future."

"Ah, yes, my future."

He looks at me for a moment then says. "I may be wrong but I have a feeling if I'd let Gaynor go on back there you might well have told her to stuff the job."

"Possibly not in those words but, yes, it had passed through my mind."

"I thought so, but I think that would be a pity."

"For me or for the company?"

"I would think both."

"I'm not so sure. I've had a lot of time these last few months to do some thinking and I'm not certain I want to go on. I missed the pressure at first but then found I was getting used to having time to do, well, nothing. You can get used to it, you know."

"So I'm told," he says wryly.

There's a pause. We look at each other, me deciding how far I want to go, him, I suspect, deciding how far he can push me.

Kenneth breaks the silence first. "What would you do if you did leave?" he asks.

"Good question. I don't know."

"How much did you really enjoy having a lot of time on your hands?"

I think of the hours spent in my search for Julie, I think of the conversations with Simon, with Polly and with Heather.

But I also think of the black times, the sleepless nights, the anxiety about the future. The emptiness of life in the Weybridge house.

Kenneth is watching my closely and I want to give him an honest answer. "Curate's egg," I say, "good in parts."

He nods. "You've still got some years to go before retirement."

"I could go early."

"You'd take a hit on your pension."

"True. I'd need to decide if that's worth it."

"Worth the loss of pension to gain free time that's only good in parts?"

This man is very astute but he has an axe to grind. Trouble is, he also has a point. Then another thought occurs. "Whose bright idea was it to put Mervyn Wilby in my place?"

"Ah, yes. Not a good move, that."

"That's putting it mildly. Was he Hunky's choice?"

A brief hesitation then Kenneth says, "Yes."

Another piece of the jigsaw clicks into place. I laugh. "Hunky brought Wilby back from Puerto Rico because he knew he wasn't bright enough to spot what was going on."

Kenneth says nothing and I follow this train of thought through. "Of course, it was only after we'd had the first hint of possible fraud and the police came calling that I was suspended. That wasn't a coincidence, was it? I bet the garden leave was Hunky's idea."

Kenneth sighs. "It seemed a sensible move at the time. Perhaps I should have dug deeper. I don't know. We don't always get it right, do we?"

"No, we don't."

He looks at me. "So, how about it? Can we draw a line

under this? Will you come back?"

It's decision time but my thoughts in the car park haven't changed.

"No, I'm sorry. I don't think I want to do that."

His lips tighten. There's a pause and then he says, "Suppose we were to offer you the Area Manager post, bigger salary, better pension?"

This does come as a surprise. "Hunky's job?"

"It's a vacancy that'll have to be filled. Whatever happens he's finished with this company."

I wasn't expecting this but I don't need to think about it. An office in London, a daily commute, the worries of a team as well as my own? It's a no brainer.

"Thank you, but no, I don't think that's for me."

He sighs. "I thought that'd be your reaction. Probably for the best. It's really your current job where you're the most use to us."

"Especially in view of some of the disasters Mervyn has caused."

He wrinkles his nose. "Several of our best clients have left us. Not good news. And I gather quite a few more are on the verge of pulling out."

"Ah, so you want me back to help stop the rot?"

"Of course. My first concern is the welfare of the company. However, I believe the company is only as good as the people who work for it. I want you back, I think the company would benefit from your return, but it will only work if you want it as well."

"You could find a better replacement for me than Mervyn."

"Of course we could, but if you go we're not just losing an employee, we're losing all the experience and contacts that you've built up over the years."

"That sounds like flattery."

"It may sound like flattery but actually it's realism. Don't misunderstand me, Richard. If you chose not to come back then we'll replace you and the company will go on. I just happen to think that it'll go on a little bit more smoothly and efficiently if you stay with us."

There's a silence. I'm thinking hard. I really don't want to resume my old life, long hours, constant travelling, stress and strain, but there is still the question of what I'll do with myself if I stop completely. An idea begins to nudge its way into my head. I decide to give it a dry run.

"Are you open to a proposition?"

"Depends what sort of proposition."

"Suppose I were to take early retirement."

"Yes?"

"I would, initially at least, have time on my hands."

"Yes?"

"You could hire me back on a consultancy basis, payment job by job, and my first task would be to repair bridges. Get those old clients back on board or as many of them as I can anyway."

There's a pause then he says: "You reckon you could do that?"

"I reckon I could. Of course a lot would depend on who you get to replace me full time but if you make a sensible choice and give me some time to work with him or her, you could soon be back on an even keel."

He sits back in his chair and looks at me for a few moments. "Got it all worked out, haven't you?"

"Actually, no, I've only just thought of this while we've

been talking. But it does seem a possible win-win situation."

He nods. "Maybe. Actually I'm not terribly keen on using outside consultants for what's really a staff job. If you keep it in-house you have more control."

"Like the control you had over Hunky and Francesca?"

He winces. "Ouch!"

There's a pause as we eye each other up then he says, "So you really don't want to come back?"

"Not really."

"Okay. So, we seem to have a bit of an impasse."

"I guess."

Suddenly he stands up and holds out his hand. "I think we'll call it a day there, Richard. Let's both go away and think about it. There's been enough hasty decisions made in this affair already."

We shake hands and I head back to my car, full of very mixed feelings. I'm cleared of any involvement in fraud but I am no closer to knowing my future.

82

It's quite late when I get back to Weybridge but it's not late in New York so the first thing I do is ring Lauren. Her obvious relief when I tell her it's all over and I'm in the clear is very warming.

"I'm so pleased, Richard, not surprised but very pleased."

I am tired now and I don't want to spoil her pleasure so I let her enjoy the moment. She seems as if she's waiting for space to say something else and I think she believes things can now get back to normal but I know they can't. Too many stones have been overturned, too many memories have been allowed to resurface. You can't put the toothpaste back in the tube.

Instead of saying whatever is in her mind, Lauren asks instead what I am going to do about the office and I say I don't know. I need time to think. She understands that so we say goodnight and I go to bed.

The following morning I call Simon and tell him I've been cleared.

"So what happens now?" he asks.

"I don't know. I really don't know. There's a bit of a negotiation underway with Swamplett and then there's the situation with Lauren. Just at the moment I don't know which way to turn."

"Anything I can do?"

"Thanks, but no, not at the moment."

"Understand." There's a pause, then he says, "What's going to happen with you and Lauren?"

"I don't know. I need to sort out what I'm going to do first."

"Are you sure?"

"What do you mean?"

"Think about your priorities, Richard. A while back you said you wondered if Lauren would ever come back from her attachment. Now she's got a permanent job so it looks like she won't. So is that it? Are you going to look for a way through or are you just going to chuck your marriage away?"

"I don't know. It's difficult."

"Of course it's difficult, but if you ask me that's your first priority, not the bloody job."

We say goodbye and I sit for a while thinking. After the tension of the last twenty-four hours I feel rather flat. What am I going to do? What do I want to do? I'm not the same person I was four months ago. Too much has happened. Back then my life was the job and a ships-that-pass-in-the-night relationship with Lauren. But now everything has changed. I still don't know whether our marriage can survive, although the past weeks have shown me that I want it to. However, if it's to stand any chance then I need to find a new balance between work, Lauren and my own space. But where to start?

Later that morning I suddenly remember I promised to ring Heather so I pick up the phone again.

"Sorry to abandon you in such a hurry yesterday but it's good news. I've been cleared. Completely."

"That's wonderful, Richard, I'm very pleased for you. So what happens now?"

"Good question. I have no idea. I need to do some hard

thinking about the future."

"Whose future? You and your company or you and Lauren?"

"Me and the company. I don't know what's going to happen with Lauren."

There's a pause, then she says, "Last Tuesday afternoon, on my terrace" – I feel a shiver run down my spine – "I was very flattered that you trusted me enough to tell me about your sister, but I wasn't really the person you should have been talking to, was I?"

"You were the only person I could talk to. I never thought I'd ever speak about it but suddenly, I don't know why, but, to use your own word, I felt safe."

"I know, and I'm pleased you did. But that was then, this is now."

There's a silence, then finally I say, "You think I need to tell Lauren, don't you?"

"Oh, Richard, do you really need to ask?"

Of course I don't. I know she's right but the thought terrifies me. How will she react after all this time? Will it even make a difference? Or have I left it too late?

For a moment I'm lost in thought and then I hear Heather's voice.

"Richard …?"

"Yes, sorry, I'm still here."

She's silent for a moment then she says. "I appreciate it's really none of my business, but I think your few days down here showed us both the value of bringing stuff out into the open. It certainly did me a lot of good."

"I know. It was good for me too but whether—"

"— Whether it's enough to break the years of silence.

357

That's what you mean, isn't it? You're worried it could be make or break."

Again I'm struck by her perception. "Yes, I guess that's it."

There's a pause, then she says, "There's one other thing, Richard."

"Yes?"

"When I say our talk was good ..." She breaks off and I hear her swallow and realise she isn't just talking about me.

"Heather, what is it?"

"I've decided. I'm going to visit New Zealand. Sometime soon. Don't know when, but I know I must go ..."

"Make or break?"

"Yes. I'm terrified but I've got to do it."

"If I can help in anyway ..."

"You already have." Another pause. "Please stay in touch, Richard."

First Simon and now Heather. It's decision time. Heather's courage has put me to shame. To plan a journey as far as New Zealand knowing that, even when you get there you might face rejection, requires a huge strength of will.

All I am faced with is a trip to New York where, initially at least, I know I'll be made welcome. What might happen after that is anyone's guess but I'll have made the effort.

I ring Lauren before I can have second thoughts. "Look, I need to talk to you. Face to face. Could you free up this weekend? If so, I'll try and get a flight tomorrow."

"It sounds serious."

"It is."

"Should I be worried?"

"No ... at least I hope not."

Silence for a moment then she says, "Okay, I'll clear the

decks. Text me your arrival time."

I swing into action and manage to book a flight to New York the next day. The only option available at short notice is First Class but I reckon my marriage and my future are worth the expense.

Then that evening, while I'm packing, the phone goes. It's Kenneth Bannerman with another proposal. We talk for about half an hour and by the time he rings off my thoughts are in a flat spin again.

83

It's a very comfortable flight, I could get used to first class travel. Lauren meets me at Kennedy and we go back to the apartment where I have a quick nap and then we go out to dinner. A very different occasion from our last meal together in New York but Lauren is clearly not relaxed.

"Okay, you're in the clear fraud wise," she says, "so what happens now? Are you going back to work as before?"

"Well, that's the question. Kenneth Bannerman has come up with an interesting idea so, yes, it could be back to work but not as before."

Lauren doesn't like pussyfooting about. "For God's sake, Richard, just spit it out."

"Okay. Here's the dilemma. The guy who stood in for me cocked up big time, lost a number of clients, damaged a lot of relationships. They need me back to try and sort it but I don't want to go."

"Let them stew then. Their problem, not yours."

"Sure, but what do I do instead? I've never been very good at doing nothing ..."

"So what's this Kenneth guy suggesting?"

"Well, it's not just him, I had an idea too."

"Gee, this is like getting blood out of a stone. Just cut to the chase, Richard."

"Okay, I suggested I took early retirement and they hired me back as a consultant to sort out all the problems."

"Great idea."

"Would have been, but he didn't buy that. Doesn't like using outsiders for stuff that can be done inhouse."

"Oh. So, stalemate then."

"Initially, yes. But he called last night with another proposition."

"At last."

"He's suggesting I go back to my old job for six months. In that time I'll try and unravel at least some of the damage Mervyn has done and the company will begin the process of looking for my replacement."

"So that'd be another six months on full salary."

"Well, probably be a bit more than that actually. When they've appointed someone they'll keep me on for a while so I can do a full handover."

"Okay, and after that?"

"I'm out. I retire but on full pension, even though I'll be going a bit early. I had to argue a bit for that but got there in the end."

"Gee, that's great."

"Yes, I think it is. Doesn't solve the problem of what I'll eventually do, of course."

"No, but you've bought yourself some time."

She looks at me then comes out with something completely unexpected. "You've changed, you know, Richard, since all this business began. I know it's been stressful but somehow you seem more, well, I guess more relaxed than I've ever known you."

I think about this and realise she's right. The slower pace of life I so hated when the garden leave was forced on me has become valued. True, I've agreed to another six months or so hard work but that will give me time to consider what I might do next.

I look up to see Lauren's eyes fixed on mine. "Okay, so you've got yourself a good deal," she says, "but I guess that's not the reason that brought you hotfoot across the Atlantic."

"No, it's not."

"You want to talk about us, don't you? How all this is going to affect you and me?"

This is the critical moment. I can't put off the decision for ever so I take the plunge.

"Yes, I do want to talk about us but first there's something else I need to tell you." She stiffens. "No, don't worry, nothing to do with you and me but very much something to do with me."

"What?"

I look round the restaurant. "Not here. Let's go and find a drink somewhere. Somewhere dark."

We end up in a downtown bar. I choose a corner booth, order a white wine for Lauren and a Jack Daniels on the rocks for me. And then, very slowly and very painfully, not looking at Lauren as I talk, I tell her about Anne, how she was killed, about the accident, that really was an accident, but how I'd always felt guilty

Halfway through I get very choked up and for a moment I can't go on but Lauren reaches out across the table and takes my hand. She squeezes it gently but says nothing and after a moment I manage to continue. The effect Anne's death had on the family, my mother's withdrawal, my father's death, the bleakness of our childhood, the absence of love. The endless nothingness.

Finally I come to a halt and for the first time I raise my

head and look at Lauren, tears wet on my cheeks.

"I'm so, so sorry."

"What for?"

"Not telling you before. Keeping it all bottled up for so long."

She smiles faintly. "Explains a lot. Sometimes, when you were very distant, I thought it was me."

"No, it was never you."

Lauren is quiet for a moment. Then she says, "Thank you for telling me."

"I didn't want to, I've never wanted to, but now I have, I'm very glad."

"So am I."

The relief of finally letting it all go is enormous. "Lauren, I know we hit an impasse that day in Bosham and, of course, that impasse is still there. But whatever happens I really don't want to lose you."

I feel her squeeze my hand. "I don't want to lose you either, Richard, and I was starting to think I had. But—"

"— I know the buts. There's no getting away from the fact that we each want to be in different places."

"Yes but it's more than that. There's something I haven't told you ..." Then she surprises me by saying, "I feel lonely."

She reads my expression and shakes her head. "I don't just mean because I'm kinda living alone in this big city right now. I mean always. I've always felt like that. And I think I always will. Alone even in company. You know what I mean, don't you? You never talk, but I don't either. We're the same. I wanted you to tell me that you accept me as I am, and now you have."

She adds, "I need this job for my own self esteem. But I

know I also need you."

"I need you too. I can't tell you how much I've missed you."

"Oh, Richard. But how are we going to sustain a marriage with me in New York and you in the UK?"

"I've been thinking about that. It might be possible."

"Absence makes the heart grow fonder, eh?" She grins ruefully.

"Kind of. Look think about it. We've existed with absence for a long time, even while living in the same house. How often did we ever have any time together apart from a few hours on a Sunday and even then one or other of us was usually trying to get something ready for the week to come."

"Well, I guess that's true."

"So what's really changed? Okay, we'll be living in different places but that doesn't mean our marriage has to end."

"Doesn't it?"

"No, it doesn't. Money's not a problem. I can visit you, you can visit me."

"Makes our relationship sound a bit clinical."

"More clinical than it is at the moment? Even before you started this secondment?"

"Gee, you don't pull your punches, do you?"

"No, but it's true. We're great when we're together like now…"

I feel her squeeze my hand gently.

"…but how often are we together like now, even when you were working in England? Half a dozen times a year?"

"High days, holidays and birthdays," she says thoughtfully.

"And not always birthdays," I say, "especially if one of us was in the middle of a job."

"Okay, so, if I've got this right, your argument is that basically we could go on with me in New York and you in the UK with very little difference in our marriage other than the small matter of three thousand miles or so?"

"I'm not saying it will be easy but surely it has to be worth a go. And who says it'll be a permanent state? Anything could happen in the future as we've found out. But for the moment I really think this could work."

She nods slowly. "I love this job, I really do. But I love you too."

I feel a lump come into my throat. "And I love you as well. So why the hell are we arguing?"

"We're not arguing. We're agreeing. Come on."

She stands up, the authoritative Lauren in control again. We go back to the apartment where we discover for certain that our last night in the Weybridge house was not farewell. It was a renewal.

LAUREN

She woke at six as usual but remembered at once that it was Sunday. There was no rush. She had the whole day to spend with Richard.

Richard. She looked at him still asleep beside her and thought back to their conversation in the bar last night. She was sad that he'd lived with such unhappiness for so long but part of her was elated that he had finally told her. She was also glad that she had finally been able to share her fears with him.

In a curious way, she realised, it made their long-distance marriage more possible. She felt they were closer now than they'd been for years. No more uncertainty – just an acceptance of the past and a desire to move on. Together.

She lay there thinking about the future, not hers so much, but Richard's. What would he do when he finally left *Swamplett, Benson and Dring?* Where would he go? Where would he live?

She lay there for a while, analysing the problem in her usual methodical way and then suddenly an idea occurred to her. She turned over and poked Richard in the ribs.

"Come on, slugabed. Time to get up. We need to talk."

I struggle back to consciousness with the words "We need to talk" pounding into my head. Seems to be a recurring mantra recently. Lauren is especially bouncy this morning whereas I'm still exhausted, from the events of the past few days, from the transatlantic flight and, perhaps, most of all, from last night's confession. We have breakfast in a small diner and walking there through the January temperature in New York soon drives sleep away.

Afterwards, at Lauren's suggestion, we wrap ourselves up in warm coats, hats, earmuffs, scarves, and gloves and walk down to Battery Park. New York at this time of year is not warm and there is a hint of snow in the air. I ask why we're doing this but all Lauren says is that she thinks we need 'another Bosham'.

I find it difficult to see the similarity between Bosham and sitting shivering on a Battery Park bench looking out across the Hudson River, but I go along with her and burrow deeper into my coat and gloves.

"Okay. You said we need to talk. I thought we'd done most of the talking last night."

She snuggles up beside me. "Last night was special but now we need to look ahead."

"We? I thought you were pretty settled."

"I am, but I won't be completely until I know you are too."

I suddenly feel warmer. The closeness we achieved last night is still there and growing stronger.

"So, do you have something in mind?"

"As it happens, yeah, I do."

"Why doesn't that surprise me?"

"Well, I was thinking. The next few months are pretty much fixed but then you'll be at a loose end, just as you were when this garden leave began."

"True." I have a sudden thought. "Hey, listen, I'm still not up for stamp collecting or building model railways."

Lauren laughs. "No, I'm sure you're not, but you could go back to my first suggestion, first sensible suggestion anyway."

I think back. "You mean, research the history of my family?"

"Yeah. I know you said no back then but now I know why. It would have been too painful."

"It still would be."

"Maybe. But not all of it. For instance, was your mother always so uncaring?"

With difficulty I think back to my early years. "Well, no, not before ... before ... Anne."

"And your father?"

"I think he was a kind man. It's hard to remember."

"Sure, but those bits are as important as the stuff that came later. And what about your grandparents?"

"I only ever knew two of them?"

"Did you love them?"

I'm struggling with long lost memories now. "I think so. I haven't thought about them for so long."

"Then perhaps it's time you did." She pauses for a moment then goes on. "I don't want to trivialise it, but what happened with Anne and all the subsequent unhappiness is only part of the story. Think of what you've achieved, Richard. Think of Simon, think of your work colleagues – well, some of them anyway. Think how your boss man values you enough to want you back. You had a shit childhood, sure, but that's way in the past. It's only stayed shit because you let it. Go back and find all the other parts that make you who you are, lay the ghosts to rest."

More or less what Simon has been telling me for years but could I really face it? Lauren hasn't finished though.

"There's another thing." She pauses then takes a deep breath and goes on. "You're feeling good at the moment. You've finally managed to speak about Anne and all that stuff back then. That's great. But it sure ain't gone away. It ain't over. Probably never will be."

I feel myself tensing. "What's your point?"

"My point is that you'll still have bad moments. That's inevitable, you can't just shrug off the pain of years. But now you've brought it out into the open, you've shared it. When it gets grim you can say so, talk about it to me, to Simon. You're not alone anymore, buster."

I'm overwhelmed. This is huge. I'm not alone anymore.

"One last thing, Richard, and then I really am done. I'm getting the impression that leisure and space have become important to you."

"Yes. Yes, surprisingly they have."

"But maybe you need to ease yourself into that. Having a project like the family history thing could be the cat's meow. And now you've started working through all that past shit, this might help the process."

"Face my demons?"

"Yeah, but with no pressure, no deadline. Work if you want to, don't if you don't."

"Is this really Lauren Kirkwood, the hotshot lawyer talking?"

She laughs. "Sure doesn't sound like me, does it, and it isn't. At least not yet. But, hey, who knows, maybe you'll convert me to the leisure habit one day."

I lift my head and gaze out across the water. "Yes, you're right. I can see the pigs flying over the Hudson from here."

"Stop jerking around, buster, I'm serious. My point is whatever you do, wherever you go, I think you'll always find some kind of project to sink your teeth into, but you may need something to kick-start a new way of life."

It's an interesting idea but I'm cautious. "I need to think about it," I say and Lauren nods.

"Okay, let's pop that in the parking lot for a moment ..." She catches my eye and laughs self-consciously. "Yeah, yeah, I know. More corporate jargon."

"Haven't heard that one before. I might use it."

"Be my guest. But moving on, you still planning to sell the Weybridge house?"

"Yes, I am. If that suits you? I'll probably try and get some kind of apartment in London while I'm still with Swamplett. You *are* cool with that, aren't you?"

"Sure. Weybridge was home for a while, a convenient base because you were there, that's all. But you won't stay in London once you leave Swamplett, will you?"

"Shouldn't think so."

"So where will you go?"

"To be honest, I haven't thought."

"Well, I think you need to get right away. Somewhere

completely new. That day in Bosham, you said you could live somewhere like that. You love it there. It's peaceful and beautiful."

"That might be an idea." But even as I'm speaking another thought comes into my mind. An idea that a few months ago would have seemed outrageous but now ...

Perhaps it's time to realise a dream.

The house was perched on a Cornish cliff. The drive dropped down from the road and splayed out onto an apron with a garage at right angles to the main house. On the other side of the building a small terrace of stone flags curved outwards affording breath taking views across the Helford River and surrounding countryside. Below the terrace a wooded slope dropped sharply towards the river's edge. It was the kind of house he'd always dreamed of.

Richard sat at a round iron table on the terrace, a cafetière of fresh brewed coffee in front of him. From time to time he looked up from the book he was reading to glance at his watch. Soon it would be time to drive through the lanes to meet Lauren off the train at Truro. He smiled to himself as he thought of her reaction when she saw the house for the first time. He was certain she would love it but he was fairly certain she would never want to live in it permanently. No matter. They were both determined to make their transatlantic marriage work.

Lauren was staying for a week and in two days' time Heather was coming to supper. As part of his new lifestyle he'd decided it was time his wife and his friend met. He was looking forward to that. He thought back to that last day in New York. When he and Lauren were talking about where he might go he'd suddenly realised it was Cornwall he wanted. And so he had come back, this time on a different search.

This house across the river from Helford was ideal. He liked being near Heather, but they were both people who needed their own space and having a stretch of water between them was no bad thing.

The final months with *Swamplett, Benson and Dring* had gone well. He'd managed to mend a lot of fences and Kenneth Bannerman was pleased. His successor was in post and the handover virtually complete. He had no idea what the future held but it no longer worried him. He'd begun setting out an action plan for the family research project and when that was done something else would turn up.

Lauren had been right about Anne. The memory of her and the aftermath of her death was still with him. Always would be, but he no longer felt so threatened by those memories. Now, when the despair struck, as it still did and would always do, there was Simon and Lauren and Heather. He didn't need to explain anything to them. They knew, they understood and in their different ways helped him through the moment.

Richard leant back in his chair looking out across the river thinking over the last few months. He hadn't succeeded in his search for Julie Orford but without it he wouldn't be here now, more relaxed than he'd been for years, so perhaps Heather had been right, perhaps it wasn't a failure at all.

The tranquillity of the Helford River wrapped him round as it had first done all those years ago. He was looking forward to having friends to stay from time to time but he was at last learning how to be at ease on his own. Especially now he'd found this house.

This house – or rather this home – did exist and he was happy in it.

POSTSCRIPT
JULIE

Far away in another place, another time, a small cottage kitchen was filled with the smell of fresh baking. She hummed as she worked.

The phone didn't ring, there were no footsteps on the gravel path bearing visitors from the past, there were no letters from old friends.

She never thought of Modbury Road school or the people who had been there. She rarely thought about the past at all.

Julie Orford (as she had once been) was just getting on with her life.